NEW YORK REVIEW BOOKS
CLASSICS

THREE SUMMERS

MARGARITA LIBERAKI (1919–2001) was born in Athens and raised by her grandparents, who ran the Fexis bookstore and publishing house. An artistic child, she nonetheless took up the study of law at the University of Athens, finishing her degree in 1943. Toward the end of the Second World War, she married George Karapanou, published her first novel (*The Trees*, 1945), and, in 1946, gave birth to their daughter, Margarita. The couple divorced the following year, and Liberaki moved to Paris. From then until her death, she lived between France and Greece, writing in both French and Greek. In addition to *Three Summers*, she wrote two further novels, *The Other Alexander* (1950) and *The Mystery* (1976); a number of plays, including *Candaules' Wife* (1955) and *The Danaïds* (1956), part of a cycle she called Mythical Theater; several screenplays, including Jules Dassin's *Phaedra* (1962) and *Diaspora* (1999), about Greek intellectuals in exile in Paris during the junta; and a translation of *Treasure Island* (2000). *Three Summers* is now a standard part of Greek and Cypriot public education; it was adapted as a television miniseries in 1995.

KAREN VAN DYCK is the Kimon A. Doukas Professor of Modern Greek Literature at Columbia University. She writes on modern Greek and diaspora literature and on gender and translation. She has edited or co-edited several volumes of poetry, including *A Century of Greek Poetry* (2004); *The Greek Poets: Homer to the Present* (2010); and, for NYRB Poets, *Austerity Measures: The New Greek Poetry* (2017). Her translations have appeared in *Brooklyn Rail*, *Asymptote*, and *The Baffler*.

THREE SUMMERS

MARGARITA LIBERAKI

Translated from the Greek by
KAREN VAN DYCK

NEW YORK REVIEW BOOKS

New York

THIS IS A NEW YORK REVIEW BOOK
PUBLISHED BY THE NEW YORK REVIEW OF BOOKS
435 Hudson Street, New York, NY 10014
www.nyrb.com

Originally published in Greek as *Τα ψάθινα καπέλα*

Library of Congress Cataloging-in-Publication Data
Names: Lymperakē, Margarita, author. | Van Dyck, Karen, translator and writer
   of introduction.
Title: Three Summers / by Margarita Liberaki ; translated by Karen Van Dyck ;
   introduction by Karen Van Dyck.
Other titles: Psathina kapela. English | New York Review Books classics.
Description: New York : New York Review Books, 2019. | Series: New York
   Review Books classics
Identifiers: LCCN 2018035289| ISBN 9781681373300 (alk. paper) |
   ISBN 9781681373317 (epub)
Classification: LCC PA5610.L9 P7313 2019 | DDC 889.3/34—dc23
LC record available at https://lccn.loc.gov/2018035289

ISBN 978-1-68137-330-0
Available as an electronic book; ISBN 978-1-68137-331-7

Printed in the United States of America on acid-free paper.
10 9 8 7 6 5 4 3 2 1

CONTENTS

THE THIRD SUMMER

TRANSLATOR'S INTRODUCTION

"THAT SUMMER we bought big straw hats. Maria's had cherries around the rim, Infanta's had forget-me-nots, and mine had poppies as red as fire. When we lay in the hayfield wearing them, the sky, the wildflowers, and the three of us all melted into one." The beginning of Margarita Liberaki's *Three Summers*, at once vivid and hazy, evokes the season and the story of adolescent girlhood that the book will unfold. The novel tells the story of three sisters living outside Athens: Maria, Infanta, and Katerina, the youngest, who tells the tale. The house, where they live with their mother, aunt, and grandfather, is in the countryside. Focusing on the sisters' daily life and first loves, as well as on a secret about their Polish grandmother, the novel is about growing up and how strange and exciting it is to discover the curious moods and desires that constitute you and your difference from other people. It also features a stable cast of friends and neighbors, all with their own unexpected opinions: the self-involved Laura Parigori; the studious astronomer David and his Jewish mother, Ruth, from England; and the carefree Captain Andreas. The book is adventurous, fantastical, romantic, down-to-earth, earthy, and above all warm. It's only season, after all, is summer.

The world inside the book could not be more unlike the world the book came into when it was first published in 1946, immediately after the terrible famine and the Axis occupation of Greece during the Second World War, and on the brink of the even more devastating civil war, barely a shadow of which can be found in the idyllic world between its covers. In fact, its cover originally featured a garden. In the story we learn that just as each of the three girls wears a suitable hat of her own choosing, so each of them has her own garden patch to tend. In Katerina's, we learn, the flowers pop up in a crazy, haphazard way. To describe it, Liberaki uses the word *pardalo*, meaning "splotched with color," a word derived from the ancient Greek for "leopard" that suggests the wildness in Katerina's heart. The whole summery world of the book is wildly, sometimes dangerously alive—one year the countryside is swept by a devastating fire—and it is nature, growing plants and growing girls, that makes it so. To its first Greek readers this novel must have offered an oasis from the unbearable realities of the day, a place to live out the life-and-death implications of war in the smaller details of flowers, birds, and bees.

Ebullient yet meditative, dreamy yet realistic, *Three Summers* is at once a story of comfortable bourgeois life, a modern fairy tale, and an almost gleeful evocation of the dizzy delights of girls letting themselves go, allowing themselves to test their limits and find out who they are. It is unabashedly a book about the girls' new sexual awareness. Maria is boy crazy at the beginning and baby crazy by the end. Infanta is remote and virginal, loving her horse more than the boy next door with whom she rides. Romantic, impetuous Katerina plays out complicated love scenarios in her mind. Social taboos are largely lifted: touching oneself, as well as sex before marriage, pass with little comment; the sisters and their friends are left free to ponder their lives and those of their elders, imagining all sorts of ways in which the future might take shape. The danger and damage life can bring are acknowledged—in the background of the three summers lie histories of divorce, abortion, abandonment, and sexual abuse—but it is the plenitude of nature and the spirit of creation that prevail. Maria's pregnancies, the mating of the she-goat Felaha, the still lifes of Aunt Theresa, and the embroidered peacocks of Infanta: these are all part of one world. Katerina, observing everyone, entering imaginatively into their lives, arrives at a new sense of sympathy and power that will eventually sustain her own creative vocation as a writer of a book, the reader is led to imagine, quite like the one you are reading.

The earthy utopianism of the novel met with immediate success. In Greece the book has gone through fifty-one printings, and to this day many Greek readers list it as their favorite book of all time. It is also widely beloved in France, where it was originally published in 1950 on the recommendation of Albert Camus, who wrote to Liberaki: "The sun has disappeared from books these days. That's why they hinder our attempts to live, instead of helping us. But the secret is still kept in your country, passed on from one initiate to another. You are one of those who pass it on." A lyrical paean to youth, a refuge from the present, a garden of promise, Liberaki's story takes us to a place where we want to be.

Margarita Liberaki was born in Athens in 1919. After her parents divorced she was raised by her maternal grandparents, the owners of a publishing house and bookstore that were central to the intellectual and artistic life of Athens. She studied law and received her degree in 1943, but her ambitions lay elsewhere. Her first novel, *The Trees*, appeared in 1945, and *Three Summers* (or *The Straw Hats*, as it was titled in Greek) followed soon after. *Three Summers*, with its emphasis on the creative impulse and Katerina as a writer-to-be, turned out to be quite prescient about the direction Liberaki's own life and career would take. While still at law school, she had married George Karapanou, also a lawyer and writer. She was pregnant with their child when she was writing *Three Summers*. Less than a year later she divorced him and moved to Paris, leaving her daughter to be raised, as she had been, by grandparents.

Living in Paris was emancipating for Liberaki. She insisted on transliterating her name as Liberaki, not Lymberaki, so that it looked like a cognate of liberation. She associated with other Greek expatriates—the poets Andreas Kambas and Odysseas Elytis, and the Marxist philosophers Cornelius Castoriadis and Kostas Axelos—as well as the likes of Camus and Jean-Paul Sartre. She wrote another novel, *The Other Alexander* (1950), before turning to the theater and screenwriting. From the exploration of the female psyche her work now moved toward Greek mythology, where she sought, as she wrote, "a more liminal space, a ritualistic Dionysian writing that tries to define

Greece's position between Europe and the East through archetypal myths." Her career from her first novels to her final screenplay, *Diaspora*, and her translation of Robert Louis Stevenson's *Treasure Island*, both of which were published just before her death in 2001, can be characterized by daring experimentalism.

Liberaki's daughter, Margarita Karapanou, who grew up between Greece and France, also went on to become an important writer, and *Three Summers* may be seen as a precursor not only to Liberaki's career but also to her daughter's. In particular it looks forward to Karapanou's most famous novel, *Kassandra and the Wolf* (1976), also a story of growing up, although much darker. (In an interview she tellingly inverted Camus's praise of the sun in her mother's novel: "Camus would come over for dinner... and he would say, 'Poor Margarita, here in the darkness of Paris, not the light of Attica.'") The relations between mother and daughter can be summed up by such an attitude, comparable to a glass half full. What has always interested me, however, is the mutual confluence of the two women's work, especially the way that Liberaki's wise-child naiveté intermingles with Karapanou's bad-girl precocity.

Both women, as it happened, were of great help in making this translation. I was sixteen, Katerina's age, when I first went to live in Greece, studying Greek poetry on the island of Kalymnos with a bunch of post-junta dissidents. I got to know Karapanou shortly thereafter and some years later Liberaki, who asked me to translate her novel. In the summers of 1992 and 1993 I stayed with them on Hydra, in their tall gray house with a bright yellow door, overlooking the port and the sea, and I came to understand how inextricably intertwined life and literature were for these women. I remember walking that first summer to their favorite swimming spot as Liberaki explained to me that although she had only one sister, the sisters of *Three Summers* were very much drawn from her own experience. Maria was happy with being a wife and mother, Infanta with being an artist, but only Katerina wanted both. She was like Katerina, she said. Her sister, Aglaia, a sculptor, was more like Infanta. (Later that evening I would meet Aglaia at the opening of an exhibition by a family friend, the painter Nikos Ghikas. Among the exhibits were the covers he had done for books by Liberaki and Patrick Leigh Fermor.)

The following summer brought new insights into the relation between mother and daughter, into their lives, their work, and indeed my own. In a breezy room I worked with Liberaki on rendering difficult passages, while Karapanou lay on the couch reading American murder mysteries and eating almond cakes I had brought from the neighboring island of Aegina. Liberaki and I would go back and forth debating alternatives, and every once in a while Karapanou would throw in a trenchant one-liner with just the right American inflection. The translation wouldn't be what it is without her. These women's lives and writings were about translating between languages and cultures, but also about translating between themselves, as well as collaborating on the translations of their books.

Liberaki used to joke that it was only taking us two summers to translate her three, so I imagine she would appreciate that it has now taken me a third to revise what I did back then. My notes from those distant visits, as well as our correspondence, show that at the time the themes of her novel were no less central to my life too. I was also figuring out how to be both a writer and a mother. Translation was a way of bridging these two pursuits. Like raising children, translation involved acknowledging foreignness: something that was and wasn't one's own, dependent and independent at once. When we translate we are asking the reader to believe that, though the work is from another language, it now exists in a new language. Perhaps a field full of poppies with three sisters wearing straw hats, I think, as I reenter the summer-lush world of Liberaki's novel. But where is this field? Where does a translation take place? How could mine be both in Greece and in America?

The title had been the first problem. I chose *Three Summers* since *Straw Hats* in America has a different class valence, more hillbilly than bourgeois, and it might send the wrong signal for a book about well-off girls in large houses attending summer parties. Even if I wanted the translation to relay the Greek sense of straw hats, it was too much to ask that it happen in a title. I had to get my readers inside the book first. Like children, translations need to be helped along before they can be expected to do things on their own. And like children it was important for them to be different from their parents—and for this difference to be noticed.

Foreign words introduced another thorny issue. In my original translation I had included Gallicisms like "Mlle" and "Comtesse" but had shied away from Greek words. The meanings of the street names, for example, had seemed part of the atmosphere of the book so I had translated them: "Spring Avenue" for "Aniksi Avenue" and "Olive Avenue" for "Elia Avenue." But perhaps such assimilation was misleading. Didn't translators, like writers, have a responsibility to teach readers about worlds they don't already know? And wasn't multilingualism an important part of this teaching? For my revised version I decided to transliterate more of the names and to include a glossary. After all, Anglophone readers over time have learned to accept "Champs-Élysées" rather than "Elysian Fields."

Punctuation can also underscore the mixed provenance of a translation. The Greek publisher of the series where my translation first appeared applied Greek, not American, conventions of punctuation. I insisted that they be changed. Revisiting the book after all these years, I feel differently. Yes, quotation marks for dialogue instead of guillemets, and certainly the table of contents at the beginning, not at the end, but the Greek practice of three-dot ellipses throughout the text, even at the end of sentences, could help to re-create—in English—the sense of stream of consciousness that the novel possesses in Greek. Roman numeral chapter headings also gave a slight sense of foreignness.

Ultimately Liberaki's novel, as well as my experience of working with her on the translation, helped me understand how interrelated writing and motherhood were and how important translation was to seeing this. Both translating and mothering were practices of hybridity, but also of unequal power. They were projects that require careful thinking about how two works or human beings are and are not the same. They demand that we take responsibility for our decisions, but also that we acknowledge structural imbalances beyond our control. In fact, noticing differences is one way to allow a child to grow up and a translation to stand on its own.

The sense of newfound independence emerging from the safety and comfort of home is what I hope my translation of *Three Summers* brings out. There is something so replenishing in this novel, something about spending time, just hanging out, not really doing much of anything, living the rhythms of a summer day. Katerina, in a memorable scene, describes what it feels like to lie in the hay in the barn pretending to take her *mesimeriano*, the mandatory afternoon nap. She draws us into a kind of resting for which we so often forget to leave time, but that is so necessary if we are going to have the strength to take risks and make a difference in the world.

—KAREN VAN DYCK
Syros, August 2018

TRANSLATOR'S NOTE

THIS NOVEL was first published in Athens under the title *Τα ψάθινα καπέλα* (*The Straw Hats*, 1946). This translation is from the thirtieth edition published by Kedros (1991). With the permission of the author I have cut some passages that seemed overly specific for an English-speaking audience, sometimes following the French translation (*Trois Étés*, translated by Jacqueline Peltier, Gallimard, 1950). I am grateful to Patrick Leigh Fermor, Andreas Kambas, Margarita Karapanou, and Margarita Liberaki for their helpful suggestions.

This translation is dedicated to my sisters, Jennifer, Sarah, and Rebecca, and my nieces, Ella, Kat, and Odessa.

THREE SUMMERS

For my sister

THE FIRST SUMMER

I. OUR POLISH GRANDMOTHER

THAT SUMMER we bought big straw hats. Maria's had cherries around the rim, Infanta's had forget-me-nots, and mine had poppies as red as fire. When we lay in the hayfield wearing them, the sky, the wildflowers, and the three of us all melted into one. "Where are you? Off hiding again?" my mother called. Shhhhh. We whispered and told secrets. Other years Maria and Infanta had told the secrets, leaving me out since I was the youngest. But this year...

This year Infanta lay a little farther away, all quiet, and Maria told the secrets to me. She talked and talked, turning this way and that in the hay, her cheeks aflame, her eyes taking on a strange glow. And when I stopped listening, watching the sun as it set or an insect as it made its way to its nest to sleep, Maria would get mad. "Hey, are you interested or not?" she'd ask. "It's not for my own sake that I'm here, exhausting myself, trying to explain things to you. Go on believing that babies are brought by storks if you want!..."

I was about to answer, to tell her that I knew that babies weren't brought by storks, that maybe I'd always known this, but her laugh stopped me, a loud, jolting laugh that made the kernels of wheat tremble as it ricocheted off the mountain opposite us and came back an echo. At such moments Maria's laugh annoyed me. I saw in it a shamelessness that took the mystery and pleasure out of things. Hearing it, I'm not sure why, I thought of the feast day of Profitis Elias last year where I had seen a small child dead, curled up in a jar of alcohol. It was just as it had been in its mother's womb.

After the midday meal I never took a nap, a habit of mine since I was small, when I got it into my head that not to take a nap was a revolutionary act showing great independence of mind and spirit. Now, where did I ever get that idea?

I would climb up into the walnut tree and make daisy chains and bracelets from horsehair. Then I would wear them and look for my reflection in the well. But I never succeeded since the sun at that hour hit the water's surface, making it glimmer like a piece of hot, melted gold, blinding me.

I made the same kind of jewelry for my sisters. But it always disappointed me when I saw them wearing it. Not because I was jealous, but simply because they did not seem to appreciate it enough. It was as if they weren't worthy of it, as if they expected the flowers to wilt, so they wilted immediately, or as if they knew the bracelets were only horsehair, and therefore they looked like horsehair, those ones from the horse's tail that switch this way and that, fending off flies.

When the sun's glare tired my eyes and my limbs felt as if I had drunk sweet wine, I would go to the barn to find quiet, a quiet full of shade and the smell of hay. People and faraway places filled my quiet time there: colored ribbons blowing in the wind, orange seas, Gulliver in the land of the Houyhnhnms, Odysseus on the islands of Calypso and Circe. She was a wicked woman, that Circe, turning men into pigs. But how impressive that she had so much power! Would I ever have that kind of power? Not for changing men into pigs, but for other things . . . I dug myself deeper into the hay. I nodded off and slept a little, though I would never tell a soul. It was always a sweet sleep, and on waking I felt as if I were returning from another world. But the meadow was there laughing, and the grapes ripe on the vine, my hand ready to pluck them, my mouth ready to taste them, and I said to myself, *Of all other worlds, and of all the stars that might be other worlds, the earth is surely the best.*

Our house was about half an hour from Kifissia. It was in the part where all the gardens were, in the middle of a meadow, set off on its own. To go to Doctor Parigori's, the house nearest us, you needed a full ten minutes. "Shopping's enough to lay you out," our old housekeeper Rodia would say.

Grandfather had built it as he wanted: large rectangular rooms with high ceilings, two terraces where we dried the corn and whatever else, the gardener's house in a separate plot, and a little farther away the stable and the chicken coops. He had paid particular attention to the garden, not only because he had studied agriculture but because he loved trees. He planted them with his own hands, raising them like children, remembering their illnesses, the frosts, the harsh winds that bent their limbs, their grafts, and the first time each bore fruit. "The trees," he would say, "are all of creation. Their roots in the earth show us how all creatures are connected to each other and to God." In the spring, he would lie down under the apple tree—Grandfather's tree we called it—and listen to the sound of the bees as they dipped into the flowers, extracting the golden pollen.

I guess poor Grandfather kept the farm as consolation. He had lost Grandmother when Mother and Aunt Theresa were only five and seven. Death did not take her. She left of her own accord with a musician who was passing through Athens on a concert tour. At his first of two concerts she fell in love with him. Then they met each other. And after his second she couldn't bear it any longer, and ran off with him. They were both foreigners, you see, so they got along. My grandmother wasn't Greek, but Polish. She had green eyes. I was pretty shocked when Rodia first told me all this. I remember it was a winter evening and we were sitting in the kitchen roasting sweet potatoes. "How could Grandmother have done such a thing?" I wondered out loud to Rodia. "Silly girl," she responded, "she wasn't Grandmother yet. Your mother and Aunt Theresa were still small." True, I guess, she wasn't a grandmother then ... "We never found out where she went or what became of her," Rodia continued. "Who knows whether she's even alive ... Grandfather won't hear a word about her ..."

In fact, nobody ever mentioned her name. Neither Mother, nor Aunt Theresa. We were the only ones who thought about her—we had discovered a photograph in an old chest. Oh my, was she beautiful. We called her the Polish grandmother in order to distinguish her from my father's mother, a lady with white hair and a bitter smile from who knows how many unrequited loves.

"What can I say, I admire her," I told them one afternoon when we were discussing her as we lay in the hay.

"Really?" Infanta said distractedly.

"Why?" asked Maria with interest.

"Well, she was brave to leave like that, without Grandfather..."

"The brave person is the one who stays," Maria interrupted. Infanta didn't argue.

I guess Maria was right. I probably just said that because I was young. But then later I realized that for the Polish grandmother far away was really here, not there.

It had rained a lot all winter. The woods were soaked and had no time to dry out; the fallen leaves rotted, became soil, and then the soil, new leaves again. And in the evenings strong winds blew, strong enough to ruffle the curtains in the dining room without anyone touching them. "Who is it?" asked Grandfather. "Nobody," we answered. "But someone knocked." "No," we said sighing, "just the wind, Grandfather."

Returning from school we would have streams of rain running down our faces. We had hoods, but we never wore them on the way home; we tossed them off and continued uncovered. Maria swayed her body left and right, her mouth half-open, as if she were drunk. Infanta marched straight ahead, always straight ahead, and when a drop came to rest on her eyelash, she wiped it away as if it were a tear. I couldn't understand if her whole face was wet why she should be bothered by that one drop. I didn't mind the rain one bit. I would run, my arms wide open to the heavens and the earth, and sing. Somehow, when I was outside the rain made me happy. But when I heard it from inside my room, hitting the roof and running down the windowpanes, it made me feel completely different. I would lock myself in, fall on my bed, and cry for hours all by myself. I'm not sure, though, if it was out of sadness.

"Katerina is a little nervous," my aunt Theresa told my mother. "She needs special attention."

"What kind of special attention?"

"You know, so she won't turn out like *her*..."

They meant the Polish grandmother. I figured it out from the tone of their voices, and from the look they exchanged. So she was a nervous woman? From that day on when somebody picked on me or when I fought with my sisters, I would let out loud shrieks. I took her photograph and that very afternoon held it up next to my face and looked into the mirror. For all my efforts to see resemblances I found very few. Her eyes were green. Mine were chestnut, one slightly darker than the other, odd but not uncomely; as Rodia said, it was a sign of good luck—her hair black, mine chestnut again, her skin fair, mine golden. The only thing we had in common was our neck and perhaps our chin. I was very proud of this—the way my neck grew out of my shoulders and continued up to my chin, showing off my face. That clean, strong line suggested I would someday be beautiful. It pleased me, and moreover it gave me a sense of security and self-confidence. Often when I was alone I would roll down the collar of my blouse so I could see my shoulders in the mirror. At night I did the same with my nightgown. I would sit and stare, completely absorbed in myself. It was as if nothing existed in the world besides myself and my reflection. One evening, though, when there was a blackout and I lit a candle, I really frightened myself. In front of me I saw my shadow spreading across the expansive wall, like a supernatural being, touching my bed and filling up the ceiling.

Aunt Theresa was right to say that this year we would have lots of poppies. The seeds seemed to have multiplied with the rain and the meadow was covered in them. Even in the garden, in the unplanted parts, there were square patches of red. They seemed to insist that something was going to happen soon. That's what Rodia says red means in a dream. I'm glad I chose red poppies for my straw hat—that way I could be in harmony with the whole world. And Maria, who chose red cherries, did all right too; their fruit is succulent and sweet. But as for Infanta's forget-me-nots, they are so rare.

I remember those years as if they were one day, one moment. On those late spring and summer afternoons we would spread out the cherry tablecloth on the little table on the porch. And when it came time for the sun to set and the day was cooling off, you would hear Aunt Theresa bumping around upstairs as if she were moving furniture, and then down the stairs she would come with her irregular gait, which sounded as if she were going to lose her balance and fall. You would see Mother come out of the house without making a sound and sit in her usual place, not facing the woods, but looking out on the open space of the old Tatoï Airport. Grandfather would also stop work; he would wash his hands and face and arrive refreshed from a hard day, ready to sit. I can still hear the sound of water running in the bathroom and in the garden. The wind felt warm. Mavroukos, staring at the running water, would start to bark, thinking the water was alive. Then in the distance Mother Kapatos would call her children, "Kostas, Koula, Hey!... Manolis!..." And Rodia would appear with a tray of tea and cakes. It was all perfect and melancholic.

Below the porch was the plot of garden that Grandfather had given me to plant whatever I wanted. I planted flowers of every kind. I didn't pay any attention to order, and I certainly didn't make designs, triangles, squares, or lines, but instead I just sprinkled the seeds randomly, whenever it was their time for planting. Often I'd try to forget where I had put them so it would be a surprise, so it would be as if they had grown there of their own accord. The colors and the kinds were all mixed up, packed tightly one against the other: yellow, red, mauve, sky blue, orange, some tall, others short, and others completely hidden under leaves. It was either very beautiful or very ugly. I'm still not sure which. Mother said it was from such things that you could understand a person's character; all you had to do was look at my garden and it was clear how disorganized I was. Everyone else called it "the crazy garden," and Grandfather, looking at it one day, said something to this effect: "You love nature, but you are not her slave. I am her slave. She makes me her servant, and therefore I can never get close to her."

Farther away, down by the cupola, Maria had her tiny vegetable garden. She had divided it into little squares, each for a different vegetable. And truly her peas were the best on the farm. They only came to five or six pounds. We could eat them all in two meals. And every time Maria would insist on taking only the smallest bite, just a taste at the end of her fork, so that she wouldn't deprive us of this extraordinary pleasure.

Infanta had chosen ten wild almond trees for her own plot. They didn't need any special care, frequent watering or digging, and as their fruit was not edible, they needed no harvesting. They were a joyous sight in the spring, and a sad one in the winter. Infanta would hold on to the branches, whether they were blossoming or bare, and rest there for a while. She was only a child then, but her hands were the hands of a grown woman.

So at that hour when the day was cooling off, I would be digging in my flower garden, Maria in her vegetable garden, Infanta would be watching her trees, and the grown-ups would be gathering on the porch around the cherry tablecloth. Not much time would elapse before Mr. Louzis, our frequent visitor, would arrive. Every day at almost exactly the same time we would hear the wooden gate creak and his heavy footsteps making the garden pebbles go scritch-scratch as if he were cracking them, and as he walked waving his arms and cane jerkily in the air, he would shake the lowest branches of the three pistachio trees lining the dirt driveway, so much so that I would often go check whether he had broken any. But somehow he never did. The only damage was the leaves that he would break off, squish in his hand, and toss to the ground as he walked, absentmindedly passing his cane from one hand to the other.

"Who could it be at this hour?" Aunt Theresa would always say. "I'm going inside just in case it's a stranger. I have no desire to see strangers." She got up hurriedly, as if someone were chasing her, and she would just manage to hide herself in the dining room off the porch, only to come out two minutes later: "Oh it's you, Mr. Louzis. And I was thinking you were a stranger."

"Please sit down," said Mother looking out over the open space of the old Tatoï Airport. "Rodia, the coffee ..."

Mr. Louzis did not drink tea, he said, except when he was very ill. "Don't make him coffee," I would whisper to Rodia secretly in the kitchen. "Why should we have to make it especially for him each time? He can just drink tea." "Why?" Rodia asked. "Because..."

In a little bit his coffee would arrive in a big teacup. Mr. Louzis sniffed it and lit his cigar. He took a sip and then a puff on his cigar, another sip, another puff, and this went on for an hour.

He was always well dressed. In the spring he wore an English suit of finely woven light gray wool; in the summertime, white linen or Indian silk. But he was very fat.

"So, what's new?" asked Grandfather rubbing his hands together. Mr. Louzis knew what was going on, not only in Athens, but all over the world. He would skip from one topic to the next with exceptional ease and a certain winning manner: from the wedding of so-and-so to the latest discovery in America, from a debate on art—was such and such really an authentic El Greco?—to the best method of grafting roses. He had traveled the world and seen many things. For the grown-ups his company was an invaluable pleasure. And for my grandfather, in particular, it meant a great deal: by putting together all that he said, the weddings, the rose grafting, and the latest discovery, he could get a general picture of the world. And in this way he no longer had to worry that he was living such a cut-off existence. And free of this worry, he could get on with living the way he liked—that is, cut off from all that. Mr. Louzis, without knowing it, gave my grandfather the right to live the life he wanted without feeling guilty. And for this my grandfather was eternally grateful.

I, on the other hand, had the sense that whatever he said carried the stamp of his loud laugh and heavy footsteps, and that things seen through his eyes couldn't help but be colored by his character, and somehow sullied. The greatest discovery became a small little nothing. And hearing my mother laugh at his jokes made me hide my face in my crazy garden and cry.

At that time we had a governess who taught us French and gave us baths on Saturday. Maria would have the first bath, then Infanta, and last of all, me. Bath day was the most exhausting day for Mlle. Zina. Just to wash Maria's hair, which was then very long, made her back ache. She used to get annoyed at me, too, because she always found a little dirt on the back of my neck, as if, she would say, I hadn't washed it all week. And the truth is that although I liked water, when it came time to get under the spigot I would always try to get the water to hit my back because it gave me the shivers if it touched my neck. It was only when I dove into the sea or the cistern headfirst that I didn't mind getting my neck wet.

So when I got into the bath last, the room was full of steam and smelling like soap; the water heater was red hot, the wood inside already embers. The extreme heat weakened my heartbeat, my eyes rolled back in my head, and it was as if I had fainted. But I didn't say anything because I liked the way it felt. It was as if I were asleep and awake, as if I were speaking in a foreign language. And my thoughts were foreign too, and although they were fuzzy, what I remembered of them was enough to fill me with shame.

The bath made Saturday different from every other day. We had tea earlier than usual and were not allowed any bread and jam in the event that it would be too heavy for our stomachs. In the evening we did not eat at the table, but had dinner in bed. We would slide into the clean sheets, our hair getting the pillow slightly damp, our skin shiny, our minds clean—the thoughts that only just before had filled me with shame had vanished, I could not even imagine that they had existed—and Rodia would bring each of us a tray with soup and boiled lamb's head. We would eat slowly, licking each bone, thoroughly enjoying the chance to play cannibals. I ate all the eyeballs—neither Infanta nor Maria liked them, they said they felt sorry for the lamb— and Maria ate all the tongues. We did not go to say good night to Mother; she came in to us. She bent over each of our beds, took our heads in her silky palms, and staring into our eyes, kissed us on both cheeks. Her skin was soft and white like the flowers in Mr. Louzis's greenhouse, and her eyes were black and shining like her hair. Mother was beautiful, very beautiful. I begged her to kiss me again, and she would either bend down and take my head in her hands again or pretend she didn't hear and leave.

"Mama, do you love me?"

"It's no time for talking, Katerina, go to sleep."

"Zezina, do you love me?"

"Are you still awake? Tomorrow I'll put you to bed a half hour earlier."

"Infanta, Maria, do you love me?"

"What's gotten into you tonight?"

They all laughed.

Mlle. Zina, who we often called Zezina, knew all the Becassine stories, but I liked *Sans Famille* best of all. At that time I firmly believed that comedy made life uglier, whereas tragedy enhanced it. I would read *Sans Famille* and cry, and feel great satisfaction. As the adventures and misfortunes of Remi increased, the stronger and more worthy of living I felt.

I loved Mlle. Zina a lot after she left. You see, while she was with us I had the sense that she was holding me back, that she would not let me do the things I wanted to do. This conviction, especially as it was unjustified, was all the more intense.

She was Swiss, and she had rosy cheeks with little red veins. I heard her talk so often about William Tell that even today I can't help but think that he is the greatest hero of all times. She also told me about the creamy Swiss milk, the snow-covered peaks, and the tarts that came out of her father's oven, steaming hot. I imagined myself sledding down from the highest peak and arriving with incredible speed right in front of the door of her father's bakery. I would leave the sled in the street. There you can leave whatever you want in the street, even money. No one steals. And I would help myself to one tart with apricots and one with strawberries. My empty mouth began to water; the make-believe smell of the hot pastry made my nostrils quiver. "There are even strawberries in the woods," said Mlle. Zina. "If you just go for a walk you fill a whole basket. But I couldn't eat them. If I put one in my mouth I would come down with a fever and chills."

It was really true. One time I remember I convinced her to try two strawberries from the garden, "just to see if you get the chills," and not a half an hour had passed before she was in bed almost unconscious.

We tortured her, poor dear. We would get her really angry so her blood would go to her head, and the tiny red veins in her cheeks would turn purple, and then we'd just laugh. But we mustn't forget that she was good, that it was she in fact who had chased away the fear that the other governess, Miss Gost, had instilled in us. Miss Gost would get up in the middle of the night and start playing the violin and hang white sheets over the mirrors. She would take us on long walks in the woods where she would make us sit obediently around her, and she would tell us how our souls had first belonged to other people or animals before us and how they would belong to them again when we died.

It really expanded my imagination to think of losing my soul, of it flying away like a bird. And if in another life I became a horse and the coachmen whipped me in the street?

"And it's for my next life that I'm learning the violin," she added with a look full of exaltation. "And if you become a pig or a cat, Miss Gost, how will you play the violin?" I remember asking her one day, laughing loudly, although my palms were sweaty from nervousness. "Nonsense," she muttered, white as a sheet. Miss Gost was always ashen pale; her hair was shiny and black, tucked behind her ears, and her dresses brightly colored.

Nights were hard on me at that time; I couldn't get to sleep, and when I finally did, my dreams were terrifying. Often I'd see a wave of sand passing before my eyes, and then it would blind me. I would try to open my eyelashes but they wouldn't open. I'd wake the whole house with my screams. Even now I'm unsure whether the wave of sand that blinded me was a dream or a product of my excited, sleepless imagination.

So we owed a lot to Zezina, who never talked to us about how our soul would leave us and instead let us run around and play, and whose insipid Swiss tales made for calm nights of sleep, all the rest forgotten. Her cheeks were rosy, not ashen pale, which in itself was something; her hair was a very light brown, with a few white hairs at her brow, which, though carefully plucked, would only multiply, forming a beautiful white crown. This bothered her immensely, though we insisted that it suited her.

Sunday was our day with Father, and it was always tense and melancholic. When we were with him all we could think about was when we were apart—that is, most of the time. So we always schemed up something crazy, something that would distract us totally: an excursion in his car to a faraway beach, some theater show that wasn't appropriate for our age, a film with horses running like mad across endless hills, or one with strange women. Once, I remember, we saw Greta Garbo kill an officer as he sat there in an armchair and then, because someone knocked on the door, proceed to talk in the most natural way, sitting on the arm of the chair next to the corpse pretending to caress him and flirt with him.

When Monday dawned we would tell everything to Marios, everything we'd seen and heard. Usually the sun wasn't even up yet and he would be over at our house ready to play, or so he said, but we knew he really came to find out what had happened. We'd start off pretending we didn't know why he was there. We'd decide what game to play. Then he would say, looking up at the sky,

"What day is today?"

"Monday. Why?"

"Oh, to figure out which classes I have homework in."

"Ahhh."

We couldn't last, though. Maria was the first to give in.

"You should have seen it, Marios ..." We'd sit down in a circle on the ground, and minutes would turn to hours, whole days, lifetimes.

The frogs have gone mad recently. It's the ones who live in the reeds on Aniksi Avenue, across from the doctor's, who start it all. You see, the large stream passes by there on its way down from Kefalari to water the fields, and the sound and the taste of the water, its color which is really a thousand colors, gets them drunk. The others hear them and answer. Then ours answer back, infrequently and measured at first, then more and more insistently, until they make a sound that wraps the whole garden like a night robe, their voice, without coloratura, like calm itself, while at other times frenzied, mad, as if in a paroxysmic fit. And there is one old frog whose husky voice makes it all seem very funny.

Usually at that time of day my sisters and I count the stars, letting the moon settle on our hair. But Maria gets this wild look.

"What are you thinking?" I ask her. We are outside, lying on our backs with our hands behind our heads.

"About bullfights."

I start to laugh.

"Yes," she whispers in my ear, "just imagine: the red sheet, the seething bulls, the men stabbing them with knives, or watching their own insides spill out. The women fanning themselves, waiting to give themselves to the winner; their pleasure, all beginning with the spectacle."

What strange things Maria said. I look at her. Of course she is twenty years old, but nonetheless ...

"Nonsense," says Infanta, and gets up to leave.

She goes to keep Aunt Theresa company. The two of them are inseparable. They embroider difficult patterns and read big books.

"Don't listen to her," Maria continues. "She doesn't know a thing about life. And she never will. She'll stay thick as a brick until she dies."

The frogs were already loud. The old frog hadn't joined in yet.

"You know everything's over with Nikos. Stefanos and Eleni are a part of our group now, and Eleni happened to like Nikos more, while I happened to like Stefanos. So we kind of traded."

And when I didn't say anything:

"What? So you're going to play Miss Self-Righteous like Infanta?"

"No, Maria, it's not that ..."

The trees bend down to strangle me, my legs turn to lead, the moon looks fake. Stefanos, Maria, Eleni, Nikos ... If things are that way, who am I to expect more?

"Why don't you pay attention to Marios?" I ask. "He loves you. When he comes here he can't take his eyes off you, and whenever I meet him in the street he asks about you."

"Ugh. He's a wimp, so thin, without any life in him." She rolls back and forth in the grass.

"I know that he's crazy about me."

Silence.

"Just between you and me, Katerina, the others are wimps too. Both Nikos and Stefanos. But it's a way to pass the time."

I'm not like Maria. I wouldn't let a boy touch me just to pass the time. Maybe I'll find someone who will watch the daisies blooming in the field with me, who will cut me a branch of the first autumn berries and bring it to me with the leaves still damp. Or maybe I'll set out to see the world alone.

"I can't understand the chattering that goes on between Aunt Theresa and Infanta," Maria adds, as if we had been talking about them the whole time. "How can she go and sit inside when the grass is so soft out here? Maybe I said something? Oh yes, about bullfights. Infanta!...Infanta!..." she calls, looking toward the house, up at Aunt Theresa's room. "Come on down! Infanta..."

Aunt Theresa's room is on the top floor, somewhat separate from the rest of the house. Aunt Theresa calls it her atelier, and she wants us to call it that too. She has a little bit of furniture, an easel, and on top of a table, her palette with the colors. In the right-hand corner there are lots of finished and half-finished paintings.

More than anything there, even more than the paintings themselves, I like to look at the palette with the colors. Those dashes of blue, orange, yellow, red, green shining there...Once when I was little I made a real mess; the magic of the colors tricked me into thinking that if I mixed them all together I would come up with something magnificent, something that no one had ever seen before. I remember I took all the tubes and emptied them onto the palette, put my hands in, and began to stir. When I had finished I was shocked. In front of me was a dull brown blob, not at all what I had expected. And as if the sadness wasn't enough, I got in trouble for it too.

Now I know that all the colors don't go together. Aunt Theresa taught me: "Red and blue make purple; blue and yellow, green."

Aunt Theresa's paintings are like carbon copies. She paints exactly what she sees, just as it is. She doesn't miss a thing—not a leaf or a blade of grass, or even a distant cloud. Although when she paints the distant cloud she makes it look like it's close up, and that ruins everything. But I do like a portrait she did of Infanta. Infanta is so beautiful... Like Botticelli's Aphrodite, Aunt Theresa says—a chaste Aphrodite. Without a doubt she is the most beautiful of all of us. Except that Maria's body is more lithe and shapely, and my eyes are brighter.

Aunt Theresa paints landscapes, portraits, and *natures mortes*. She's done lots of trees from our yard and from the nearby forest. But when I see them on the canvas, although they're the same shape and color as the real ones, it's as if they've lost their relationship to each other, as if each one is by itself, in its own landscape cleverly joined together by someone. As for her *natures mortes*, fruit is her favorite subject, particularly apricots and cut-open melons. "They're so convincing they make me want to eat them," she says, laughing. Me, I don't like them. Generally I dislike *natures mortes*, especially ones with fruit because fruit is for tasting, feeling, and smelling.

Infanta sits for hours in Aunt Theresa's atelier. She says she likes the view from up there, and the quiet. Down below there are Mother's nerves, Grandfather's complaints, our voices, Maria's laugh.... But that quiet is unnatural, and sometimes even frightening. Like scenes remembered from nightmares in which you are hurt, or being chased, when the earth opens up to swallow you, or you want to speak but you can't because your voice is stuck in your throat and no sound will come out, and you are trying to scream for help...

Nevertheless, Aunt Theresa is a kind person, kind and cowardly. She jumps at the slightest sound; her lip begins to tremble if the wind blows harder. "Someone is coming," she whispers. For her, "someone" is something bad. "Hmm, I think I heard something too," I say to scare her, but also because for me "someone" is anything unknown.

"She's still frightened because of what happened back then," Rodia said one evening, and then she told me the whole story.

We were baking some sweet potatoes in front of the fire. It's the only way to get Rodia by herself and make her talk. Because I want to know everything. I'm not indifferent like Infanta.

"Mrs. Theresa was a young thing when it happened," began Rodia. "The same age as Infanta, and she looked a lot like her too. They had all gone on an outing, your mother, your father, Aunt Theresa, and her fiancé, a tall young man with shiny hair and thick lips."

"What about me, Rodia?"

"You weren't even born yet. Mrs. Anna was three or four months pregnant with Maria. Anyway, there they were. After they had eaten and drunk, your mother and father lay down under some pine trees, and Aunt Theresa and her fellow decided to go for a walk. On the way they found a cave and went in to have a rest. But it seems the young man had other things on his mind . . . how should I put it . . ."

"Come on Rodia, tell me!"

"He made Aunt Theresa a woman against her will. There you have it. He took advantage of her."

"Ohhh . . ."

I can imagine her at that moment. Outside, the sun strong, the trees motionless, resin dripping freely like wine from the trunks, the pebbles hot as coals, the insects quiet. Inside the cave is refreshingly cool, the moss damp, drops of moisture hanging from the rocks, not falling. How long can a drop hang like that in the air? And Aunt Theresa unable to give herself to him, to the experience. A shiver ran down my spine.

"But Rodia, isn't it true that when a woman loves a man she gives herself to him?"

"Not before she's married, my child—never. It's a sin. And besides, it was the way he did it. Mrs. Theresa didn't want to. So what was he doing? I remember her—the poor thing—after it happened. She was like a crazy woman for a while. From then on she never wanted to see him or hear about him. She couldn't even get near another man . . ."

Now I understand why Aunt Theresa's voice trembles when she says "someone's coming." Why her trees on the canvas are separate from each other as if they belong to different landscapes. And even why her fruit has no taste, feel, or smell.

Nonetheless, lately she has been painting a lot. She stands facing the window. She surveys the property, her eye focusing on the woods, where the pine trees are short, round, close to the earth, others spindly with graceless branches reaching to the sky, all with a crown of haze, a dim crown hovering above them at midday.

"It will be a panorama," she says.

Half shutting her one eye, she draws back from the easel to see better.

"A panorama," Infanta repeats.

Infanta never hunches her back when she embroiders. It is always perfectly straight. When a crown of midday heat encircles her, she chases it away with one quick motion.

"And how do you like this?"

She spreads her embroidery out on her knees. There are peacocks, lots of peacocks with their tails fanned out. Their legs are hidden, because peacocks have ugly legs, and they know it. For a whole year Infanta's been working on it, and it'll take another two more years to finish. It's going to be for Aunt Theresa's big armchair, the one next to the window.

"Sometimes I try to count the stitches but I get too dizzy..."

Just thinking how many feathers each tail has and how many colors each feather... It's a form of protection, though. When Infanta embroiders she doesn't feel scared. Or uneasy. Or anything else.

"It will be a masterpiece," Aunt Theresa says loudly. "You are approaching perfection, Infanta."

For both of them perfection is their goal. They often talk about it. In painting, in embroidery, it doesn't matter. Because when you embroider something beautiful you become beautiful inside, and the more beautiful it is, the more beautiful you become.

"That's why you must live alone, Infanta."

"Alone?" she asked.

Now that she knows, she doesn't ask anymore. She sits proud, upright over her embroidery with the peacocks. And each day her eyes grow more and more distant.

I used to think she had Marios on her mind, because she blushed when she heard his whistle and saw him climbing up the hill from his house to ours, and because when he arrived instead of joking with him the way Maria and I did, she whispered a hasty greeting and went up to the atelier.

One day when I caught her following him with her gaze from behind the half-closed shutters until he disappeared around the corner of Aniksi Avenue, I couldn't refrain from asking: "Infanta, if you want to see Marios why don't you come down when he's here? Or maybe it's easier to idealize him . . . at a distance, especially when his back is turned?" "Idiot," she replied, "I was looking at the meadow. Got that? At the meadow."

We never talked about it again. Even if I had asked, Infanta wouldn't have answered. Who knows, I might have been mistaken. Maybe she wasn't thinking about him and really was looking at the meadow.

As for Marios, it's obvious he is only interested in Maria. I figured that out years ago. We were high up in the big fig tree playing knights and castles, having no idea that it would be the last year we would play that game, that we were growing older by the day, by the hour. I saw Marios touch Maria by mistake in the middle of the game. He quickly looked down at the ground where he was standing. We were high up, the queens of the castle, and he was the conqueror below. He grew paler, and paler . . .

"Marios," I yelled, "what's the matter?"

"Oh, the sun is getting to me," he stammered. And then after a bit, "I'm never playing this game again."

He didn't even want to roughhouse with her anymore because she would throw herself on top of him, and when she wasn't winning she'd even bite and scratch him.

So from that year on the games stopped. We turned to studying and serious endeavors. Every once in a while in the evening Marios comes over, neatly dressed, and somehow formal. He doesn't want us to muss up his hair like back then. Ever since he started university he takes himself so seriously. He reads really thick and heavy books, and when we suggest a walk or excursion he says he's very sorry but he has to study or he has to go to Athens to the laboratory. Marios's going to be a doctor, a surgeon to be exact. "Medicine comes naturally to the Parigori family," Mrs. Parigori always says. And then as if by chance she slips in the fact that we are lucky to be their neighbors: "You never know, after all we are only human . . . Something could go wrong."

Thank God nothing ever does. We are all very healthy. Even Grandfather, who is seventy-five years old, never goes to the doctor. He has a big medical dictionary, and if he feels sick he opens it, and reads, and figures out his own diagnosis and cure. Rodia is the only one who has a problem. Her feet hurt when it's damp. But the doctor says he can't do anything about that. The same way he can't lessen the pains of Tasia, the gardener's wife, when she gives birth. For each of her three children she turned the world upside down. Even though their house is at the far end of the property, her screams reached us—even Grandfather in his room. He had to close the windows and doors and put cotton in his ears.

I really felt sorry for poor Tasia. As I watched her belly grow I got more and more anxious; I wanted to explode, as if I was the one carrying all that weight inside me. Maria was very interested. She would go near the house when the pains began and hide in the bushes and wait. In a bit she would see the doctor arrive with Mother Kapatos. She wasn't a real midwife, Mother Kapatos, but she knew a lot about it, and Tasia wouldn't give birth without her. They were mortal enemies, swearing at each other all the time. One would be jealous of the other and at the slightest excuse pick a fight. But things changed the minute Tasia was in her eighth month. She would prepare sweets and send them to her. She'd bring her children milk. On the eve of the birth the official visit took place. "Why do you go out of your way?" Mother Kapatos would ask. "Now why shouldn't I drop by for a visit? We live so close, we're neighbors."

And it was true, Mother Kapatos's house was only two steps away, at the edge of the woods. Poor, half tumbling down, one room and a kitchen. What's a woman to do with five kids? Mr. Kapatos, the husband, spent most of his life in jail with small breaks—vacations let's say. As soon as one sentence was over he tried to get a new one; his family was used to this. "Where's your father?" "In jail," the children would answer, as if they were saying "in the country." And the littlest one confessed to me that they do much better when he's not around because "he hits and has a fierce temper."

So Maria would hide and listen. The last time she was even able to get a look. She had snuck in at the side of the house by the window while I waited anxiously a little further away for a firsthand report. She came back upset and very red in the face. She tried to smile with her mouth, but her eyes were all teary. I didn't understand anything she said.

Now Nontas, Tasia's last child, is two years old, and we are two years wiser. We see things differently. It's only Infanta we're not sure about, because she never talks about that stuff.

Who knows what will become of Infanta.

"She's the most modest and beautiful of all," says Mother. "She'll get the best husband."

And Aunt Theresa laughs enigmatically.

II. AT THE PARIGORIS' HOUSE

THE DAY is hot, the mind empty, the leaves motionless, the body and soul, too. We try to give meaning to what we see. At times the dead are living, and at other times the living, dead. I go visit the cows. They look at me as if it's the first time they've seen me. The hens gather around me looking for crumbs that I don't have. Romeo, Infanta's favorite horse, turns his backside to me. Mavroukos's gravestone, which is always cool, is hot today. My old buddy would have been sweating. He used to get hot in the summer and hang out his thick tongue and pant, his bulldog face taking on a tragic expression. Then he would climb up on the ledge of the cistern and wait for me to push him in because he didn't have the courage to jump in himself.

From the half-open door of the dining room I watch Mother set the table. She always does this herself, with the greatest care. She handles the knives and forks as if they were made of glass, spacing everything evenly, in the middle the decanter of olive oil and the salt—Grandfather forbids pepper, he thinks it's bad for the health and the bread in a basket, already cut.

She looks as if she is thinking hard as she sets the table, as if she's studying each of her movements. I look at her full body, her shiny black hair in a bun that hangs heavily at the nape of her neck.

"Mother…"

To be sure, her waist has filled out and further down she's quite plump. Her cheeks aren't rosy, but she still is young and beautiful.

"Ah, you scared me," she says. "How did you come in without my noticing?"

And seeing my bare feet, "Barefoot again? Where are your sandals?"

I explain to her how I first watered the garden and then went to visit the cows and Romeo and the hens. I didn't say anything about Mavroukos's grave.

"I don't think I'm ... Oh, Mother, I'm so bored today. I don't know what's wrong with me. I don't...."

My voice begins to shake.

"Are you sick?"

I lie down on the couch on my stomach. She comes over and puts her hand on my forehead. I wish she would smother me in her breasts, like when I was a baby and she was still nursing me. If she knows I'm not sick why does she ask? If she really wanted to know what was wrong I might tell her. She is about to ask—her voice gets warmer, sweeter—but she draws back. There's always a certain trepidation between us. We can't give away secrets that we don't have.

"The sun must have got to you," she concludes.

Too bad, Mother ... And I would have told you so many things about the Land of the Houyhnhnms and about Mavroukos's grave and about the things I can see from the top of the walnut tree.

"Rodia," she calls. "A lemonade for Katerina."

She glances at the table and adjusts a fork that's too far from a plate. A deep sigh escapes from her chest. To have children of your own and not know what they hide inside them ...

"What is it, Mother?"

"Nothing."

"But ... you sighed."

"I didn't sigh. I breathed."

And a little later: "I can't understand that restlessness of yours. Where did you get it from? Both your father and I are ..."

"What about our Polish grandmother?"

She turns abruptly, her eyes fierce; she isn't looking at me the way a mother should.

"How dare you!"

Her face is bright red.

"Yes, so there!" I shouted. "You all hate her. But I love her. Because she was beautiful, because she played music not the way you do, because she knew how to ride a horse across the fields."

I roll back and forth on the couch like a little animal. My lip trembles. It's because I'm nervous. Mother turns white. Perhaps she's thinking that she sacrificed herself for no reason, that she should have got remarried and started her life over again, as the saying goes.

I feel sorry for her. I want to go over and kiss her hand, to say thank you, thank you...

"Katerina, come over close," she whispered. "Sit next to me. Since you know the whole story... One shouldn't criticize one's parents, but the Polish grandmother was not a good mother. She went off with a foreign man, gallivanting around the world... without a home, without a country...."

"But she was free, happy."

"No one knows that. But come now, calm down, my little one. Did I tell you about the yellow dress—the seamstress is coming tomorrow to fit it."

She caresses my hair and kisses me. I must try hard not to give in to her.

"Well, I love her," I say. "And nothing will change my mind."

At that moment we hear the doorbell. It's Leda, Marios's little sister.

"A message," she says. "Marios is inviting all three of you to a party next week. But he told me to give the message to Maria." "We'll have a great time," she whispered in my ear—she's thirteen—"There will be older boys, friends of Marios's from university."

The Parigoris' house was the last one on Aniksi Avenue. Two stories high and large, it contrasted sharply with the other houses in the area, even more so because it didn't have animals, vegetables, or fruit trees. On the north side there was a row of cypresses that blocked the wind; in the garden there were mimosas, acacias, flowers of every kind. In the front there was a huge, round flower bed with deep green grass, carefully manicured; and in the middle, six rows of roses fanning out like spokes—red ones, white ones, pink ones, yellow ones, and others whose colors are hard to describe, reminiscent of the pale color of tea or of clouds forgotten long after the sun has set. For two years in a row Mrs. Parigori's roses had received first prize at the state fair. And another year she had exhibited a strange cactus that looked like a human head. Mrs. Parigori really did love flowers—digging the flower beds, watering them, decorating the house with them. Mr. Parigori used to say—it was his stock joke—that he had fallen in love with his wife when he saw her arrange a vase of flowers. Of course no one believed him. He was at a gathering of friends, the story went, when he saw her hands with their long, pale fingers take a handful of cyclamens and spread them gently, sparsely in a shallow glass vase, and their stems underwater, an ashen green, and her hands even paler, moving about like a woman's naked body in the sea. One month later he asked her hand in marriage. Laura was shocked. She didn't love him; she didn't even know him very well. Her mother, however, insisted: "He's rich, he has a future, and he's a good boy. Of course he's not our social equal"—the Montelandis boasted that they were one of the first families from the Ionian islands—"but people of our social standing would ask for a dowry and you don't have one."

So they got married. He brought with him his love and the promise of a comfortable life, and she, her connections with the best of society and those long, pale fingers. A successful combination. Not even three years had passed before Mr. Parigori was known as the best doctor in Athens. He worked hard: hospitals, house visits, conferences. In the evening though, when the sun went down, he liked to return to his house in the country, to stretch out in his armchair—near the fire in the winter, on the porch in the summer—to smoke a cigar slowly and watch his wife. When Marios was born, his happiness changed, took another form. Laura's voice, her movements, became more distant; it was the cry of his boy, his first steps, that were closest to his heart. "What a sweet boy he is," he whispered. And he grew annoyed when he heard his wife say "the sweetest boy in the whole wide world," because he wanted to be the only one to think and say such things.

As for Laura, in the beginning of their marriage, her husband consumed her totally. He, that is, and the care of the house. Later the hours began to drag. A little reading in the morning, a little sewing, some gardening... But the afternoon was endless. The evening, even worse.

It was therefore necessary that Marios appear on the scene. When she felt the first kick inside her, the first sign that he was really there, it was as if a long road appeared before her, straight and difficult, with no turns. The kick came on Good Friday, in the afternoon, in the fifth month of her pregnancy. Every so often the bells of the nearby church tolled Christ's death. She was resting on the window, leaning out to see the heavy sky. Always clouds on Good Friday, it can't be a coincidence...When suddenly, thump, thump... She leaned over and looked at her belly and placing her hands gently but firmly on top...thump, thump...That's what it was. She broke down in tears and sobbed like a child. Out of joy, of course. Although, in some far away corner of her soul there was also a nostalgia for the things she would never again experience. The road she had seen before her was straight and narrow. She would gain in depth and lose in breadth. That night John gave her a good dose of valerian. "Pregnancy often affects a woman's nerves," he said.

When Marios was three or four years old she would take him by the hand and go for walks. The ravine was nearby. In the spring its banks were covered with white and purple crocuses, and all year round there was maiden-hair. Mrs. Parigori would stretch out on the grass with a slightly old-fashioned novel—she didn't like modern ones—and the little one would throw stones into the stream. He had figured out that each one made a different sound as it hit the water, so he never grew tired of the game. He sometimes also liked to throw in bits of straw to see where they went. Some would merge with the water and sail off into the distance, others would be swept up by the wind before they even hit the surface, and others would get caught on a big rock that happened to be in the way. "Go help them along," his mother told him one afternoon when she saw him sadly eyeing the bits of straw that had gotten stuck on the rock. He didn't want to. He was scared he'd come to the same fate. "Now don't be a coward. The water is only ankle deep. Go on." He broke into tears and clung to her neck.

He wouldn't let go. Laura felt his two little hands strangling her. She looked up at the banks of the ravine—high, high up. "A bit of physical exercise would do Marios good," she told her husband that evening.

Leda was born when Marios was nine years old. She was a pale child, with mousy hair, gray eyes, and a difficult personality. She did whatever she felt like, which drove Mrs. Parigori to despair, but amused her father. She ran around with the kids from the neighborhood catching cicadas and may beetles or stealing fruit from nearby gardens. Lately she had taken up with the Kapatos kids, who were particularly good at stealing fruit. When Mrs. Parigori found out, she grounded her, but to no avail. Leda still went off on her afternoon jaunts. As for Marios, he is deep in his books. He also has a complete skeleton to study on. When he touches it, he tries not to think that Maria's body is like that inside.

When dancing, Infanta never lets go in the arms of her partner, whereas Maria overdoes it. Mrs. Parigori's garden is phantasmagoric. I'm wearing my yellow dress and I'm very pleased with myself. "The color of hate," Petros whistles at me. "I guess you wanted me to wear red, huh?" "So you don't love anyone?" "No one," I sigh, and the petals of the oleander fall at my feet. "Not me, not even a little?" He puts his arm around my waist." "If you want to dance," I tell him, "I'll get up. Otherwise, take your hand off me because it makes me feel seasick." He laughs loudly. "What a joker you are, what a joker."

How could Venetian lanterns and Negro spirituals ever go together? Not to mention Mrs. Parigori's roses in full bloom, about to wilt, with no prize this year?

Leda had the idea of wearing a Pierrot hat, even though it wasn't carnival time. No one can stop her. In the end she's free to do as she pleases and she knows it. That's why she wore the hat. I'd like to wear a Pierrot hat but I haven't the courage. Then I'd have to kiss all the boys and let them squeeze my waist. What would that be like? The petals of the oleander fall at my feet. On their way down they brush against my hair and tickle my ears. I laugh. "Why are you laughing?"

Stefanos asks. I can't say that I'm ticklish because I'm sure he'd misunderstand.

"I was just wondering what would happen if we were all real Pierrots."

"There's no such thing as a real Pierrot. They're all fake."

"Leda, come and kiss your grandmother good night," Mrs. Parigori calls out.

"I'll be right back," Leda tells Alekos. "Now don't dance with Margarita."

Thirty cherry drinks and thirty lemonades on a tray make a pretty sight. "Which would you like?" "One of each, thank you." I take a red one in my right hand and a yellow one in my left. *Just think, Petros mentioned my dress. There you go, he wanted me to wear red. Well, let him wait. Stefanos is nicer. But he's with Maria.* They're dancing like limpets stuck to a rock. Maria touches her cheek to his, with the utmost naturalness. *How can Maria be so natural?* Her dress which is the deep red of a watermelon doesn't cover her. But you can't blame Maria for that; no matter what she wears she never seems sufficiently dressed.

Infanta is an angel. Infanta is wearing white. *Why are you so restrained, Infanta? Why do you never give in to the dance, to the evening as it unfolds?* The boys bow to her and she dances with them stiffly. "The most beautiful are always the coldest," Alekos whispers to Marios, and he looks over at Infanta, trying to figure her out.

"Maria's a good dancer," I hear Stefanos say, and I watch his eyes following her amidst the other couples. "Oh, she's a little heavy," I say, because he has white teeth and a wide chest. "But, of course, compared to Eleni she's much better." "Would you like to dance?" "Why not?" We dance around with everyone else. I like the wild dances. "Do you have skulls and things like Marios?" "No," he laughs. "I study law." "Ah, law."

It grows dark. "The lanterns should be lit," Mrs. Parigori says. "It's still early," Leda argues. "No, it's time." And to Aunt Theresa who is sitting by the window, "Youth, a summer evening, and darkness are a dangerous mix." But the lanterns are only on the veranda and the garden is big. Suddenly everyone decides to visit the garden. "But at this hour you will see nothing," Mrs. Parigori complains. "No, no," they insist. They all rush off together. Then they separate like the little garden paths. Two by two. Telling secrets, whispering, touching...The girls' skirts brush against the boys' pants, and the wind blows the girls' hair across the boys' foreheads. But the girls hold back. "After I've washed my hair," says Eleni, "I can't do a thing with it." "It's divine," says Emilios, trying to kiss a curl in the dark, which has boldly managed to fall across his chin. "Don't, don't, Nikos will see us," she says laughing into her hands. "And here I thought Stefanos wasn't supposed to see us." "With Stefanos...now...there, do you see them?" And she points behind a tree where a boy and girl are tightly wrapped in an embrace: Stefanos and Maria kissing shamelessly. I see them. Marios too. It must bother him. I take him by the arm. "Marios, she doesn't know what she's doing. Don't think that she does..." He's shaking all over. "She doesn't love anyone," I tell him. "It's just that she wants to live." "To live?" "Yes, she has this idea that this is what life is about." "Have you ever watched bees?" she says. "They flit from one flower to the next taking the best from each." "I hate her. I really do." "Me too." I feel Marios's eyes on me. Why did I say me too? Because of Stefanos? I feel ashamed. "Because she makes you so miserable," I add.

"Infanta...Infanta," a voice cries. It's Aunt Theresa. "Where is Infanta?" she asks anxiously. "Oh...somewhere around here." "What's the matter?" "Nothing, I just brought her a jacket. She had a cold yesterday." "I hadn't noticed." "Infanta...Infanta." We find her sitting on a bench with Emilios and Nikitas. "What were you talking about?" Aunt Theresa asked. "About horses," said Nikitas. "Infanta knows all about them." "Yes, she can even gallop," I add. "You should come over one day and race with her." Aunt Theresa gives me an angry look. Infanta smiles. She is so beautiful, my God so beautiful... In the waning light with her white dress and her long neck, she looks like a swan. She's put her hair up. Her neck is almost womanly. She lets her blue jacket hang off her shoulders. With her right palm she touches it distractedly; the material is soft like the fur of a cat. "My, it's hot," she says after a bit and tosses it onto the bench. She gets up and goes over to the veranda, leaving Aunt Theresa with the two boys. *Why are you so restrained, Infanta, why, when it only makes you unhappy?*

The wine is strong. "An hors d'oeuvre?" We've lost all feeling in our legs, and are very content. We sing the Greek song: "Have you seen Anthoula, the fairest of them all?" And on the radio an American woman syncopates the beat, "I saw her late last night..." She continues, "boarding a boat..." Here she reaches the climax. "Bound for a foreign land." The woman's voice cracks. A sob. Heartache here, heartache there. An orange moon appears from behind the mountain and falls on the reeds, the stream is gurgling, the frogs begin their nightly song, an owl gives a shrill hoot landing on the roof. I wish I could take it all in, hold it in my arms or be held in its arms. Something is swelling inside me, getting larger and larger... I sigh. "What's the matter. Katerina? Are you sad?" everyone asks. "No," I answer. "I'm perfectly happy," I'd have whispered in Mavroukos's ear if he were still alive, because he too would often lower his head between his paws in the evenings, and sigh deeply. Inside of him something was surely swelling and overflowing. "It's time to go," Aunt Theresa says.

One always has to leave just when the party's getting good. "It was wonderful," we all say to Mrs. Parigori, "wonderful." "Good night." "Good night."

On the way home we're all quiet. Finally, when we're just about there, Maria says, "I didn't like Eleni's dress at all."

III. FATHER AND MR. LOUZIS

YESTERDAY we went to see Father. He lives in Athens on Aristotelous Street, with Grandmother and his brother Agisilaos. Their house is neither old nor new. It's on the first floor, and across the way on one corner there's a clinic—it's a maternity clinic and there's a sign with a blue cross and the word "quiet"—and on the other corner there's a taverna with a courtyard and a climbing vine that blossoms in the spring. I mention the clinic and the taverna because when I think of my father's house it's the mixed-up smell of medicine and wine in the street that I remember, and also the idea of women giving birth as they listen to people singing in the taverna and of people singing as they listen to women screaming.

I remember one day when Maria, Infanta, and I were looking out the window, we saw a car pull up in front of the clinic and a young couple get out—the girl didn't look any older than Maria. "It won't hurt at all, you'll see," the guy was telling the girl, and she was smiling, though her forehead was covered in sweat. A few hours later the same car came and picked them up. He helped her in. Her eyes had a deep sadness about them, and her hand seemed to want to touch her belly, to check it, but she kept pulling it away, ashamed. "Must be an abortion," Maria said, letting out such a screech you'd have thought they'd taken *her* insides out.

Father's house is not very nice. It has a long, graceless corridor with doors that open into the bedrooms. The dining room is dark. And the kitchen is a brownish gray, which no matter how much you scrub never changes color. Every once in a while a cockroach appears and scampers across the black and white tiles. "This week I'll exterminate them for good," Grandmother says. "I've got a new cure." And she repeats the threat every now and again.

But I like my father's bedroom. It's strange. It has the normal furniture for a bedroom but instead of clothes, combs, brushes, and other such items, there are tools, wires, ham radios, the hull of a model ship... There are also books in French and English full of machines and numbers and algebraic equations: stacks of books that all seemed the same to us. But two are different and are set apart on a small shelf—*Robinson Crusoe* and *The Jungle Book*. It seems no matter what we do in our lives we always have these stories with us. Once a week when we would come in from the country for a visit he would read them to us from beginning to end. All three of us would lie on his big bed with half-closed eyes, listening. Now we are older and embarrassed to ask him and he is embarrassed to suggest it. So there are huge silences full of *Robinson Crusoe* and *The Jungle Book* as if he were still reading and we were still listening. Those silences make us all very sad.

"What are you inventing these days, Father?" we ask in order to interrupt the silence.

"A radio with a system that..." He begins to explain how it works. We like to listen to him even if we don't understand a thing. When he talks about thunderbolts, rain, and other natural phenomena, though, it makes more sense. In fact he's much easier to understand than our science teacher. It's because he has his own way of seeing things, a simple, straightforward way, and so his explanations are also like that.

"What is the rainbow made of?" he asks out of the blue.

And when we don't reply, "There you go, you know all that ancient Greek and you don't know about the rainbow..."

Father has a nine-to-five job. He's a banker. But he spends all the rest of his time with his machines and his books. It seems that even in the old house when he lived with Mother he did the same thing. It was perhaps the main reason they separated. That, and his unfaithfulness. When I was little I couldn't understand how someone as pure as my father could ever be unfaithful. Now I understand.

I can't remember much about the old house. It was near Lykabetos hill and it had a terrace that looked out on Faliron. Father lived with us and we had a bloodhound named Dick. I also remember two Chinese vases in the two corners of the living room. But nothing else. Maria, however, remembers a lot. Sometimes she tells us stories, and Infanta and I feel sad.

Almost every week on Sunday we went to the sea with Father. He had an ancient car that looked like a bomb, which we called "Kara-ïskaki." Once when we were driving in Athens a street urchin had called it that, after the revolutionary war hero I guess, and it stuck. Father's car was not just any old car, so it deserved a name. It was brown, gray, or maybe khaki, and its insides were lined with dark red leather, a luxury that contrasted strikingly with the rest of its appearance. It was high above the ground, open-topped, with its motor up in the front, separate from everything else, giving it a dog face. The back resembled the tail of the hoopoe bird and had a little wooden chest inside where we tossed our bathing suits, fishing gear, and whatever else we happened to have with us. All in all, it was a car with personality and a provocative appearance.

Often our cousins, Andrikos and Ellie, came with us. Andrikos was little, but Ellie was the same age as Infanta. She was a dark-haired, small-boned girl with an ugly nose, but the most beautiful eyes. She had a sweet way of talking, and she talked a lot. We really loved Ellie. We could talk about the most ordinary, everyday things with her without them ever sounding stupid. When they came to our house in the country for holidays we would all sleep in the same room. We'd make solemn promises and wake up in the middle of the night to whisper secret wishes we'd never admitted to each other, and which mostly we made up on the spur of the moment. Or we'd tell each other's future from the moon: such and such would happen if it was at a slant, such and such if it was straight up and down. We really had a great time together.

So Ellie would come on Sundays, and sometimes Uncle Agisilaos, too; that's when the fun really began. Uncle Agisilaos was like a big kid, loving and irresponsible. He had a way of being unpredictable that was thoroughly charming. You could wait for him in Kifissia and he would be looking for you in Faliron knowing perfectly well that you were in Kifissia. That's the way he was in everything he did. He had no sense of time, and no sense that there was such a thing as evil in the world. It was as if he lived on a desert island playing with pebbles all day long. Father was also a little like a child playing with pebbles. He too seemed to know nothing about evil. The only difference was that if you were waiting for him in Kifissia, he would be there to meet you.

Father and Uncle Agisilaos looked alike. They were both rather short with black hair and their eyes were always sparkling with the reflection of the sea. That's because they're from Mesolonghi, and they spent their childhood fishing there. Before they set out they would hang a white sheet from the window to see what the weather was like. On the water they talked only about necessities: the fishing line, the bait, the way the fish were biting. And in the late afternoon when the sun had become orange and the sea an orange reclining woman, they ceased talking altogether.

Not only did Father and Uncle Agisilaos look alike, but they had the same obsessions. For example, they would only put gas in Kara-ïskaki when the red light came on. For this reason we often ended up in the middle of nowhere late at night out of gas. Once Mother and Grandfather came out searching for us because they were sure we'd been killed on the Sounion Road. Instead they found us whooping it up. We had spent the day at the sea. We were driving along, our skirts pulled over our swimsuits, holding a bucket full of fish, when suddenly the motor turned over once or twice and the car stopped in front of a sandy beach. Father tried to get it to start again but nothing happened. We all got out happily. It was already getting dark, so we lit a fire and grilled the fish and sat around and sang and ate. Uncle Agisilaos thought of fixing coffee. Everything he needed was in the trunk: a gas stove, a pot. There was also an empty gas can. Father took it and stood at the side of the road with the hope that someone would stop and give us gas. Every time a car passed he would raise the can in the air. One or two cars stopped, but they didn't have any gas. After a long time, when the songs and jokes had reached a high pitch, we saw two headlights in the distance. Father held the can up high. The car stopped and out stepped Mother. She was disheveled and in tears. We grew silent. Only Uncle Agisilaos ate a final fish, tossing it up in the air and catching it in his mouth.

"What's going on? What happened to you? Are you all right?" Mother screamed.

"Just wonderful. We're making coffee," was Father's reply.

"Miltos, you haven't changed a bit."

Mother strode furiously down to the beach to see for herself if we were all right. Near the fire there was a towel with cheese and bread. Her high heel got stuck in the cheese. Mother bent over and took off her shoe to remove the cheese. At the same moment Uncle Agisilaos began serving coffee as if he were sitting in a living room, offering the first cup to her. Mother looked at the cup and then at Uncle Agisilaos with contempt. In the meantime Maria, Infanta, and I had gotten to our feet and were standing completely still. Mother grabbed us and pushed us toward the car, where Grandfather was waiting. At the last moment I managed to give Father a kiss. He was still standing there with the can in his hand. We all squeezed in next to Grandfather; Mother sat next to the driver. When the car started, Father lifted up the can and said, half to the driver, half to Mother, "Do you by any chance have some gas?" Mother turned to the driver and said, "Let's go." Father was left at the side of the road with the can, while Uncle Agisilaos lit a cigarette and enjoyed his coffee.

Those Sundays will remain with me exactly as I lived them. I can't forget a single detail. It was then that I got to know the world of the sea. Having grown up with ants, lizards, and frogs, we found the waves shocking. We let the crabs sink their claws into our flesh so that the salt got all mixed up with our blood. When the fish touched our bodies, we could feel how cold they were. And we hoped that we would come upon a whirlpool so that we could experience the sweet taste of death but not actually have to die.

Maria did the sidestroke, the "ladies' stroke" as it was called. She would stay in the water for a little and then lie in the sun on her back, becoming more and more relaxed, not speaking loudly or laughing, her face growing sweeter, her gait, childlike, her breasts smaller, her eyes brighter, more transparent. *How pure you are on Sundays, Maria . . .*

Infanta had also changed. It was as if she were looking at everything askew. She stupidly laughed at anything and made superfluous gestures. She teased Father and Uncle Agisilaos, and wouldn't keep still for a minute. Of course it probably made a difference that Aunt Theresa was not around.

Ellie and I used to swim far out. By the time we got back to the beach our skin would be tight, our breath easy. We would soak up the sun, eat bread and pears, and praise God. Then Uncle Agisilaos would start telling his Mesolonghi stories . . .

Our place in the country is small, whereas the sea is immense. On Sunday nights I could never sleep.

On Mondays the routine began all over again. We were completely consumed with the approaching birth of our rabbit's first litter. We made her a nest in an old fruit packing case, and lined it with hay. She added her own soft fur. We all waited. The rabbit sniffed around, smelling her nest and chewing on a green leaf we gave her to distract her from the pain—we were sure she was in great pain, and would have been disappointed to learn this was not so. When her time came, she took up the appropriate position and gave birth, hardly groaning at all.

Infanta didn't pay much attention to all this. She was more concerned with Romeo's needs: his food, his currying, his exercise. Often at teatime she would devise ways to steal sugar, like putting a lump in her mouth and then running off to give it to Romeo.

The story of how she acquired that horse is a rather peculiar one. One day, the year before last, I think, we had gone to Mr. Louzis's estate, the three of us and Mother. We were invited for the first strawberries. Actually we children were not really the point. Mr. Louzis was more interested in Mother. At times his eyes would rest on her shoulders, her hair, and stay there. Mr. Louzis's estate was grand, and his house the largest and most luxurious in the area. It was even bigger than David's, which had been closed for four years anyhow, ever since David and Ruth had gone back to England.

It had rooms with high ceilings and decorated walls, valuable paintings and rare porcelain. In the winter he burned huge logs in his fireplaces and his face became redder with yellowish highlights. He even had a housekeeper who made creamy desserts with pheasant eggs. She was a woman with either white or blond hair and eyes that were blue and angelic, but with a devilish glint. We were scared of her and took great efforts to never be left in a room alone with her. "Miss Katerina, come and see the black rabbit." I pretended that I was playing with the dog. "And a carnation as big as a chrysanthemum."

"What wonderful desserts Mrs. Aphrodite makes!" Mother would say. "Just watch out she doesn't poison you," I retorted one evening as we walked home, and everyone broke into laughter.

So on that particular day Mr. Louzis showed us around the whole property. He had fruit trees of every type, a vegetable garden, and beautiful flowers. In the greenhouse I saw some white flowers that had petals as thick as flesh and a very heavy scent.

"If you will allow me, I would like to send you a pot of those flowers," he said to Mother.

"I would be pleased to receive such a gift," she replied.

"The only difficulty is that they need a great deal of attention," he said. "And heat, a great deal of heat."

"I will take good care of them," Mother replied.

When we arrived at the stables and pushed open the wooden door, Infanta let out a loud cry, something between an "ah" and an "ooh." She was staring at a young colt with a cinnamon-colored coat. His head was magnificent, rather small with huge, sweet eyes and a long neck. His body was perfectly shaped, nimble, with sleek legs that he lifted every once in a while as if asking permission to run. Beneath his shiny coat you could imagine his red blood. He was a horse of great force and pride.

Infanta went up to him, placed her hand on his head just above his nose, and her eyes grew misty. "Watch out," said the man minding him. "He's very nervous and sometimes ill-tempered." Infanta didn't take her hand away. She rested it there with even greater confidence, and with the other she began to pat his neck. The horse grew restless and began pawing the floor. It was about to turn around when Infanta looked deep into his eyes. The horse calmed down immediately, letting out a soft neigh as if to caress her. Infanta began to cry.

Outside on the porch Mr. Louzis and Mother were waiting for us. They sat opposite each other. Between them there was a table spread with an apricot linen tablecloth. On the table was a glass bowl of cut strawberries, sugar, and sweet wine.

Maria and I ate with gusto, but Infanta barely tasted them. Her eyes were still misty, and when she tried to speak she sounded choked-up. Suddenly she coughed two or three times as if clearing her throat and said very loudly, "I want that horse."

We turned to look at her. Her lips had gone white.

"I want that horse," she repeated. "The colt with the cinnamon-colored coat."

Mother found herself in a very difficult position. She made desperate signs in Infanta's direction, raising her eyebrows, and lowering them. She didn't know what to do. Infanta took no notice. She was staring far off into the distance as if at the horse's sleek legs running, running…

Then Mr. Louzis laughed. He turned and looked at Mother, who was blushing.

"Since she wants him, she should have him."

This time his eyes rested on Mother even longer.

"Now, now. It's just a childish whim. Two days won't have passed and she will have forgotten all about it."

"I want that horse," Infanta said again.

We were all horribly embarrassed. I bent down and ducked under the table to retrieve an apricot doily. Maria nudged Infanta with her elbow, whispering, "Have you gone mad?"

Luckily Mr. Louzis never stopped chuckling.

"I see that your daughters have character," he said to my mother, and she blushed even more.

In three days Infanta had her horse and we sent Mr. Louzis two plump newborn piglets in return.

Infanta never lets us ride her horse. In the beginning we were surprised. We thought surely she was being unfair. But we soon got used to it. Every day she takes him for a ride wearing her cinnamon-colored trousers and shirt, which blend in with the color of the horse, their single silhouette rapidly disappearing from view.

At first it wasn't that way. Romeo had a difficult temper. He didn't want to be ridden, and when anyone mounted him he saw to it that he was in control. But Infanta was also stubborn and didn't give in easily. When he misbehaved she pulled on his reins until he foamed at the mouth. Her own lips formed a thin, white line. She dug her spurs into his flesh. They struggled. Two or three times he threw her. Once on the way up the mountain he broke into a wild gallop. She straightened up, pressed her knees tightly against his sides, and drew in the reins so that her hands were touching the bit. Then she bent so far forward that she was lying against his back.

It was one of those days when the mountains are close enough to touch and even the most difficult task seems manageable. The day before it had rained, so the woods gave off the bitter scent of damp undergrowth and pine trees, the animals had taken cover, the ant trails had disappeared, and a silence full of significance had settled. The horse, the only moving thing in the midst of all that motionless nature, was running, running... Infanta tightened the reins. Since she too felt a part of the stillness, she couldn't bear all that life beneath her. Angry tears filled her eyes, tears that stuck and stung. Digging in her spurs only quickened the horse's pace. The slope was steep, the earth soft and red—still damp—and the horse's hooves sunk into the earth, just enough to secure his footing. Nothing was in his way. The sun had disappeared. His coat no longer glistened; it had become a dull gray green brown like everything else around him. Infanta stood out in her cinnamon-colored clothes. From a distance she seemed to be gliding through the air, hanging from some invisible point that kept moving farther and farther away. She was breathless; she couldn't get rid of the agonizing stillness—her whole body was numb.

Suddenly she raised her head, kicked Romeo hard with her spurs, and cried out, "Bravo, Romeo, faster, Romeo!"

The trees, the bushes and everything whizzed past.

"Faster, Romeo, faster!"

The wind rushed into her lungs, straightening her body. She crouched down again, feeling free, her body nimble.

"Run, Romeo, run."

The trees all blended together, the speed filling in the spaces between them making them seem like one endless tree. Opening her lips, at last she let herself breathe.

When she came home that night we saw a whole new world reflected in her eyes.

Romeo and that long story have nothing to do with Father or with the Sundays we spent with him. They are connected to Mr. Louzis. Sometimes when I think about Father and see his face before me I also see Mr. Louzis's face. It appears in an insidious way, positioning itself next to Father's, uninvited. Does Mother really find Mr. Louzis's jokes funny?

Yesterday when we went to see Father, he seemed odd. As if he had something on his mind that he wanted to tell us but he couldn't. He started . . . then stopped.

"Did you say something, Father?"

"Something, but now I've forgotten . . ."

And then after a bit, "My how you've grown. You, Maria, are almost twenty, and you, Infanta, eighteen. And my little one, Katerina, already sixteen. How beautiful you have all become."

We looked at each other in surprise. Father never talked to us this way, with such tenderness. Not that he was cold. To the contrary: his eyes had the sweetness and calm of animals lying in sunny pastures. It's just he couldn't express it.

"You know . . . I . . ."

"What, Father?"

"Oh, nothing. Was I saying something?"

Soon Grandmother came in to announce teatime.

"And I've fixed you a treat," she said.

She always prepared something, but every time she announced it as if it were an exception.

In the dining room Uncle Agisilaos kissed us and told a joke, and then left whistling a tune.

"All afternoon he was waiting for tea and now that it's ready he gets up and leaves," muttered Grandmother. "My children will never grow up."

For a moment while Father went in to get his handkerchief she turned to look at each of us in turn and said in an official voice, "Whatever your Father does you must love him."

"Of course we will. Whatever he does, we will love him. But what is all this about?"

When we arrived in Kifissia and took the road down to our house, I saw a shaft of light, the last of the day, falling on the oleanders, making them even more beautiful than usual. And I thought to myself how different our road was from Father's, how separate his life was from ours. And this made me sad.

"How's Miltos doing?" Mother asked when we arrived home. She always asked about Father.

"Fine," said Infanta.

"He's making a fantastic radio," I said.

"I think he's gotten involved with a woman," Maria said.

Mother grew pale, just a bit.

"How can you talk that way, Maria? Have you no respect?"

And then a little later, "Why do you think that?"

"Oh . . . some half-formed thoughts of Grandmother, some attempts by Father to tell us something . . . Who knows, we may even have a marriage on our hands!"

"You don't know what you're talking about!" I screamed, glaring at her.

I hated Maria at such moments, I really hated her. I wanted to leap on her and pull her hair out strand by strand.

All evening I was a wreck. I wanted to cry. Anything would have set me off—a voice that was too loud, a touch . . . But later in bed, lying there thinking, I began to wish Father would marry and become a little happier. Perhaps the prayer Rodia had taught me made me change my mind, or maybe it was just because I was half-asleep. I was always a better person just before I fell asleep.

After that Sunday Mother seemed preoccupied. Often in the evenings seated at the piano she let her hands fall to the side. Her mouth would take on a bittersweet expression, and her eyes would stare off as if remembering something.

We would wait for her to play.

She plays the piano without passion, using the same restrained tone all through a piece. Something is missing from her playing, something that is connected to Aunt Theresa's painting and the distant and close-up clouds.

At that hour Grandfather would be reading about trees and flowers or organizing his seeds in little boxes. His head would nod to the rhythm for a bit and then come to rest in the position it was accustomed to, bent a bit to the right. He was afraid of music. For him, it was magical. The Polish grandmother had worn a black velvet dress the evening of the concert, and a white camellia in her hair. Her eyes, usually closed when she listened to music, had opened, by chance catching his. He had felt her hands tremble, her desire. He had guessed what lay behind the quick rise and fall of her breast, the rhythm of her breath. He was losing her. "Bravo, bravo, bravo!" he heard her cry as the musician bowed to the audience. Later... But let's see, these tomato seeds are better than last year's, the tomatoes will be plumper. And about grafting the fig trees, I must tell Georgos to be careful, or perhaps I should do it myself...

In the meantime Aunt Theresa shifts around uneasily. She sits in one armchair then gets up and moves to another. She can't get comfortable. Dusk makes her anxious, because at night she keeps dreaming about the fiancé with the thick lips, though she never thinks about him during the day. A chill runs through her body. She wakes up dripping with sweat. And in the morning a dizziness, an exhaustion like a woman who has spent the night . . . But only momentarily. Just until she gets out of bed and opens the window.

Memories . . . memories. The air is heavy with them. I can't stand it anymore. I no longer fit in that big room with the piano, the little boxes of seeds, the peacock embroidery. I run outside and lie down on the grass. I look up at the moon between the two eucalyptuses; it touches the ledge of the cistern, and I can see the silhouette of a frog in its circle of light. But the frog is not on the moon. Like me, it is on the ground looking up.

IV. A WALK

THE LAVENDER bloomed. It happened suddenly, one morning. The evening before we had stroked the buds, which were still green and hard. We had begged them to open that night, and the next day from the window we saw six bushy rows of purple playing with the sun and hundreds of white newborn butterflies fluttering around, chasing each other, making love, only to die the same night.

Maria began to cry. She went and embraced the stems, burying herself in their aroma, letting her tears flow freely. "I'm going for a walk," she said after a bit; Mother asked her to pass by Kritikos's to see what had happened in the end regarding the mating of Felaha, our goat. Kritikos had a billy goat and he was supposed to lend him to us for a few days. He was asking I-don't-know-how-much wheat in exchange.

"Tell him that he's asking much too much," Mother said. "It's not as if we're going to eat the billy goat. Offer him half."

"Why don't we use Mother Kapatos's billy goat?" I asked.

"Because Kritikos's is stronger and the kids will turn out better," said Mother.

So Maria got ready to go. She wore a sleeveless white dress that was open at the neck, and atop her black hair, the big straw hat with the cherries.

"Why are you looking at me like an idiot?" she said when she reached the gate.

"You're different today, Maria. You have a strange glow about you. Not exactly you, not your eyes, but your skin, your cheeks, your arms, your legs, everything."

"You, my child, have a wild imagination," she said as she closed the gate behind her.

Outside the thyme was in full bloom and the sun was burning hot. Felaha, tied under a pine tree was chewing away. It would be the first time she'd gone with a billy goat, the first time she'd borne a kid. "If you only knew what was in store for you," whispered Maria as she passed by. "If you only knew…"

She began walking rhythmically. Her waist bent with each step, and she felt her body below her waist bending as well, and the motion pleased her. It made walking easier, as if she were flying, and each time she touched the ground she felt as if the earth was a thick substance that grabbed and then released her.

The cicadas sang on and on. Every once in a while a bee passed in front of her. It made a few circles around her head and then flew off for more thyme. The birds had quieted down and everything—the pine trees, the earth, the animals—was a wave of heat. The vapor rising from the trees dimmed the sun.

Just fancy asking for so much wheat…Unconsciously she quickened her step, as if she were trying to use up a secret store of energy. She could feel herself sweating a little under her arms, at her neck, between her thighs. But she wasn't scared of the heat. She welcomed it. Under her skin it was as if the cells were dancing. And further in, the blood.

She took the road that went down to Helidonou. It was a strange road because it was really five, each one parallel to the next and separated by a row of olive trees. Looking down you saw six rows of olive trees divided by spaces of earth. A whole crowd of people or a line of carts could pass by here. As Maria went down the slope she switched from one road to the next. She would be on the left side looking over at the rows of olive trees to the right and then without trying she would find herself on the right side looking at the olive trees to the left. This zigzagging took longer. But she wasn't in a hurry.

The houses were closer together again here. About forty all in a clump, crowded together out of loneliness, like people. The gardens were beautiful this year. The heavy rains that winter had done them good. They were full of green and the trunks of the trees were shiny. Tiny tomatoes were beginning to appear. You could already see the yellow stamen on the male pistachio trees, and the female ones waiting. The males would go to the females. All the females could do was ready their juices, receive the male, and bear fruit. They waited, in the burning heat, sensitive to any gust of wind that might bring them the seed.

Come to think of it, not one of them was a man. Not Nikos, not Stefanos. And Marios was such a weakling... Of course she had never kissed him, not now that he was older, and his eyes did look as if they wanted something. Perhaps his body too...

Stefanos, a few days ago, had unbuttoned her blouse, a green blouse the color of pine needles. They were lying in the forest. It all seemed very natural. She didn't move. She watched each of his movements calmly, coolly. Later she closed her eyes and said to herself, *Now I am closing my eyes*. She heard the sigh that came from her chest and met up with his nervous fingers.

Last year in the forest Nikos had unbuttoned another blouse, a yellow one the color of fresh hay. They were lying in the forest. It all seemed very natural. She closed her eyes, sighed, and the same sadness filled her. Something was missing. And the faces of the boys, bent over, searching, full of anxiety. There was really something very comic about them. She laughed. Both Nikos and Stefanos had gotten mad. "Are you crazy?" they had asked. She got up, one hand mechanically buttoning up the green, the yellow blouse. "If you could have seen your face in a mirror!" she sang out. "Oh my..."

Those evenings on her way home she would stop at the church of the Panaghia, the Virgin Mary. She would lean her bicycle up against a cypress, sit down on the cement pavement in front, and light a cigarette. She would wonder if what she had done was a sin. It hadn't hurt anyone. But why did she feel so sad afterwards? Perhaps the sense of incompletion, the desire for a truly generous offer, the way the pistachio trees receive the seed, keeping it inside them until they bear fruit.

By the time Maria had arrived at Kritikos's the sun was high in the sky. The sheep had returned from the pasture. They were all gathered under the pine trees motionless, with their heads down, some standing, some lying, packed tightly together. The breeze caressed their wool, making it flutter, but they didn't even notice. This is what inexistence is, total inexistence. Among them there were a few goats with their brown horns and their slanted eyes; they looked like devils amidst angels.

The house, surrounded by a low stone wall, was near the animals. Maria pushed open the wooden gate. The scent of dung and milk, thyme and billy goat met her. It rose and mixed in with the heat until it became something you could actually touch.

In a corner by the wall a young man, naked to the waist, was washing. With one hand he poured water from a watering can and with the other he scrubbed his body vigorously, as if he wanted it to hurt. He wasn't using soap. The water dripped from his hair, leaving a few beads on his shoulders that glistened in the sun and ran down to his trousers, getting them slightly damp. His belt was undone, and hung on either side. The beginning of his waist showed, slightly paler than the rest of his body. His hips were limber like those of a hunted animal. He had strong hands and a gentle body, white in those places the sun never reaches, like a baby's.

"Excuse me . . ."

She stood at the doorway, undecided.

He turned his head toward her. For a second he didn't talk, he remained there looking at her, from head to foot, as if she were an animal he was about to buy and was guessing its value.

"What do you want?" he asked.

"Kritikos, I wanted to ask him about Felaha, about the billy goat, that is . . . if he'd take half . . ."

"Father is at Gekas's at this time of day, having a drink. But you can tell me. It's the same thing. You're Mr. Dimitris's granddaughter, aren't you, from the house in the meadow?"

"Yes, from the house in the meadow. Kritikos was going to give us the billy goat for a few days and Mother said—"

"Is your goat 'wanting'?" he interrupted.

"Wanting what?"

"The billy goat, what else. I mean is she in heat?" His eyes fastened on hers.

"I don't know," she said without lowering her eyes. "How should I know?"

Then he became embarrassed. He remembered that he was talking to a girl, and one from the house in the meadow at that, and he blushed.

"You must be tired," he said after a bit, and his voice was no longer brusque. "Come in and rest."

She tried to leave.

"We can give you the billy goat..." The young man looked up, calculating, counting on his fingers. "In ten days," he said finally. "It will be a good time."

She climbed the step that separated her from the cool room and found herself sitting on a wooden chest covered with a sheepskin. The shutters, made from a single piece of green wood, were shut.

"In ten days," she repeated distractedly.

They were silent, facing each other, she seated, he standing. His presence weighed on her. She felt him there so alive with his dark hands and feet, with his white skin in those places the sun never reached. A golden flame danced inside her. Her knees felt cut off from the rest of her body, as if the fire were coming out of the earth and rising slowly through her body, beginning at her feet and continuing on up. Now the flame had reached her breast. She had difficulty breathing. She wanted to cry for help, but he would think she was crazy. He was so sturdy, like a piece of well-chiseled stone. His nose, his chin, his forehead were composed in straight lines, his shoulders and soul, too. Not a single curve. Whereas her body was all round, with sweet, smooth curves and rises, gentle like the earth itself, longing to partake of the other.

He was shocked to be standing before such roundness. He wanted to cry. He wanted to fall into her arms and cry and cry... as if his soul had been gathering clouds for years and now the time had come for rain.

At the same moment a bee came in through a chink in the door, a bee as gold as the flame inside her. It buzzed around, withdrew, and then came back and landed on her hair. With a mechanical gesture she tried to whisk it away, but it wouldn't leave.

"Ouch!"

It had stung her on her arm, leaving its stinger in. She leaned over to look at the sore spot, and shivered.

The young man looked worried. He came over beside her. Then he went out to get some damp earth. With one hand he held her arm tightly and with the other he began rubbing the bite with mud. The skin became red all around, and swollen.

"It will keep swelling," Maria said.

"It's nothing," he said to her. But inside he was sorry, deeply sorry to see the skin so sore.

Their heads came close to each other. Maria's hair touched his ear. Her cheeks were red, her eyelashes wet.

"Oh, it hurts," she said. "And I'm cold."

She looked him straight in the eyes. He bent down his head and continued to rub the sore spot patiently. By now a strong and primitive energy was passing between her body and his. Oh to cry, to cry, lying on top of her.

"I'm cold," Maria said again.

The shivers had gotten stronger. Her shoulders were shaking. That one bite had poisoned her whole body. She felt like she was burning up, and then she would get cold, her eyes filling with tears and the shivers wouldn't go away. He put out his arm and wrapped it around her.

"I can't bear to see a person cold," he said, and his voice was shivering more than Maria's body. "Even an animal. In the winter with the snow I want to embrace all the shivering animals and warm them with my breath."

He stayed there with his arm around her, feeling her body's spasms, her shoulders shaking. He was holding her tightly. It hurt, but she liked the pain. She turned her eyes toward him, his strong hands enclosing her roundness, which was warm and good like the earth. A goodness he had never known before. And when their bodies became one on top of the sheepskin he began to cry. It was time for the rain. She brought him toward her with all her strength, she wanted to hurt more, more, she wanted this moment to have the beauty of perfection. It seemed to her as if she was suddenly on the top of a mountain with all the world's beauty spread out before her. She screamed. Then she became calm like the river that flows through the same river bed for centuries.

Finding herself again on Elia Avenue, she looked at the five parallel roads, chose one, and began to walk peacefully, slowly, without zig-zagging from side to side or lifting her eyes from the ground. Maria was thinking, and when she thought she always looked down. The red soil, the ants going back and forth, the anthills, the sticky resin, all helped her think. She looked at them, learned from them, and drew her own conclusions. Everything that was good in their world was good for her too, and if something bad happened, she took note. Of course sometimes things got confused because when one animal ate another, it was bad for the animal that was eaten, but it also meant that other animals and plants were saved. She knew a great deal about their world, how an ant that doesn't pull its weight is ousted from its community, how the grasshopper brings disaster, how the cicada knows from birth how to sing, and how each of these animals is born, mates, gives birth, dies, becomes one with the earth and is born again from the earth. She even knew about the queen bee and how she had special servants that brought her food so she wouldn't get tired; and how when the time came for her to marry she would leave the hive and buzz and dart around the air, strong from all the attention and care, behind her an army of drones; how she would fly for two or three days without a break and the drones would drop, exhausted, dead, one by one until only she was left, and then she would build her own hive and become queen. The first part was rest and gathering strength, then looking after the body and attracting the males, then choosing the strongest after destroying all the rest and finally birth, innumerable births. Maria often thought about this process. She found it heroic and beautiful, with a hidden tragic element. Perhaps it was her own fate...

She tried to reflect on what had just happened and why. Her time had come, that was all. The man was a simple coincidence. He had passed over her the way clouds pass over the earth. She had been asking for that pain and agony for a while now, when she lay with her sisters in the yellow hay, or when she heard the frogs sing, or when, lying in bed, she listened for a cry in the night. Odd how recently at night she had been waiting for something tragic to happen, she couldn't get it out of her mind, she wanted it, just as when she was a child she would call out from a nightmare, and her mother would come to her and shake her, saying, "Wake up! It's only a dream," and she would sigh with relief and disappointment. "So," she would say to Infanta the next morning, "you were strangling me in my sleep last night. Yes, your two hands were around my neck and you kept squeezing and squeezing until..." and she would close her eyes luxuriating in the memory.

Now the sun was exactly overhead; there was no shade on the road. It must be midday. *I should hurry*, she thought. *They will be worried.* She had totally forgotten about home. She envisioned the midday meal: Grandfather, Mother, Aunt Theresa, Infanta, Katerina. How could she face them? She wasn't embarrassed now while she was alone, nor before God. God after all was the bees and the cicadas and the ants. And what she had done, in their world, was not something bad. But the others? The humans? They would guess. Her mother's eye was so sharp at times it seemed it was measuring the depths of her soul. And Aunt Theresa would have her suspicions. Aunt Theresa didn't like her at all. She was sure of that. Only Grandfather and Infanta wouldn't notice. They were always off in their own worlds. As for Katerina, she was curious and saw everything. "You have a strange glow about you, Maria," she had said to her that morning. "Not exactly you, not your eyes, but your skin..."

Now that glow had overflowed. She could feel it. She was shining all over. She went to look at herself in the stream, but the water was rippling. She waded in and splashed water on her arms and throat, on her face. Her lips were on fire, and her eyes had an odd heaviness about them. But her body was light. A shiver ran through her every once in a while. "I have never seen skin as soft as yours," the man had said, "nor skin as hot."

Going home, she found Elia Avenue interminable. The steep hill gave one the feeling of martyrdom. Maria recalled the night of suffering that Christ had passed when he begged not to drink the bitter cup. Why did today remind her of that night? Hadn't she had a joyous experience? She stood proud in the heat, ready to bear all the burdens of the world, her body and soul strong. So why did she keep thinking that from this day on the sacrifices would begin?

When she pushed open the wooden gate of the house, she felt calm. Rodia started to scream that she should hurry because all the others were seated. From the kitchen there was the smell of roast beef. The first fresh figs of the season were in a bowl. She entered the dining room at ease.

"What happened to you?" asked Mother, staring at her sternly. "We were worried."

"I lay down in the forest and fell asleep."

Everyone lifted their head for a second—half a second. Then they all began to eat. She kept her secret to herself. One by one she looked at them, and it seemed to her that each of them had a secret, too. Katerina was perhaps the only one whose secret hadn't fully ripened yet.

And when the bowl of figs had been emptied and Grandfather had lit his pipe and a sleepy midafternoon silence had descended on the room Maria said loudly, "I want to get married."

Everyone looked at her, this time for longer than a second. Aunt Theresa got up flustered, she took a few steps as if she wanted to get something, a plate, an ashtray, but then she forgot what it was. Infanta turned white. Her mother waited for an explanation. Grandfather didn't stop smoking. Her youngest sister drew near as if in support and asked her, as if she were the head of the family, "Are you in love with someone?"

"No," she said, "but I want to get married."

Her voice sounded calm and decided.

V . . . .

SO THE days slipped by without our noticing. Up until now our memories and expectations were enough. But one day we woke up. No longer could we stand in the sun with our eyes half-closed, letting our skin tan, watching it get darker and darker. Nor was our morning exercise satisfying the way it used to be.

VI. MARIA'S WEDDING

SINCE yesterday it's been about to rain, but the rain won't come. It clouds over, then the sun comes out, then it clouds over again. That's how it's been. A few drops begin to fall but they stay hanging in the air. The trees lean in one direction, then in the other, unable to make up their minds, their roots wanting water, their leaves wanting sun. It grows dark. The sky is heavy, everything is heavy. The animals are afraid. The hens settle on their roosts. The rabbits huddle together and lick themselves. The goats look around uneasily. When Mavroukos was afraid he would tuck his short tail between his legs, his eyes pleading, one tooth showing. He wouldn't leave my side. Of course, in the place where he is now he has nothing to fear. The gravestone above him stays put; no wind can lift it.

Thunder. Lightning. We shut our eyes because we can't bear the brightness. We suddenly feel cold, colder than when it snows in the winter. Silently we stare out the window, not daring to move, holding our breath, about to suffocate. We can't bear another minute.

Then the rain comes. We laugh with relief.

"Welcome," says Grandfather, "very welcome."

What he means is that the rain will be good for the trees.

"Yes, very," says Aunt Theresa, as if she were glad for the trees, when it's really because she wants to wash her hair with rainwater.

Mother doesn't say anything. She met Father on a rainy day.

I'd love to run out into the rain. But I would get wet. So I sit curled up on the couch like a cat, not thinking a thought, just listening to the rain. Something is brewing inside me that I don't understand. It fills me with joy and agony. I only feel better if I sing or draw many circles one inside the other, or four-leafed clovers.

"Go, get a book or your embroidery," says Mother. "I don't like seeing you sitting there with your arms folded."

"I can't."

"What do you mean you can't?"

"I mean, I can't."

She raises her icy eyes. Mother never actually gets angry, she stops herself just before that point, which is worse, it's as if she's smothering you. *You should beat me, Mother, for my impudence.* I get up to ask her for forgiveness but then I get embarrassed and stop. I look at her out of the side of my eye. She looks sad. I go over to the window and tap my fingers on the pane. I play a tune that's popular these days. My left foot keeps the beat. Her eyes stroke my back; she has already forgiven me. Then I can't bear it anymore. I run out of the room to cry. The rain is pouring down on me, my hair is sticking to my forehead. Mother can see me from the window, but she doesn't call me. Time passes, and little by little I feel the sense of relief that comes with tears.

"Katerina, have you gone crazy?"

It's Maria. She comes out of the house in her raincoat and takes me by the hand and pulls me inside. She is very gentle when she is not totally consumed with herself.

"You'll catch pneumonia. You're soaked. Come in and I'll dry you off."

I let her pull me in. She takes off my clothes piece by piece and wraps me in a white bathrobe. Her steady hands pat my body and warm me.

"Let me be," I say, "what does it matter to you?"

And when she looks at me surprised, "What does it matter to you if I get sick? What's it to you?"

Perhaps if I got sick Mother would love me more. She would lift up my head and give me water to drink. She would beg me to eat. At night in the dark she would caress my forehead. My room would smell of medicine and flowers. And one evening when I had a really high fever I would say...

"You know, sometimes you are very naughty." Maria whispers. She rubs me more vigorously than before.

"Maria, who are you going to marry?" I ask her then.

"What do you care?" she says, and laughs.

"Of course I care. At night before I go to sleep I think about you and Infanta, Mother and Father, and a little about Aunt Theresa and Grandfather. I ask myself what our lives will be like later, what we will do. After all we'll have to do something, won't we, Maria?"

The rain had stopped. I didn't notice exactly when. Only the trees were dripping and the drops seemed red, yellow, green in the air, the colors of the rainbow.

"What are you trying to say, Katerina?"

"That we shouldn't let the sun burn our skin and the rain soak us, that…"

"That we should take control of our destiny, not God, eh?"

I grow quiet. I didn't mean to say that. I respect God.

"That we should take charge?" Maria says again and then waits for my answer as if her life depended on it.

"Often I think of Prometheus and…"

She bursts out laughing, and laughs like I've never heard her laugh again.

"You really are crazy!" she cries. "Maybe it's Prometheus you want to be. What do you think we are anyway? We're just ants, you hear?"

She gets serious for a bit. She wrinkles her eyebrows. An invisible shield protects her body. I feel that she is defending herself. But from what exactly?

"As for me, I'm not interested in Prometheus and such tales. I want to live like the animals and plants. All the rest is fake."

"What rest?" I ask. "I don't understand. As for Prometheus I only mentioned him because I remembered an essay we had to write for school: 'How do you view Prometheus?'"

I stand up and close myself in my shell. I don't wrinkle my eyebrows but I stretch my neck taller and taller. Maria looks me straight in the eye. She knows I'm lying.

"You expect great things from life," she whispers. "Not me. You see, I know that what is really important can be found in the little, everyday things."

She closes the door behind her noiselessly. My bathrobe has slipped off my shoulders. I look at my naked body distractedly.

Toward evening the rain began again. We didn't expect it, nor did we expect Marios. Nevertheless, there he was. He shook out his raincoat in the kitchen and then appeared in the door of the dining room, where we were all seated around the table waiting for dark. For a moment his silhouette, as he stood there, dominated everything. It had a strange hold on the chairs, the sofa, and even on the painting of a reclining woman dreaming that hung on the opposite wall.

"Good evening," he said.

We greeted him enthusiastically because we all loved Marios. I even went and got a fluffy towel and began rubbing his wet hair.

"You're going to hurt him that way," said Maria, and Infanta turned and looked at her and then looked at me.

Marios laughed.

"No, no," he said, "it's good for me. Harder, Katerina. That's it . . ."

"If he's a doctor he must be scared of colds." I explained. Everyone thought that was funny and laughed, and I wished I hadn't said it.

"Do you think he's like you, staying out in the rain?" says Maria.

I think back on the afternoon. I was such a different person then. My only comfort was solitude. I could have done great things, gone without food or sleep. Now I wanted people around me to keep me warm. I felt safe because with one step I could pull on Aunt Theresa's skirt, and Rodia was cooking rice and it smelled good. One problem with my plan to take a trip around the world is that Rodia won't be there to cook.

"Marios, will you eat with us tonight?" Mother suggests. "Whatever we have."

She leans over and tells Maria to prepare a pudding. Maria gets up. In a while Marios also gets up, just to check if the rain has stopped, though everyone can hear clearly that it hasn't. He opens the door to the balcony and goes down the steps to the garden.

The kitchen is in the back part of the house; it is lit by the fire from the oven. The flames play with Maria's face, making it change expression, though inside her nothing has changed. A shadow across her eyes makes her seem sad, another enlarges her mouth as if she were laughing, then many flicker together playing on her skin, her forehead, her cheeks. And even though the flames and their shadows are all the same, each one makes Maria look different, making her seem to feel things she doesn't feel, see things she doesn't see and will never see, and all this creating an illusion that is only skin-deep. Her hair seems red, at times golden, and when she moves away from the fire it gets darker.

Marios wants to hold that highlight in his hand, but reflections can't be held. A sadness overcomes him. How is it possible for someone to read about anatomy all afternoon, to put everything that he learns in perfect order, and then suddenly for him to get it into his head that he wants to hold a reflection? He sits outside the kitchen; his forehead gets wet without him noticing. Maria is moving back and forth. She takes two eggs from the third shelf, she breaks them in a deep plate, and begins to beat them. Her feet in her summer sandals are firm on the ground. Up to her middle she is motionless, though her right hand and shoulder are moving. Her breast becomes a wave. Marios would love to get lost in that wave. His throat is dry. If he raised his head a bit he could quench his thirst with rainwater.

Maria doesn't know he's looking at her. She tosses the beaten eggs into the milk in a saucepan on the stove. She takes a spoon and begins to stir. Her eyes fix on the flames. She forgets herself. She leaves the spoon in the pan and, putting her hands on her waist, she arches her back. It's times like this she would like to be in Kritikos's cottage. One afternoon she had started to go. It was after a long midday nap of strange dreams. As soon as she awoke, hot from sleep, she dove into the cistern to cool off. But the cold water didn't make the dreams disappear. She ran to her room, quickly slipped on a dress, and went out.

She stood in the middle of Elia Avenue. If she went to him, if she went inside his house once more she would never be able to leave again. And she knew she didn't want to stay forever. She sat on the root of an old olive tree and cried a bit. Her body was full of longing.

Marios could see that her body was full of longing. Perhaps...

"Maria!"

She turns abruptly, frightened. For a second she seemed to hate him.

"How did you get in here? Why did you come in here? Are you spying on me?"

"I was admiring you, Maria."

His voice is soft, timid, because he wasn't able to catch the reflection. Maria knows this and despises him for it.

"You're wet again. Come on in and dry off."

Marios climbs up the last step and sits in the chair by the door. At that moment a change comes over him. He finds a new strength. He can concentrate completely on what he wants to say.

"I'd prefer if our children were more like you," he said. "You're healthier, more beautiful."

His voice is calm, a calm that frightens Maria. She starts to laugh but her laughter gets caught in her throat. She starts to walk toward him but her feet won't move. They seem nailed to the floor.

Marios slowly draws his box of cigarettes out of his pocket and takes one...

"I forgot my lighter at the lab," he says. "Do you think you could give me a piece of coal?"

Mechanically she takes the tongs and chooses a piece of coal. She takes it to him. For the first time she feels that she, the stronger one, must obey him, because she will carry his children. This thought passes like lightning through her brain as she extends her hand to give him the red hot coal. There is still one last chance, to throw the tongs out the open door of the kitchen, to watch the red hot coal dance into the night and fall to the ground. Just one toss. *If I take this last step, if I give him the coal, I will become his wife. But if I throw it*... Her hand shakes. The step is completed, her hand approaches Marios, who, upright, bends over to light his cigarette.

"You know I'm not a virgin," she says, then, as if to get back at him.

Marios grows pale, very pale indeed. He doesn't know what to say, perhaps he is ashamed that Maria is not a virgin.

"I love you, Maria," he says after a bit.

Then she rests her hand on his shoulder and looks him in the eyes. She has the air of someone who has made up her mind.

One morning at dawn Nikitas arrived on his gray horse. We saw him from the terrace before he reached us. He had stopped the horse at the top of the hill. After a moment he gave her a kick and took the incline at a gallop.

We had just woken up and were stretching our arms and legs in the sun, dancing around. Although Maria and Infanta may have been very serious during the day, they still danced around in the morning. We wore soft rose-colored nightgowns, the same color as the dawn.

"He's come to go racing with me," said Infanta.

"How do you know?"

"You'll see."

"He may be on his way to Mr. Louzis's."

"No, he's coming here."

We didn't have time to say anything else because Nikitas had stopped in front of the wooden gate and was waiting for Georgos, the gardener, to let him in.

From up high we could only see his blond head and the smooth rump of his horse. The mare was named Victoria, but Nikitas called her Vicky. She was a beautiful specimen, with a shiny coat, bright white in some places and darker, almost gray in others, and the gray bright in some places and darker, almost black, in others. That horse made me realize how similar white and black really were.

We had known Nikitas for years. He lived in another part of

Kifissia, in Kefalari, and was a friend of Marios's, Stefanos's and Emilios's. We had gone to his house and he had come to ours on rainy autumn afternoons when everyone—Stefanos, Eleni, Margarita, Emilios—gathered around the phonograph playing records and dancing. But he had never come over by himself, especially not at this hour.

Infanta's eyes were bright; the thrill of the race shone in them. And although they were always dry, as if she couldn't cry, for one moment a moist veil covered them. They were green like the depths of a grassy lake, and every once in a while little flecks of brown appeared turning green and then vanishing.

She lifted her shoulder-length hair with both hands and let it drop absentmindedly.

"I'm going to get ready."

When we came downstairs, Maria and I in our summer dresses and Infanta in her cinnamon-colored trousers and shirt, we saw Nikitas on the veranda and Aunt Theresa asking him, rather coldly, how it occurred to him to race with Infanta.

"The girls suggested it that night at Marios's, and . . ."

"Yes, we did," I said upon arriving. "Good morning, Nikitas. How are you?"

Nikitas wore a blue shirt, the color of his eyes. His forehead was wide and round, and his blond hair was short. When the wind blew it stood on end like porcupine needles. He wasn't handsome, but he had beautiful hands.

"Good morning, Infanta. How are you?"

But after that we couldn't think of anything else to say.

"I'll go get Romeo ready," Infanta said at last.

We watched them leave, at first slowly, without talking.

At this time we were all consumed with Maria's wedding. Grandfather was a new man and called in builders to build another house on the property. He oversees everything himself, the stonework, the measurements. The day we set the first stone we killed a cock. Its blood splattered the foundations. They say this brings good luck.

In the meantime Mother is getting the dowry ready. Aunt Theresa and a seamstress from Athens help her. Maria goes on long walks by herself, and then when she comes back she tries on a blue nightgown or a white petticoat in front of the mirror and explains with great precision what she does and does not like: "This pleat a little to the right, this tuck less obvious, and the belt, tighter, like this." She turns from left to right, and even gets another mirror so she can see how it looks from behind. She smooths her hands over her body, as if she were caressing it, making sure the line is to her liking. She doesn't hide the fact that she is admiring herself. If she were alone, she might even throw off the last piece of clothing and dance naked in front of the mirror, totally satisfied by this image of beauty that is her own. Having no other desire for the moment she would feel a perfect separation from all other living things. She would be the only thing left in the world.

"Don't you think the yellow suits me better, Mother?"

Maria's voice is full like her body.

"Yes, yellow goes with your dark hair."

"Dark women are always more attractive," the seamstress throws in. She herself is as dark as a gypsy.

All that can be heard is the sound of scissors. The room is full of white, red, and blue snippets, and others with flower patterns. I hang around in the midst of all this not knowing what to do, picking up a snippet and then dropping it. I lie down and listen to the seamstress tell her stories. The poor dear had three loves in her life, all failures. Oh, to be able to give shape to such experiences, to make them live after their death ... I get all excited when I hear people talk about their lives, about things that have happened to them, even the simplest events. I feel that in the telling they have greater significance than they had in real life.

The fact that Nikitas comes over in the morning now and then affects us all. Human lives are connected, so it matters, and if he stopped coming maybe it would matter even more. "Good morning, Nikitas. How are you?" Infanta says when she sees him arrive. "Good morning, Infanta. How are you?" Nikitas answers. Then they grow quiet, mount their horses, and leave. They never mention who wins. And to tell you the truth we weren't much concerned either because our main interest was Maria's wedding.

The house is coming along—the dowry, too. Everyone is happy. Maria is calm. Father too seemed pleased when he heard the news. I think he was moved because he immediately started talking about a new invention of his, not stopping to ask about the details of the wedding. Or perhaps it was just indifference. As for his own affairs, he didn't say a word. Nonetheless something was in the air...One day when I went to see him at his office, still dizzy from the bright sunlight outside, I dimly made out a woman in the shadows, a beautiful blond, who on seeing me approach, greeted Father hurriedly and left. That night I told Mother. She asked me whether the woman was tall or short, whether she was beautiful, what color her eyes were. "I didn't get to see her eyes," I answered, "but her hair was blond and she was beautiful." Mother seemed to look sad. "Not exactly beautiful," I quickly rejoined, "more garish."

Marios comes over often in the evening and keeps us company. There are days when he's cheerful and others when he's sad. Maria is always the same. Except that a grudge seems to be growing inside her.

"Don't think that I'm already yours," she told Marios one evening in the stillness of the garden.

A desire to escape... She knows it's her last chance.

"I don't. You're free. If you don't want to get married ..."

She lowers her head, surprised by her own words, by everything. She searches his eyes in the dark. She takes his hand and squeezes it.

"Don't take this seriously, Marios. I know I'm going to become your wife and that's how I want it."

Marios leaves. He's both scared and hopeful. On the way home he tries to remember what the great philosophers and doctors say about the nature of woman. The theories get all mixed up in his mind. He can't match them with real life. He sees that his father no longer tries to understand his mother. One day Laura Parigori opens the door to a beggar and gives him her dress. The next day she gets angry with the servants for opening the door to "one of them."

Maybe it's that Laura feels a certain disgust for misery. Back on the island of her childhood everything was beautiful. She lived in the best house, every object—the chair, the candlestick, the plate—was a work of art. In the evenings they would gather around the big lamp and talk about music, art, poetry... A fine warmth would envelop her at those times. Her mother would sing. She used to have a lovely voice. She hasn't sung since she moved to Athens. Instead she puts on her makeup even though she's nearly sixty-five and goes and sits in the fashionable coffee shops and plays cards. Laura sometimes tries to talk to her about the old house, reminding her of the chandelier in the living room, the window that looked out on the sea...

And once she started to say something to Yannis about it. It was summer. She was on the veranda. Yannis listened the way one listens when someone is telling a story about something that happened long ago. Then she stopped, perhaps out of fear that his distant manner would make her own memory distant.

And that memory elevated her in the eyes of God—she knew it—so it had a special place in her heart, the way a certain corner of her old room near the window also had a special place. It was the corner with an armchair, a little desk, and a shelf with books, dried flowers, and old photographs. There was a box full of shells somewhere behind one of the photographs. Back then she and the other children would set out for long afternoon walks along the shore. Some shells shimmered and could be detected from afar; others were buried in the sand, and you had to dig to find them. Her friend Ernestina found the most. But Spiretos secretly gave all of his to Laura as they were leaving. She thanked him with her eyes. She was facing the sea. He was facing her. She watched him. His body and his face seemed to dissolve in front of her, but his black eyes grew larger and larger, becoming two dark, steady, solitary points in the sea.

One time Leda found those shells and wanted to keep them. Mrs. Parigori grabbed the box from her and gave her an angry look. "Mother is strange. At times she scares me," Leda said to Marios that evening. Marios gave a short laugh because he remembered his walks in the ravine as a child when he'd been afraid of the rushing water and had clung to his mother, but she hadn't taken him in her arms. A book would be lying open at her side. Later at night in bed when she drowned him in kisses, his heart wouldn't warm up; the loneliness had spread inside him when the shade had fallen in the ravine. The darkness came so quickly at dusk that many times it would be night before they could climb the slope to the open field. Marios would often step on sharp stones or scratch his big toe on thorns.

When they reached the open field, Marios would begin to sing. Laura would hug her book under her arm. She wanted to run across the field to the other side and fall down and sleep. She would sing too, a melancholy tune.

"As if returning from a land of fairy tales," said Mr. Parigori, who would be waiting for them on the veranda. Laura's cheeks were red and she had wild lilies in her hair. Marios held some in his hand and had a pensive look about him. "So what's up? Did you see any dragons, any water nymphs?" Both of them were confused and couldn't say a word. "So what's the matter, Laura? Is it your nerves again?" He muttered something else while she distractedly arranged the flowers in a vase. Then he took Marios on his knee and showed him photographs of all the animals and plants of the world, telling him about their habits and ways of life.

His mother's words always left Marios feeling uneasy. There was something bitter about them. Whereas his father's words gave him a sense of ease, almost happiness. Nonetheless he preferred his mother's.

One evening—it was odd—on hearing Maria laughing down by the cistern, he thought it was his mother, even though their voices aren't at all alike.

The wedding took place at the end of the summer. It was a warm, sweet day. There was neither sun nor clouds. It was neither hot nor cold. The leaves hadn't begun to fall. Some were green, others yellow, and others reddish.

All the relatives came, even Father. Father hadn't seen the property for three years; that is, since I was seriously sick when he came every afternoon and sat by my bed.

"How are you, Miltos?" Grandfather asked on the morning of the wedding. Aunt Theresa greeted him coldly and politely and Mother said, "I wish them all the happiness in the world..." "Me too," said Father with difficulty, unable to look Mother in the eye. Later they pulled away from the others and walked together for a bit along the road. It was the first time I had even seen them next to each other. Mother was a little taller than Father, just a bit.

"He seems like a good kid..."

"Yes, he's a good kid, a fine family, and a scientist as well."

"Do they love each other?"

"He has loved her since he was a child."

"And she?"

"Well, since she wanted to marry him? Children are so peculiar, Miltos. You never can tell..."

Anna sighed and looked off into the distance. Wasn't she partially to blame for that? For someone to open up to you, you must also open up to them. She was never able to take that first step with anyone, not with her father, not with Aunt Theresa, not with Miltos, and not with the children. Even when she was playing the piano in front of them she made sure she used the same restrained tone all through the piece so as to not give away her feelings. Though when she was alone at dusk and the last light of day fell on the white keys while the rest of the room was already dark, she would forget herself and take the first step. But then there was never anyone there to respond so her overture meant nothing. One afternoon Katerina had abruptly opened the door and rushed into her arms in a whirlwind. "How did you play that, Mommy? Play it again. Play it again." Katerina's cheeks were red and her eyes damp. "Play it again, Mommy, come on." "I wasn't playing. It was the radio," she whispered, and the iciness was there again.

"You can't tell with them," she repeated. "They have the strangest ideas..."

"Today's children make demands on life," said Father. "They have courage and independence."

"And that is very dangerous."

"And very wonderful."

Father could have invented the most magnificent machine in the whole world. But instead he works at a bank.

"I was scared of great things," he said quietly.

"And yet back then ... when we were in love you could have done so much."

"Perhaps, then."

They had reached the pavilion with the jasmine. Mother paused a moment and looked around her. She laughed, a little nervously.

"Do you remember?" she asked.

"Yes, I remember." He laughed too, sadly. "Anna, I'm thinking of getting married," he said after a bit.

In the meantime we were getting ready and dressing Maria. She hadn't wanted to wear a white dress and veil. "That's too old-fashioned," she declared. "That's for when girls were as pure as lilies." Instead she wore a light blue dress with a white flower pattern.

"Now I'll become as pure as a lily," she said, laughing. But when we also began to laugh she got serious and looked straight in front of her. "It's good to be pure, isn't it Katerina?"

Infanta was looking out the window thoughtfully.

"Not Infanta's kind of purity. Do you see what I mean, Katerina?"

"Yes, something that's inside us," I said, picking up the comb and beginning to comb her hair.

Infanta turned toward us as if she wanted to say something of great importance. Her face was long and thin, too thin, her cheeks were pale.

"Has Nikitas come yet?" she asked.

"We'll find Nikitas at the church with Petros and Emilios."

Those three would represent Marios's friends, and Margarita and Eleni were to represent Maria's.

I like brushing Maria's hair, bringing the brush under the hair and watching it get blacker and shinier. Her hair has a splendid vitality.

"Will you have children, Maria?"

"Five or six," she answers simply.

She stands in front of the mirror. Her legs are long and shapely, her body rests on them perfectly. Her thighs are round and full, her waist slim, and her breasts free and proud, like petals on a stem. I help her put on the light blue dress. As soon as she's wearing it her face and body acquire a calm. Her breasts and thighs are less obvious and her hair less shiny.

Infanta's dress is a light pistachio color, mine is coral, Infanta doesn't look like she's going to get dressed. She stares out the window, totally absorbed. We go over to the window and look out at the garden and the pavilion with the jasmine where Mother and Father are silently sitting next to each other on the wooden bench. Suddenly Father leans over and kisses Mother's hand.

At church they found all their relatives gathered. The neighborhood church was small and poor with old, dark icons painted on the whitewashed walls. It had a courtyard with two cypresses and an old priest who always mixed up his words. Often at dusk, returning from a walk, I would go in and sit in the pew by the window and watch the sun, which outside was diffuse and immaterial, passing through the stained glass windows and becoming red, yellow, and green rays. I would bathe in the light and would feel a new light being born inside me.

Marios's mother came up immediately to greet us. She seemed moved. She started to embrace Maria tenderly, but at the last moment she changed her mind and, holding her by her shoulders, kissed her on both cheeks. She was wearing a white dress, very youthful, adorned at the waist with a bouquet of obviously artificial flowers. She also wore a string of pearls and pearl earrings. Her hair was light brown, combed up with great care. It only puffed up above her forehead, making a soft wave before it was abruptly stopped by a hairpin. Her eyes were blue, without a spark, as if the world around her didn't have meaning for her. Laura Parigori lived in the past. She fed off nostalgia. And on those days when that well was dry, and she was left there leaning over trying to draw something up, then she turned to books with the same anxiety. And when she wasn't reading she was thinking about what she had read, and it was as if she were very far away. Sometimes at dinner she would forget to eat, other times Yannis would talk to her and she would answer yes, yes without having heard a word he said. All this made her think that she wasn't intended for this life. But then she couldn't imagine any other, more appropriate life.

"You are very beautiful today, my dear," she said to Maria as she looked her up and down. "Pale blue suits you marvelously, even if I would have preferred white."

"Mother, are you already talking like a mother-in-law?" said Marios laughing, a glint in his eyes.

And Aunt Aglaia bent down and whispered to Aunt Aspasia that in the past brides had worn white, but she had never seen a mother-in-law wear white.

"White with pink and purple flowers ... She's pretending to be a young thing. Just fancy, the other day I saw her in the center of Kifissia with a rose in her hair. And another time ..."

Marios and Maria stood next to each other, straight like tall candles, listening to the words of the priest. Marios seemed distracted, but Maria listened to every word, as if she were listening to a lesson at school that she wanted to learn well.

I began to weep so hard I couldn't hide it. I heard Father take out his handkerchief and blow his nose loudly. Mother, nearby, cried silently to herself, trying not to let it show. Grandfather remained calm. Only at the end did he lean down and mention something about great-grandchildren to Grandmother. Once or twice Nikitas turned to look at Infanta. And Petros stared at me the whole time. When we came out of the church, he approached me and said:

"Finally you decided to wear red."

"It doesn't mean a thing," I retorted. "And I'd appreciate it if you didn't make a fool of me by staring at me in church."

"I was not looking at you. There was a beautiful angel painted on the wall behind you."

We all kissed Marios and Maria, wishing them every happiness.

Then we slowly descended the road to our house. Uncle Agisilaos began telling jokes, and Ellie, who hadn't said a thing all day, confessed to me that she was in love and that she too would like to get married. Aunt Theresa added that when two people join together in holy matrimony neither one has any hopes of ever achieving perfection.

"But what is perfection, Aunt Theresa?" I asked.

She didn't answer, but only speeded up her step. In front of us were Marios and Maria. They were holding hands. They seemed calm and happy.

That first night, though, Maria didn't sleep a wink. She kept Marios warm but remained cold herself. Only her palms were burning. She rubbed them over her body to warm herself up, beginning at her neck and ending at her feet. Her pulse was throbbing. She could feel it everywhere, in the palm of her hand, in her belly, in her temples, in her chest, as if her whole body was a clock ticking away monotonously through the night. She grabbed at her heart to stop it, she pressed on her temples, but the beat only grew stronger. And it was as if it didn't come from inside her but from a foreign body, and it annoyed her that it was keeping her awake.

Next to her Marios had fallen asleep. He had taken her warmth and shut it up inside himself. His face was calm, his black hair had fallen across his brow and touched his shut eyelids, and on his lips a smile was floating like a child dreaming of wonderful toys.

The few morning clouds had disappeared. The air was clear and crisp because it was the day after the full moon. Every nook and cranny in the room was lit up. The moon rays even fell on the pillow, in her eyes. She rolled over to the left to find some shade, then to the right; she tossed this way and that. Light surrounded her. It flooded her face and crept across her throat. Her hair dipped into the light as if into cold water, and she felt cold, very cold. In a while the moon came to rest across from her. Its face was smiling, and then angry. And sometimes it was really two faces kissing each other. She tried to find the exact place where the lips met, as she had done as a child.

She would sit at the back of the house, on the cement step outside the kitchen, waiting. A vague light, timid at first, a light with no color, would light up the mountain range across the way, making it clearer and clearer as time went by. Later, she never knew exactly when, it would begin to turn red, and then after the red turned to orange the moon would come out. At that hour no one could get her to move from the step. While the man and woman kissed in their faraway heavenly world, she would be dreaming. "Look, it's laughing," Katerina would say. How could it be that she saw two sad faces while Katerina saw only one and it was laughing?

She couldn't sleep. She lay there on her back with wide open eyes looking out at the sleeping garden. It was a night without wind. Marios stretched out his arm and embraced her. She must stay still while he slept.

Her insomnia seemed to her like lethargy. She saw and heard and thought as if a shroud was covering her senses, erasing differences, so that she could no longer tell vision and sound apart, and ideas became vague, distant, and foreign.

Near dawn she thought about how she loved Marios. That was why, after all, she had married him.

VII. AUTUMN

Autumn came after Maria's wedding was over. The days got shorter. In the afternoon, tired of the cool shade of my room and needing sunlight, I would go for a walk, hesitating at the doorstep, surprised and saddened to find that the sun already seemed to want to hide behind the mountain.

At that hour, though, everything took on a tremulous beauty. The pine needles stood out independent from each other, while the grass below seemed to be one solid body, a single skin covering the whole earth like an orange peel. The goats grazing nearby had a supernatural power as if they had been sent by some higher being. Their coats gleamed, their look had a peculiar steadiness about it, a frightening motionlessness. As the last rays of sunlight fell on them, it seemed to me as if they suddenly disappeared, as if their bodies dissolved into the mist that enveloped the trees. But it was only because I had closed my eyes. When I opened them they were still in the same spot, chewing, as if reborn from the mist. The faces of Georgos or Tasia or any other worker who happened to pass by were striking, beseeching. Mother Kapatos's shrieks, "Kostas, Koula, hey! . . . Manolis! . . ." were like those of the witch in the fairy tale. The cistern was getting ready to accept the reflections of the stars and the frogs' loves. The water's surface rippled slightly.

Everything took on a tremulous beauty, and I tried to capture that beauty, the way someone tries to hold on to an object. But it always escaped me, so I'd go running off, whipping the air with a switch I'd fashioned from a willow branch, trying to forget.

The sun would vanish abruptly. The meadow after a day of reveling in the sun reached a climax, turned a brilliant, gold red, and then became suddenly dark. At this moment the olive trees would show the faces and arms they had kept hidden all day.

Autumn sunsets always come earlier than you expect because every day is shorter than the day before. Many times in the afternoon I would take the road toward Mr. Louzis's, which was full of blackberry bushes, and this hour would find me far from home. Other times I would be caught up in a book and I would just manage to run outside to the meadow before the sun vanished completely.

The books I read at this time filled my life, and thrilled me. I wanted to tell someone but I didn't know where to begin. So when I was outside I would sing different songs, as I happened to remember them, all mixed up—it was kind of like my crazy garden, if it's possible to compare a song to a garden—and instead of words I would put in the names of the heroes of the books I had read, sometimes repeating them two or three times, and I would talk to them. "Alyosha," I would say, "Alyosha, could a soul as perfect as yours really exist? Alyosha, Alyosha..." And I would wonder how Mary who was so good and honest could love two men at the same time, and I cried because Liza died—she shouldn't have, nobody should die—and I would cry as if she were the dearest person to me in the world.

I broke off two or three berries from the hedge and ate them for comfort. Without realizing it, I had arrived at Mr. Louzis's property. I looked at the cypresses that blocked the icy wind on the north side, just the tops, that is, because there was a wall around the compound with barbed-wire fencing covered in climbing flowers. In the spring there were little pink and purple roses and wisteria, and in the fall there were golden yellow flowers with copper red leaves as if the sun were reflecting off them. If I wanted I could push the gate open and go in. Mrs. Aphrodite would offer me pudding, maybe even ice cream, and Mr. Louzis would tell me some jokes. But then he would surely ask after Mother. "How is your mother? Does she still have those headaches that she sometimes has in the summer?" "Headaches? Mother never has headaches." "Yes, she does. What about that pressure she complains of?" "You must be mistaken, Mr. Louzis."

So I didn't push open the gate. I just bent down a little to find an opening in the leaves to peep through. Although I went often to Mr. Louzis's and I was free to look at everything when I was there, somehow from the outside peeping in I had the sense that I might see something new. Perhaps because from the little holes between the leaves everything appeared in fragments: a piece of the stairs, half a window; and when I shifted my position, the rooftop, the foot of a visitor.

Once I saw Mr. Louzis kissing the gardener's daughter. She was concentrating so hard on cutting the roses that she didn't notice him, until she was startled by a kiss on the back of her neck. It seemed he had kissed her before, because she didn't say anything when she turned around. She only laughed loudly, showing her gold tooth, her neck wrinkling up like a face in a grimace.

That's when I realized that Mr. Louzis and the Comtesse de Noailles couldn't possibly be relatives. Besides, Mr. Louzis himself had never mentioned it. Others talked about it, referring to the photograph with the dedication that hung over his fireplace in which the Comtesse de Noailles was looking off into space, wearing a thick ribbon, perhaps velvet, which hung low on her forehead, giving her a thoughtful and nostalgic air.

The first person to suggest that they might be relatives was Mrs. Montelandi, Marios's grandmother. She had come over to visit us one day and had brought the conversation around to the trips she used to take to Paris every year when she was younger, and to the people she had met there. One of us, I don't remember how or why, mentioned Mr. Louzis. Mrs. Montelandi, as soon as she heard his name sat up in her chair, began stroking the double row of pearls that hung around her neck, and, throwing us an inquisitive look that was also full of respect, began asking us for details about Mr. Louzis: Have you known him a long time? Where did he used to live? Was he always this rich? When she finished she added with an almost indifferent tone that Mr. Louzis frequented the salon of the Comtesse de Noailles when he lived abroad, and that she had even heard people say they were related in some way.

Aunt Theresa could not hide her joy.

"He comes here too," she said, "and rather often."

"Is he from the Ionian islands?" asked Mrs. Montelandi, trying to let Aunt Theresa's remark pass unnoticed.

"Who?" asked Aunt Theresa, as if there was any doubt.

"Mr. Louzis."

"Ah . . . Mr. Louzis . . . no, no. He's not from there."

The photograph of the Comtesse de Noailles hangs all by itself in the drawing room on those afternoons when the sun sets quickly. Everyone else is out in the garden, while inside the blinds are drawn shut, forgotten since noon. It is almost dark—which is even sadder than total darkness. And some dust has gathered on the piano. In this dim light her eyes probably appear even more nostalgic.

The way back was beautiful, full of that sweet feeling of exhaustion and the damp smell of wheat. The mountains of Parnitha and Pendeli loomed grand and silent. I was frightened by them, in awe of them, and I felt so tiny, like an ant, and calm, like a flower that closes its petals and goes to sleep.

The minute I opened the gate to our house the train to Europe passed through Tatoï. It whistled two or three times, and I could hear the sound of the wagons on the tracks. That was the train the Polish grandmother had left on. In Athens at the station all would have gone smoothly. The musician, seeing her coming, would have taken a few steps toward her, bowed, and kissed her hand. But when the train passed through Tatoï, what would the Polish grandmother have done? Leaning out the window, perhaps she would have tried to see the lights of our house beyond the meadows and the woods that separated us from the tracks. "Does anyone you know live around here?" she would hear him ask. "It's beautiful land. But it's dark—how can you see anything?" She would have lowered her veil over her eyes, full of nostalgia for what she was leaving, for what was already distant, inaccessible . . .

That's what I would think about when I heard the train passing, and other things, too. I would lose my calm, also my respect for Parnitha and Pendeli. They weren't so far away. I could easily reach them. Everything lost its calm; the flowers even seemed to be moving and the roofs shaking.

Mornings were different now. Day broke with less brilliance than in the summer, but everything was somehow clearer. The air smelled of crushed apples, and left in your mouth the juicy, tart taste of apples eaten unpeeled. It was a delicate air, sometimes chilly. The sky was blue—a deep, rich blue—with white clouds racing by. But the more the day progressed the lighter the blue became until it was almost gray-white. And by midday it seemed an ashen covering had descended, pressing on foreheads, weighing on hearts, bringing a certain gloominess. Breathing was harder, but then at some moment the covering would lift, become deep blue once again with white clouds racing by.

Often on such mornings Nikitas would come over riding Vicky. Infanta and Romeo would be waiting for them. They would go off on a two- or three-hour ride and then come back laughing, and very thirsty. I would put down the book I was reading and come out of my hiding place—it was a shady spot beneath three or four trees that had grown close together, making a little room—and I would go to the well to draw up cold water because I always liked watching people or animals quench their thirst. Their return would break my morning into two parts as different as two different seasons. I would fill two glasses and two buckets without hurrying, enjoying their anticipation, and then after they had drunk, their joy.

Nikitas lit a cigarette and walked over toward the pavilion. His blond hair and blue eyes made him stand out like a bright spot in an already bright atmosphere.

This was the hour when the discussion of the magazine would begin—in the meantime Petros would have arrived. We would settle ourselves in the armchairs, the wind blowing, and tease each other and laugh. But their decision was serious: they were going to publish a magazine.

Nikitas wrote poems and Petros something he called essays on aestheticism. Beauty is this and this, he would write, or Art is this and this. The relation between Truth and Beauty is ... Often he would refer to great poets and argue who was greater. At other times he would write about theories and modern trends, making projections about the future. "You must transcend your own time," Petros said. "You must be original," Nikitas said.

I listened carefully. Their ideas worried me. Unconsciously I tried to keep their words at a distance, to hear them as if they were foreign, so that I could still have my way of seeing things. They wrote, I didn't. I didn't have anything to write. Although I had written good essays in elementary school—the teacher had even read them to the rest of the class—in middle school I was the worst. I was always forgetting the connection between the beginning, the main theme, and the ending. I didn't write like they did. I also thought about how the books I read couldn't have been written using their theories and rules, nor could those who wrote the books have been trying to be original. I attempted to tell them this one day.

"What if writers were free," I began, "completely free, and if..."

"Is Margarita coming?" Petros broke in.

I thought he was just being mean.

"How should I know?"

It wasn't long ago that Petros asked me if I would go steady with him, and if I agreed he would go steady with me. It seemed like a funny idea so I laughed. I had no desire to have thoughts of Petros floating around in my head, making me miserable. I knew how girls suffered when they had someone on their mind. On the other hand I didn't want him thinking about Margarita.

"You know she stayed back a year," I said.

"Who?"

"Margarita."

"Is that supposed to be news? We've known that since June."

Nonetheless, even though I knew how girls suffered when they had someone on their mind, one night I couldn't sleep because that same afternoon on the road to Mr. Louzis's I had met David, the astronomer, as they had already begun to call him.

It was almost six months since he had returned from England

and he still hadn't visited anyone, not Mr. Louzis, not the Parigoris, not us.

In the beginning he had closed himself off with some builders who demolished the left turret of the house and put a revolving iron dome in its place. "It will open mechanically and then we'll see the heavens," said Kapatos. When he wasn't in jail he was a builder, and everyone in the neighborhood supported him in the hopes that he would get himself back on the right road—besides he never committed crimes near home. Then when that task was accomplished and the various instruments had been installed, David had started writing—at least that's what they say—a study of a certain star. No matter how you explain it though, it was terribly impolite of him not to have visited us, even formally, since he had been gone such a long time and we were family friends.

At first I didn't recognize him. It had been four years since I'd seen him and he had grown a beard. I was walking along singing, whipping the air with my switch, when he suddenly appeared from behind a blackberry bush at a curve in the road. I was about to greet him, welcome him, but instead I just looked at him and went on walking.

It was a strange moment that floated in space and then flew away before I could catch it, hazy, and yet perfectly clear because it captured all my old hatred and jealousy for the colorful rubber balls and the striped jackets with gold buttons that used to be sent to David from England. Also, I had been scared of his eyes when I was really little because they were so black and shiny like the witch's eyes in a painting by some famous painter that hung on Aunt Theresa's wall. I remember how their similar eyes made the two of them merge in my mind sometimes as a sort of alternative kind of being, a scary being, other times as mother and child, and still other times as the same person with two different faces that could be changed like clothes.

And his house also had something sad about it: so tall with three floors and two turrets, one to the right and one to the left, with a very few narrow windows just where you didn't expect them, one off in the right-hand corner, the other down to the left, the other floating in the middle. It looked like a castle out of a Mickey Mouse cartoon, one in which the mice would have wild parties at night and dance quadrilles in the holes of a huge, half-eaten cheese.

It was dark gray with a border of red bricks around all the windows. It didn't have a garden or a fence. Its land was sown with potatoes and onions.

In the morning, against the backdrop of sun and sky, David's house looked a little silly, but at dusk and at night it had an exceedingly serious air to it. This was because dusk, like a painter, gave a certain overpowering tone to the landscape that united all the colors and effaced discord so that in the end one couldn't imagine anything suiting the night better than David's house, nor anything suiting David's house better than those fields sown with potatoes and onions.

When I reached it on the way to Mr. Louzis's I knew I had gone halfway.

I remember the inside fairly well, not so much from seeing it, but more as if I had read a description of it in a book or had heard people talking about it. The deer antlers hanging on the wall in the entry hall; the lion feet on the table and chairs in the dining room (there was no window in the dining room); the books in the library all bound in exactly the same way so that you thought it was many copies of the same book and that if you had read one you had read them all. But none of this prepared you for Ruth's colorful room.

It was rose-colored the last time I saw it and the time before that, white. At other times it had been blue or yellow. Of course the walls and the floor didn't change colors, it was just all the rest: the curtains, the bedspread, the tablecloth on the small table, the two or three pillows that lay on the floor, the chair covers. I nearly forgot the doll. It never moved from its place on the pillow where it sat coquettishly, but its dress changed often.

"It's a personal need," Ruth would say. "When my mood changes"— she had her own way of speaking, a mixture of colloquial and scholarly Greek, all with an English accent—"I have to change the color around me to match." In the same way Aunt Theresa "compensated" when the cards didn't come out right in solitaire, and then afterwards tried to convince herself that they had come out right all by themselves,

Ruth changed the color of her room, not so much because her mood had changed but because she wanted to change her mood.

On the dressing table between the bottles and makeup, there were all sorts of tiny animals, made of porcelain, ivory, clay, grazing next to each other, a valuable porcelain elephant next to a cheap, colorful cat bought in the flea market, the sky blue borzoi next to a stumpy wooden dog. The same kind of things were also on the shelves between the books, which were never the same since Ruth gave them away as soon as she had read them. On the walls the faces of movie stars who she happened to admire at that time smiled down; sometimes they were famous, other times they were unknown, perhaps just playing the role of postman or maid, but bound for glory. And every year there would be photographs of the most recent tennis champions.

On the whole, though, Ruth was a very simple person. And with her small build, her blond hair down to her shoulders, and her merry eyes, it was hard to imagine that she was forty-five years old and had a son as old as David. Her childish looks and manners, her blue eyes, and her pale complexion made me wonder how she could be a Jew. Even when I told myself that she was an English Jew, so of course she could have blond hair, I couldn't get rid of the image I had from reading the Old Testament of Jews as dark-skinned, pensive people with dark shiny hair. I thought of them as having olive oil skin, yellow fingers, a repelling yet intriguing nature, sweet and sneaky voices, a bitter soul.

Ruth, on the other hand, was always laughing. She had two deep lines on either side of her mouth, but none around her eyes or forehead. She was pleasant to be around, and she wanted everyone, even children, even David, to call her Ruth. By doing this and leaving her hair down she thought she would never grow old.

She had met David's father in England, in a big port. Their first meeting was sort of romantic. One rainy evening when she had forgotten her umbrella and was running like a soaked cat, she slipped and fell. At the same moment a gentleman leaned down and tried to help her up. "Come, come my child," he said, "it's nothing"—in the dark he had mistaken her for a small child. Ruth, though, began to cry loudly, saying that certainly she had broken her backbone and that no one should move her from that spot. The gentleman, after failing to persuade her to move, was obliged to pick her up by force whereupon he saw, through the thick curtain of rain that made the streetlights yellow, that she had a slight scratch on her knee and that she was not a little girl at all.

Ruth never stopped playing such childish tricks, just as she never stopped changing the color of her room, nor having around her the miniature animals she loved and the photographs of the actors she admired. Though this was the excuse for small quarrels with her husband, it was also the main basis of their happiness and the reason he was still as in love with her as he had been on the first day they met.

She too was as in love with him as she had been on that first day. Leaving aside that he was a shipowner and had to deal with ships, seas, and freight, as well as his mania for good English tobacco and whiskey, she saw in him the direct descendants, on the one hand, of the heroes who fought at Marathon, and on the other hand, of the philosophers who could live off bread and water and sleep in a barrel.

The fact that he was a Greek Orthodox and she was an English Jew had given a special charm to their relationship right from the beginning, the charm of the slightly forbidden or sacrilegious. And as they did not always live together—his office was in an English port and she preferred the climate of Kifissia—the few months they spent together always had an air of adventure.

She was immensely happy when she was expecting his return. But she was never sad when he left, nor was there any particular goodbye ritual. She would be combing her hair or drinking her milk, and he would lean down and kiss her and say goodbye, while he distractedly stared at a vase of the season's first chrysanthemums. And seated there, she too would kiss him and say goodbye, arranging the folds of her bathrobe. It was exactly the way they had said goodbye a few days ago when David's father, instead of going to England, had gone off on a walk to the main square to drink ouzo with Mr. Louzis.

We had not experienced all those things for four years. We hadn't heard Ruth's chattering, the calm step of David's father, nor the music box in the front hall under the deer antlers, which would play two tunes, one after the other, after you wound it up: the monotonous Byzantine hymn to the Panaghia and Christ that Ruth loved so much, and an English love song with words from Shakespeare that also sounded like a prayer. We hadn't had all this for four years, and we hadn't realized how much we'd missed it. But my meeting with David brought it all back. That night after I had seen him I couldn't sleep—all the old images passed before me: Ruth's animals dancing to the tune of the love song, the sun-drenched field with the potatoes spreading out in front of the wall of the dining room that had no window, and David's eyes, black and shiny, the same as the witch's, filling me with that old childhood fear.

From that day on, my walk as far as Mr. Louzis's took on another meaning. Every time I set out and thought to myself that I might meet David, I felt a flame dance inside of me. "When I think of him, my heart beats," Eleni used to say about Emilios. But if there had been someone to tell me I'd meet him for sure, I'd never have set out or I'd have run home. In the evening, looking at the light and the shadows that played in the water of the cistern, I would imagine our future meeting, down to the smallest detail: what he would say to me, what I would say to him, what I would be wearing, how he would look at me. Perhaps we would sit down on the roots of an olive tree. It had been three days now since Emilios had kissed Eleni under a pine tree. That astronomers existed, I knew—just a few days ago I had seen the photograph of the most famous astronomer in the world in an American magazine. He was fat with a baby face, and wore glasses—and I also knew that poets existed. But in the same way that Jews for me could never be blond, even when I had Ruth right in front of me, poets and astronomers couldn't have houses and beds, nor drink their morning coffee with milk. But David loved coffee with milk, and ever since he was small he would hold his cup very politely—an obedient well-behaved boy with his striped jacket and gold buttons. His house was funnier now than then, on the one side a turret, and on the other a round, iron dome that shone in the sun like an old tin can! Perhaps I should have greeted him. He probably misunderstood my silence, attributing it to my old dislike for him. He must have learned that a few months before he left, I persuaded all the other kids in our gang not to speak to him in an attempt to deflate his grand image of himself. The few times he came to our house or we went to his, he would act all distracted and either disappear or go and talk with the grown-ups on the veranda. Mr. Louzis said, "He's an extremely clever child." David's tongue loosened when he spoke with Mr. Louzis, and his distant and ironic stare would reach as far as the pavilion where we would be sitting. He would say good night to us very politely, bowing before us as if we were ladies, though he wouldn't kiss our hands. "What a wimp!" Maria would say. "How unpleasant!" I would say. And we would all agree that he was stuck-up.

Ruth hadn't come back yet. Too bad. If she were here she would have invited us over. But of course if someone said, "Do you want to marry David? He wants to marry you," I would have responded, "No, no, no, a thousand times no." When I see him next I'll run up and ask him about the heavens and stars. Perhaps it would be more polite to start by asking him about university, and telling him about Maria's wedding and all that has gone on here. If Petros only knew where my thoughts were now…

Yesterday afternoon, seeing Kapatos return from David's with his shovel on his shoulder, I let some time pass, and then walked that way.

At dusk, Mother Kapatos would pull up a chair and sit in front of her house, her back against the wall. And her tired glance would not dare to wander far. It would fix on the mound of old tin cans, rusty wire, and other junk her children had gathered and stacked in front of the door. Farther away the trees bent in the wind, and Gekas's taverna was full; farther away was Ruth's room of many colors, then Athens, then the rest of the world.

Kapatos's sons, so young and poor, seemed to find consolation in gathering things that had volume and weight. In the pile by their house you could find wire too thick to bend and pieces of cans as sharp as knives. But the most valuable thing was a boat, a real one, and fairly large, too. Who knows how it ended up in the woods near here, but they found it there and dragged it home. It sits on top of the pebbles and thyme, next to the rest of the rubbish. It seems to have widened over the years. Away from the sea it looks like a drowned man whose stomach is swollen with water. But it also manages to retain a fine silhouette and a nostalgia for the sea, especially when you look at it sideways, like a woman after thirty years of marriage, wide-hipped and heavy-breasted, can still have shapely hands and legs, and a perfect nose. The boat wouldn't float: its timber creaks and must be cracked; but this doesn't matter because for the children it's a toy and it's unlikely that it will ever see the sea again.

About this time Kapatos arrives and eats a plate of food. Then he crosses himself, lights his cigarette, and leaves. No one speaks to him. Even Koula gives him his plate silently, as if to a dog who has no master. In the old days they were scared of him because he would beat them. Now that he doesn't have the strength nor the temper to do that, they simply despise him. They don't let him sleep in the house. When he's in jail no one goes to visit him. And when he's about to say something, their silence rises like a wall in front of him and stops him. Then he looks at them with his one eye, his left, which resembles a blue bead, while his right one, closed and covered in a wrinkled eyelid, looks inward. If the conscience like the heart resided in a certain part of the body, Kapatos's conscience would certainly reside in his eye.

I found them all in their usual places, the way you find actors on stage, one sitting, one standing and talking, a third staring sadly into the audience, using the same gestures and words they used yesterday at this time. Mother Kapatos was sitting with her back to the wall. Kapatos was lying two or three meters away waiting for his food. Koula was going to and fro fixing it, the boys were out, the boat was empty, and the oldest daughter, Amalia, was reading.

Amalia had just finished high school with many sacrifices and she was planning to become a teacher and move far away. She had a passion for learning. Her eyes, even paler than Kapatos's, took on color and life when she talked of books, in particular about those Russian books her big brother sent her from Kavala, where he was a tobacco worker. Those books talked of a different world, a world for men and women whose dream was not a house and garden but something less concrete and yet more grand.

"How was work today?" I asked, looking at Kapatos.

This was a time of day when they didn't mind an outsider dropping by for a chat. Only they made sure they never had to address each other. If the conversation led to this, they would keep their eye fixed on the outsider and refer to the other in the third person: "He says that he doesn't know, but..." This of course was not the case between Mother Kapatos and her children. There, there was complete understanding. They knew that for their sake she hadn't taken a single day off in twenty years, and that her eyes were sinking deeper and deeper into her skull, losing their glow. Her eyes were cast-iron black and her face was old before its time. She had no front teeth, though she was only forty.

"We're almost there. We've just about finished our part of the job. Now specialists will have to come install the telescope."

And as he saw a questioning look on his wife's face, still seeming to respond to me, he added, "Telescopes are certain kind of tubes which when you put them up to your eye make it possible to see what's happening in the heavens. They say that the moon has mountains and valleys..."

"If we can't even get our life right here on earth, what do we want with the heavens?" Amalia threw in, once again looking at me.

And I wondered if that was meant for her father or for everyone in the world.

"But that Mr. David is a difficult person," continued Kapatos. "He's working us to death.

"He's always been that way, every since he was little," said Kapatos. "He was a difficult child. I know—oh did he make Kalliope suffer when she worked there! By the time she got him dressed he would have kicked her ten times, sometimes he'd have bitten her, too."

I felt joyous. That's all I'd wanted, to hear about David.

"And his mother would never let anyone beat him... Beating is catastrophic for children, she said. A crazy Brit, what do you expect? Oh, I forgot to ask about Tasia. It looks like she's pregnant again, doesn't it? We'll be having another baby soon."

"So what exactly did David do to Kalliope?"

"The upshot is that she couldn't even manage a month in that house. And all the others who worked there the same, if not worse. A nice house, good pay, they'd say, but those children . . . and they'd hand in their uniforms."

"It certainly seems as if he hasn't changed at all," I said just to hear their response, waiting anxiously.

They didn't respond. Perhaps they didn't hear. Mother Kapatos had her eyes glued to the little mound of junk; Kapatos started to get up because he saw Koula coming with his food. In the distance you could hear the boys, out of breath, getting nearer all in a pack, a sound like the hooves of galloping horses. Soon they were there with an empty nest in their hands. They had shoved the birds out and even shot one with a rubber band. They couldn't contain their joy. Amalia wet her finger with spit and mechanically turned two or three pages, and then closed the book because it was completely dark.

"Don't just read Dostoyevsky," she told me as I got ready to leave. "There are also contemporary Russians."

On my way back I had a cuckoo for company. I whistled at him, he whistled at me, I whistled back, and he answered. While I walked on the sharp stones, he flew from branch to branch. Amalia will become a teacher. She'll go to a faraway village to educate children. While she's writing the alphabet on the blackboard the rain will stream down the windows and the potholes in the empty schoolyard will fill up. David is writing a study about stars and he's let his beard grow. Before I went to the Kapatoses I was thinking only of him. Now Amalia's life is also on my mind. Also Nikitas's, and Mrs. Montelandi's, who had such a beautiful voice in her youth. Because sometimes the seduction of other people's lives causes me to lose the thread of my own, and I become Amalia and Mrs. Montelandi, as if those particular people leapt forth from the millions of people out there, standing out like bare mountains at dusk. And the seduction is no less when those particular people, instead of leaping out, bury themselves amidst all the others, losing their distinction, a mob of unknown faces passing under my window. I can't remember what David's face looks like, I can't see it the way I did in the afternoon when Kapatos passed by with a shovel on his shoulder. It's chilly. Somewhere nearby it must be raining.

THE SECOND SUMMER

I. LAURA PARIGORI

WHEN LAURA Parigori opened her eyes that Sunday morning, she realized that she had left the light on. The book she had started the night before was lying on top of her, its pages slightly crumpled. She could barely remember the page it was open to. She must have fallen asleep while reading and then slept soundly right until that moment. "Strange," she whispered, "and I thought I had insomnia."

Often Laura dreamed that she couldn't sleep. She would wake up exhausted, her body worn out from the idea of not sleeping.

She threw off the sheets abruptly and stood up. She was wearing an antique nightgown. A wide lace collar hung across her shoulders and chest. And although from her middle down the fine material clung to unattractive curves and lumps, the lace with its embroidered flowers and birds gave her round, expressive shoulders the glow of a girl at her first dance. Her breast was full of tenderness and abandon.

She glanced at the door and hurried to turn off the light. Yannis was odd about things like that. He could buy her the most expensive dress and spend money on her slightest desire, but he would complain if he saw the water running for too long or a light on in an empty room. Sometimes when Yannis stayed the night in Athens at the hospital, Laura would turn on all the lights and walk around as if it were day. She'd also turn on the radio as loud as it would go, and run into the garden where the light and sound would reach her altered and unreal.

At that moment the bells from the church of the Panaghia began to toll. And soon the street was full of the sounds of women talking and children playing. The first service was over and the second about to begin. One by one, the villagers came out of the small whitewashed door, continued down the path between the four cypress trees, out onto the cobblestones of Aniksi Avenue, which then wound its way like a white ribbon between the red fields.

"What beautiful countryside," Laura said, leaning out of the window, sighing. "And good people, too."

She would watch them every Sunday as they passed by, the wife of Gekas, the owner of the taverna, always leading the way. She went to great lengths to be the first out of church. It was strange that a woman in a dumpy calico dress with plump hands could appear so attractive. "As long as the taverna, the wine, and my hardworking husband are fine," she would say. Everyone had their suspicions, though, and thought that Gekas was really making his money the two times a week he went to Piraeus. What did he do in Piraeus? And why did he never mention it? "His sister is there," Mrs. Gekas would say. "He's so fond of her..." The more money he made, the more picky she became about her friends. She cut off relations with the wife of Michalis, the construction worker, and Kalliope, the egg lady, and instead put all her energy into cultivating friendships with the Kritikos and Kouvelis families, since they had the largest flocks around.

"What beautiful countryside..." murmured Laura, sighing again.

The morning rays came in through the open window and played on the wall opposite.

She couldn't bear the bright light, which made everything seem naked and the same. Leaning out of the window, she went to draw in the shutters. Once again she had forgotten that this house had blinds and that they opened and shut by pulling a linen cord. Why couldn't she get used to this after all these years? Why did she always lean out instead of standing straight and proper like the maid?

Immediately the room became familiar again; certain corners were lit up, others were dark, a coolness settled on the photographs, each book turned its appropriate color and shape. They were all things she loved dearly and wouldn't trade for anything in the world. Besides, she didn't have that kind of transformative power. Things were the way they were. She couldn't change the color of her eyes, or trade in her pudgy feet. Her feet had always been that way. Her breasts were beautiful, though. Only Ruth could change colors and moods. How she loved Ruth! Ruth could really make her laugh. When that lump in her throat became unbearable she would leave the house and either turn right toward the woods where she would lie on the ground and cry, or left toward Ruth's where she would laugh until dusk.

Anna was also nice. But ever since she got divorced she didn't laugh much and she would only talk about her property and sew.

"If I was divorced..." Laura was about to say. But old memories like sunken ships at the bottom of the sea suddenly rose up from the depths of her soul: hazy, trembling, a broken steering wheel, a bent rudder, masts jutting into space, the drowned treading water.

The time the foreign doctor had come to stay—he rose early, took a walk in the garden, ate a great deal, wrote an article on vitamin C. "Gnädige Frau," he would kiss her hand. She dreamt about him. And later when she met the small artist, his tiny slit eyes brimming with life, his nervous short legs, his exaggerated movements—like a rat. Yannis would have thought him ridiculous. And then there was the young man who kissed her as they danced, not knowing of course that she was Mrs. Parigori. Sometimes going down Deliyannis Street in the carriage she would see a man passing by, his step strong, proud... "Stop!" she wanted to cry to the driver. The bells jangled, the reins hung loose, the horse skidded a bit as he stepped on the asphalt scattering pink and white oleanders to the left and to the right.

Nobody had ever suspected anything. She remained with her eyes wide open looking at the wild lilies, the water running in the ravine. Marios used to cling to her, but then he stopped needing her. Leda had never needed her. Suddenly something made her want to run and sing out of tune. Nothing would change. No one would ever know. The men would leave as they had come, her heart a house with changing tenants. This is what made life interesting, like a novel.

"Laura, are you ready?" Yannis's voice interrupted her thoughts. On Sundays they ate breakfast together in the dining room.

"Almost," she called out louder than necessary.

"Why are you yelling? I'm right outside your door."

The door opened and Yannis stood there laughing. He sat down on the rumpled sheets.

"I do like Sundays," he said after a bit.

"If only they would leave you alone. God rested on the seventh day, but not you. There's always a telephone call, or a..."

She looked at him tenderly.

"I'm coming—just a minute," she said, putting her robe on over her nightgown and going into the bathroom.

Yannis glanced around the room. He had built the house with the fruits of his labor exactly as he wished. Only this room was somehow out of place. Perhaps it was the photographs with the old-fashioned clothes, the furniture from Corfu that Laura had brought from her father's house, the chairs with the thin legs... It all made him feel the way Mrs. Montelandi did when she looked at him.

The dining room, on the other hand, was bright and comfortable with practical, modern furniture.

"How did you sleep?" he asked, sitting across from her at the big table.

"I had insomnia, that is..." And changing her tone abruptly, "Where is Leda? I haven't seen her this morning."

"She must be running around outside. Don't worry."

Leda's escapades were his joy. She had her own particular way of doing everything—such freedom. Marios resembled him, shy and hardworking, but Leda had found the perfect combination of the Montelandis and Parigoris.

"Listen, Yannis," said Laura, "I want you to talk to her seriously. She's always off with those Kapatos tramps."

"All right, all right."

He thought of the photograph of his father he carried in his wallet crumpled up amidst his notes and prescriptions. His father had come from a poor family and worked his way up to boss in a printing shop. When he was young he must have been a tramp.

"Yannis, for goodness sake, there is such a thing as different social backgrounds. The other day they caught her carting off someone's fence to make swords."

"All right, I'll speak to her," said Yannis.

He didn't like to discipline her. But the truth was that Leda could pick up bad habits from those Kapatos kids. He'd already heard her saying "damn," which just wouldn't do.

"I'll go down and see if I can find her. At this hour she's usually down by the boat pretending to be Bouboulina trying to save the Greeks from the Turks crying 'Enemy sighted! All hands on deck!' The other children fixing their eyes on the distant hills. The intensity of children's play is strange, medically speaking—"

"I'm on my way down too," interrupted Laura, "to see Marios and Maria."

"How is Maria doing?"

"She's beginning her eighth month."

"So, in a month or so ..."

"Yes, about that."

By this time they had reached the door.

"One minute," Laura said, "let me get my umbrella, the sun is strong."

And they walked down the hill just as the second service was ending.

"Little white boat, floating by the shore, where are you going, who tends your oar?" Maria was singing softly sitting in a chair on the veranda with her two hands folded on her belly. Her feet hung, swinging back and forth to the song's rhythm. Before getting pregnant her feet had reached the tiles; even her heels, she mused.

She wore a light blue dress with yellow flowers. Katerina would say "yellow worlds" because she had just discovered a plant by that name and she kept chanting it over and over. Why should anyone get so excited about a plant called "yellow world"?

Marios was watering the trees. They were Grandpa's wedding present to them, along with the house: forty apricot and twenty cherry. Each Sunday morning Marios would put on a pair of shorts, no shirt, and go out barefoot to play gardener. He would dig with all his might, sweating hard, and when the water came down the trench and slowly filled the holes under the trees, he would lift up his head and take in deep breaths. It was during those moments he realized that he experienced true happiness. Whereas the big events—like when he graduated or got married to Maria or learned he would be a father—brought worries along with the happiness. He would get a lump in his throat, his heart would pound, his eyes would fill with tears, and he'd be at a loss for what to do.

Maria's melancholy voice reached him all the way in the orchard: "Who knows what lies around the next bend..."

He looked in her direction. She had her eyes half-closed and was leaning her head back as if resting it on something, but the back of the chair only came up to her shoulders.

He started to run to her. He had already thrown down his hoe when he stopped; the hole was overflowing. He blocked it off with dirt, letting the water pour back into the trench and then dug an opening to the next tree. For another minute or two he hesitated. Then with slow steps he walked toward the veranda whistling softly, feigning indifference.

He approached her quietly, barefoot, while still keeping an eye on the water.

"Maria dear, why is your voice so melancholy?" he asked.

She was startled, as if she had been far away. She turned and looked at him with eyes even deeper and darker than they had been last year.

"But I am happy," she said absentmindedly, unfolding her hands and bringing them to her heart as if to get rid of some burden.

The pain of happiness, Marios thought.

"Shall I bring you an armchair?" he said. "You're not comfortable in that chair, it's too high off the ground."

"No, no, I'm just fine. The armchair hurts my back."

"Whatever you wish."

He caressed her hair and started to leave.

"I've got to go or the water will overflow."

She smiled at him the way a mother smiles at a child playing hooky.

"Maria, I hope you don't think I don't want to stay with you and talk..."

"Go on now. The water will overflow," she said laughing, already swinging her feet back and forth. "'Little white boat...' Sometimes I like to be alone."

She was dreaming of the child God would send her. God...well... if God was the one who sent children. She was thinking about how she had cried after the first and second months of marriage, sure she was infertile. Her mother had laughed. "It doesn't always happen right away, silly girl," she said, remembering how it was three months before she had gotten pregnant with Maria. How happy Miltos had been then! Anyway...

By November Maria was pregnant. Marios was thrilled. It so happened that they had quarreled a bit the morning she learned the news; the maid hadn't ironed a shirt properly or something like that. Marios was not finicky, but it bothered Maria, who liked her clothes well washed and nicely ironed. And so they began to squabble, and Marios paced back and forth, dissatisfied. He had already forgotten that the cause of it was just a shirt. Then Maria told him the news—and suddenly everything changed.

The only hard part was that the more time passed, the less she wanted to be touched. Strange creatures, women! The first evening of their marriage she was cold as marble, and the second and the third, the same. Later, though, it was she who wanted him. As soon as they lay down, she would curl up close to him like a cat and tell him sweet things. She would cover him completely with her arms, as if a warm, pink cloud at sunset had settled over him. Her whispery voice would excite him and then all of a sudden he would embrace her, knowing that her voice was soft enough.

It was a period when they went out rarely, didn't talk to anyone, and even between themselves said little. The two mothers complained about their aloof manner. Anna even broke down in tears one day when she took them a sweet and Maria forgot to kiss her goodbye. During this time Maria still wore tight nightgowns and brushed her hair before going to bed. Marios, pretending to read the newspaper, would watch her carefully from the bed where he sat: the slope of her neck as she pulled her skirt over her head, the curve of her waist as she bent down to unbutton her shoes, her face all golden in the mirror from the reflection of the lights. Her eyelashes spreading unnaturally long shadows under her eyes gave her an air of seriousness and mystery, a diffused intensity. Maria raised her hand and closed a box—it went click in the night—Marios waited.

But ever since she told him of the child she rarely came near him with her whispering. The day came when she didn't even want him to lie next to her for fear that he might knock her by mistake.

The truth is, she suffered a lot the first few months of pregnancy; she was dizzy and nauseous. Of course he couldn't understand. He would forget and light a cigarette in front of her even though she had told him that it bothered her. At such moments it was as if she had lost her mind. She would say things to hurt him. Her eyes had the same hard glare they had that rainy day in the kitchen.

Then she would calm down, her face and her whole body giving off an air of absolute self-sufficiency that drove Marios crazy. He would say something to get back at her but she wouldn't hear him. She would look off into the distance, as if unaware. She did it on purpose, though, to irritate him. She was stubborn, cruel perhaps. He wanted to torture her the way she tortured him, so she'd understand. Then he would suddenly remember that she was his wife, that he loved her, that she would soon give birth to his child. His eyes would fill with tears. He would go down on his knees before her, all gentleness, hugging her legs ... "That dirty cigarette ... Next time you will just have to beat me." Her once distant look would slowly light up. She would laugh. And he would join in. "I don't understand why we fight," they'd say to each other. "Why ... what for?" They would think about this for a moment, and then laugh again. Everything would be back to normal.

The change that the child brought to Maria's life happened to coincide with Marios's return to work. In the first few months of their marriage he lived for the moment. He was imprisoned in the present. His studies and the hospital were beyond comprehension, something out of someone else's life. His dreams for the future were colorless and without meaning. He was like a drunkard who, taken with the pleasures of the moment, sees nothing else. They would wake up late. In the afternoon they'd take a walk and suddenly it would be evening. The days were short like hours and Marios wondered how he ever found time to do all that he had done before. Chaos and nothingness merged with eternity, staying with him like the scent of cyclamen and heather that filled the forest, and like the sound of her voice echoing in the ravine.

But when Maria heard the call of the child, he heard the call of the outside world. Dusk was coming on and he was looking out the window. Instead of seeing the pine trees bending in the wind, he saw clearly in front of him the hospital beds, the operating room, his father wearing gloves. He saw himself doing his first operation, and a shiver of excitement ran down his spine. He wanted to be there right now. Surely one day he would be famous. He had a sure hand. In Athens the lights would already be on and the cars would be darting to and fro. "Tomorrow I'll go to the hospital," he said aloud. She got up to turn on the light. Now he couldn't even see the pine trees. The night seemed like an eternity, and in the morning he had the impatience of a schoolboy on the first day of school.

From then on their life took the shape it would have for the rest of their lives. Maria accompanied him to the garden gate. She had just woken up and was not yet dressed. Her nightgown showed below her long robe and her hair was still uncombed. Her eyes had something of the mistiness of dreams, and when Marios bent over to kiss her, a nighttime scent, a womanly scent, drifted up from between her breasts. "I could have waited another week," he said sadly. "There was no reason it had to be today."

He glanced down the road, which went past the woods. He would take that route to get to Aniksi Avenue, where his father was waiting for him. He had called him last night. The cold air seemed to slap the earth, everything underneath making him want to run away. "But now that I've made up my mind . . ." he said.

She stood erect at the gate, watching him as he left. "Go on inside," he called out, "you'll catch cold." She waved to him and turned to go in. It was the first day she had spent alone since the wedding. She felt a sadness and a certain relief. There were so many things that had to be done. When Marios was around she couldn't do anything. She was so lazy, wandering about, and they woke so late. Now it was only eight. By noon she could accomplish so many things. She could visit her mother to discuss baby clothes. A warmth filled her as if she'd drunk a lot of tea after a walk. She went into the bathroom singing, and threw off her clothes, letting the cold water run over her body. She felt a shiver of anticipation. Unconsciously she pressed down on her tummy, but nothing showed yet. "Ah, it's nice to be expecting a child," she said looking at herself in the mirror.

Only later did she begin to get bigger and feel the child kicking and the weight. Her feet and face swelled up. Then the winter came— hours of housework and sewing by the fire. She tried not to think of the birth, but when she was with other women she couldn't resist the temptation to ask; she always brought the conversation around to that. She'd pretend to be indifferent, as if she wasn't afraid. "It's a pain that defies description," Mrs. Parigori said. "But you forget it immediately," added Mother. Aunt Theresa, of course, had nothing to say on the subject.

Sometimes when she was alone she would get anxious. And if she died? Jokingly, she would say this to Marios. "A strong woman like you! What a thought!" He would laugh. "In any case we'll have the best doctor, and my father will be there." But inside he too was a little scared.

The vomiting and dizziness had passed. Sleeping, though, was becoming more and more difficult. She lay on her back because she was uncomfortable on her side. She couldn't even curl up her legs. Spread out on her back, her eyes wide open, sleep would creep up on her without her noticing, the sweetness of those first few minutes when dreams lasting a second seem to take up the whole night.

In a month or so . . . Who says time passes quickly?

She folded her hands on top of her belly again. She looked at them and then at the garden. The cherry trees, bright red, were heavy with fruit. The sun was high and hot, but there was a breeze, and with it the scent of lemon verbena. It was pleasant.

At that moment Mrs. Parigori's umbrella appeared in the distance, and then Mrs. Parigori herself in a pale green dress. She walked with tiny steps, bouncing slightly on her high heels, making untidy, spastic motions because her umbrella kept threatening to fly away. She would try to hold it with both hands, but then her handbag would slip off her shoulder. She stumbled, but she never thought of closing the umbrella. It was also green with four huge roses.

"Mother!" cried Marios.

"Ah, yes," said Maria, who had been watching her approach for two minutes.

She got up to greet her. Marios had already arrived at the gate.

"The wind is enough to drive a person mad," said Laura. "We don't have such wind on Aniksi Avenue."

They climbed up onto the veranda to sit, but there was already too much sun. It was steadily moving up the steps; in no time it would be at their feet. They rose to go inside where it was cool. Meanwhile they sent word that Anna should join them. Soon Yannis arrived with Leda. The two families always ate their Sunday meal together.

EXCERPTS FROM MRS. PARIGORI'S DIARY:

May 26th. Today I saw Maria. She's getting very heavy and her face has swollen up so that her eyes are two small slits. That Maria has the patience of an angel. She never complains and always seems satisfied. Marios, on the other hand, is just like Yannis.

"I hate dissatisfied women," Maria said, as she stood up after lunch to close the shutters. She had seen me staring out the window absentmindedly.

Her comment didn't come out of the blue. We had been discussing the subject at the table. Yannis and Marios were saying that dissatisfied women live in their own imaginary world, that is, they're deluded.

"So there are no women who are rebelling inside?" I said.

"Rebelling against what?" asked Yannis.

"I'm not exactly sure. Against their womanly fate, perhaps. I don't know, a desire for something else, something impossible, something they don't dare do..."

"That's just cowardice," said Katerina, but she didn't manage to finish her sentence before Anna threw her a fierce glance.

"Dissatisfied women are simply unsuccessful women," said Maria, her cheeks flushed. And she went on and on about the animals in the forest who enjoy the lightness in their gait, their claws as they attack, their teeth as they devour their prey. She wandered so far from the topic that we all forgot what we had been talking about.

Marios is lucky. Maria seems to believe in submission. When she folds her hands on top of her belly it is as if she were proud of her weight, as if she wanted it this way. She's sure to have half a dozen children.

May 26th. A year earlier. It seems to me that Marios is in love with Anna's eldest daughter.

A day doesn't pass without him going over to visit and then he always seems to come back sad. What's going on? Could it be she doesn't love him?

The same year, a few days later. Marios and Leda had their friends over for a party yesterday. I prepared all sorts of nice things to eat and decorated the yard with Venetian lanterns. This new generation is enough to drive a person crazy. They have such a free way of acting and talking...

I don't like the way Maria acts with the boys. She takes them all by the arm, laughs provocatively. She was wearing a showy dress that didn't cover her properly, and when it got dark she disappeared two or three times behind the trees with Stefanos. She mostly danced with him. She didn't seem to notice Marios. Perhaps it's better that way. He will forget her.

One day, one of many, ten years earlier. I must be dreaming. I have been at the Edipsos baths since yesterday, all by myself. I traveled on the same boat as a man with large melancholy eyes and a limp. I could fall in love with such a man.

Yannis says that the waters of Edipsos will do me good. Ever since I gave birth to Leda I've had a little phlebitis; some days my legs are very swollen. Of course I never had thin legs, so now I can just blame it on the phlebitis.

I got upset when I saw him in the dining room. At first I just saw one of his eyes, hidden amidst numerous unknown faces, and then later, after I had pulled my chair a bit to the right, his whole face. He is very pale and seems very sad.

Here there are people from different social classes, and all the cliques that are formed here mirror those classes exactly. Successful businessmen and their wives make up the core group. They have yachts and take short jaunts along the coast, and in the afternoons they hire cars and go for excursions in the country. Women who live in the provinces during the year and who meet every summer at Edipsos form another group. They gossip about the first group, feigning contempt, though if one of those ladies happens to talk to them, they can't hide their joy. These women, however, snub the third group, whose husbands are civil servants or own small businesses in Athens or in the provinces. But their scorn is returned since the only dream of these women is to meet the women of the first group with their yachts and beautiful jewelry. In the first party the men discuss international problems; in the second, Greek politics; and in the third, nothing much. As for the children, they all play together. But where oh where is the Corfu society? There are a few older ladies from good families, but they never talk to anyone, not even to each other. Perhaps they worry who will make the first overture. They enter the dining room with vacant expressions on their faces. I'm afraid theirs is a world that is fast disappearing. For this reason when I saw my old friend Ernestine (the one who collected the most shells, and is married now to one of those big businessmen) and she introduced me to that group: "Mr. So-and-so, Mrs. Parigori etc.," I brought the conversation around in such a way so that I was able to add "née Montelandi, from Corfu."

The first day is almost over and I still haven't managed to meet him. As soon as the sun set, he took an armchair and went and sat all alone by the sea. When I happened to pass by with Ernestine, he lifted his head and looked at me. I know now he will be in my dreams.

I will see him coming over to embrace me—though I'm not at all sure that I'd let him get away with such behavior in reality. I wonder what my children are doing now. My mother promised to stay in Kifissia to look after them. Marios is fifteen years old and I can't say that he's disobedient; he already shows a certain aptitude for medicine. Leda, on the other hand, is as mischievous as they come, and she is always trying to climb into the well. I must wire Mother tomorrow to see how they are.

Laura looked out the window, as if to ask the night why life was so strange. There were times when she had such a bitter taste in her mouth. She leafed through another two or three pages in her diary and closed it. Then she caressed its edges and spine. At Edipsos she had laughed when she had realized that the bellboy she'd taken for a child was really in his forties. She'd noticed that bellboys and jockeys looked like children regardless of their age. It amused her. How pleasant those evenings were at Edipsos: the ship whistling before it emerged from behind the mountain, and then coming to a stop and anchoring just in front; the fishing boats too close to the shore; the sea full of tiny lights... Maria had surprised her today. She was a courageous woman. Perhaps she had never had to battle with her dreams. Laura opened her journal to a clean page: "Today I saw Maria. She is getting very heavy." Then she began leafing through earlier pages. On the days that she wrote she also read, always starting from the end and going backwards.

Without stopping her reading she leaned over to take off her shoes. Wearing high heels all day long had tired her out.

II. DAVID, THE ASTRONOMER

"WHEN it comes to love, you two are both retarded," Maria told Infanta and me at one point last year. Without answering, Infanta had thrown her a haughty look; she could even keep her cool when Maria was running after her up the circular staircase that led to Aunt Theresa's room, whistling and singing maliciously "the theory of perfection, tra-la-la, the theory of perfection." I, on the other hand, would get hurt. I couldn't bear such insults; and besides, deep down it bothered me that I hadn't fallen in love. Only sometimes in my dreams—Stefanos, Petros, Emilios, or Nikitas. But when I woke up the feeling would last at the most five minutes and then fade away. "You listen up, Maria," I shouted and started after her. I caught her quickly because she was laughing, and with teeth clenched I threw her down in the lavender and tickled her mercilessly. She was as weak as a child when she laughed. Only when I had gotten out all my anger and she had apologized did I start to laugh myself and it would turn into a nice day.

What would Maria have to say about this year?

All in all I had only spoken with David three times this winter, and none of what I intended ever got said. The first time was when Ruth returned from England and invited us all over for tea. Of course he was forced to notice me since we were sitting opposite each other at the table. He even said, "I think I saw you one afternoon on the road with the berries. Was that you?" "I don't think so," I answered. "I often go there, but if it had been me I would remember." Then the conversation turned to more general matters. Ruth was talking about the growth of the workers' party in England, stressing how dangerous it was. "The British aren't to blame," she added. "It's the Russians who had the idea in the first place." And Mrs. Parigori, after a moment of silence, added that the roots of this evil really went back to the French Revolution. Meanwhile Mr. Parigori, Mr. Louzis, and David talked about the same topic, but as they were men they approached it differently. The workers are right. The state should protect them. Then they'd have no cause for complaint.

For a moment I thought of Amalia, but then my mind was completely taken up with David again. And since I couldn't look him straight in the face I watched his hands. David had full control of his face; he never changed expressions no matter what he heard or said, but his hands gave him away. Free and spontaneous, they sometimes seemed happy, other times sad, and often indifferent or ironic. For irony one finger would stay in the air while the rest of the hand closed; for sadness both hands would settle on the table, one on top of the other, like wounded birds folding their wings. On the whole they had something feminine about them, even uncanny. His fingers were long and thin, very long and thin, the skin tender, smooth and dark, not a hair on them.

His voice fit perfectly with his hands when he was rushing to say something: shrill, high-pitched, feminine. It had an infinite number of tones for expressing emotion. The whole range danced before one's eyes the minute he spoke.

His face on the other hand remained unchanged, one might say expressionless if it weren't for a glare that sometimes flickered in his eyes. I caught a glimpse of such a glare when I asked him to wind the music box and he refused, saying it would bother the grown-ups. The thought that I was perhaps one of those women destined to a life of unrequited love filled me with a pleasant, bitter melancholy. But when he bid me good night the same glare enveloped me like a sudden gust of warm air.

The second time I saw him was in Kifissia in the pastry shop. And the irony is that my own desire to see him almost made me miss him.

Mother had asked me to go buy some pastries for two or three friends of hers who were coming from Athens, but at first I refused.

It was the hour when I usually went for my walk to Mr. Louzis's estate.

"Let Infanta go," I cried.

Mother looked at me sternly.

"Infanta has a cold," she said.

"Let Infanta go," I said, "why always me?"

I felt my voice tremble and tears come to my eyes. Thirty times I had gone toward Mr. Louzis's and not once had I met David but today, today surely I would ...

"Every day you go for a walk for your own pleasure, and when I ask you for one little favor..."

Mother's look was fiery to begin with, but then it cooled down. It was clear she was hurt; she thought my response was out of lack of affection. You could hear the complaint in her voice, but soon she had regained her usual composure.

"Come back soon. The guests will arrive around five."

And as she left, a gesture she made reminded me of a lady from another epoch lifting the train of her long skirt.

The only thing left for me to do was to take the bicycle, ride quickly to the pastry shop, and then go for my walk. David would be standing in front of the potato field; the afternoon sun would make the old tin of the observatory look like a golden cupola from an oriental tale.

And then, just as I was giving the order to the waiter, figuring out the bill in my head so that I wouldn't waste a minute and nervously squeezing the leather wallet in my hand, I saw him in the left-hand corner behind the store window seated in a wicker armchair. He was staring outside absentmindedly, eating an éclair.

The "fifteen minutes of fantastic feats" they had in the movies that always filled me with suspense and horror—cars spinning in the air and then hanging in trees like hats, motorcycles racing round and round a circular wall and then, after arriving at the top, continuing to circle with the naturalness of a cockroach scuttling across the floor—those fifteen minutes lost their shock value and were nothing in comparison with the sight of David eating an éclair behind the store window of the pastry shop.

I don't know how it happened, but he got up and greeted me and I found myself sitting next to him. Without asking me, he called to the waiter, "Nestor, an éclair for the young lady."

"I'd prefer a meringue," I said, but he acted as if he hadn't heard me. "I'd prefer a meringue," I repeated when the waiter arrived with the tray. "The meringues aren't good here," replied David. "Only the éclairs." And he motioned to Nestor to leave.

A vague disgust arose inside me slowly, getting lodged in my throat, making me choke. It was just like when, as a child, I had tried to swallow a whole plum. Why should I have been dying to see him all this time? Perhaps it was just a mad fixation. I watched him to see what impression I was making on him, if he could tell I was nervous. He was bending over slightly, trying to light his pipe. The tobacco must have been moist—it wouldn't light. His movements revealed his annoyance. At one moment when he had dropped his lighter, he shoved back his chair noisily as if he were angry. And whereas before it was the tobacco that wouldn't light, now it was the lighter itself. I blushed as if I were to blame for all this. I didn't know what to say. And to think I'd been dreaming of him for two months. My books, my secret corner, everything at home suddenly seemed like paradise. Then Nestor, in order to please us—all the other tables were empty— turned on the radio as loud as it would go. A jazzed-up version of a Bach piece was playing. "I have to go," I said, and got up abruptly. "Miss, you forgot your pastries," cried Nestor, running after me.

From then on I went to Kifissia for my walks. The oleanders hadn't bloomed yet. The fallen leaves smelled of cold and rain. The afternoons in the sun were beautiful though.

But David's corner behind the store window in the pastry shop was always empty; so, after Ruth invited us over again and David didn't even come down to greet us, I decided never to go back to Kifissia. That evening, I remember, I went and ripped the velvet dress with the lace collar that I had begged Mother to make me. Maria guessed something was wrong, but she didn't tease me the way she would have before. She looked at me tenderly, very tenderly. Pregnancy had changed her. She had became sweeter, softer. During Lent we went to David's. Ruth commented, "Greek Easter is the most beautiful holiday; even better than Christmas in England." It was then that we realized winter was over.

And hardly any time had passed before the wind began to carry the scent of violets and lilac. This always left us feeling divided because the lilac reminded us of spring orgies and awoke in us all pagan instincts, whereas the violets steeped us in a mystical pain, reminding us of the true meaning of Christianity. "Don't forget that it is Spy Wednesday," Aunt Theresa came out on the terrace to reprimand me. I was laughing and dancing around with a daisy stem because the he-loves-me, he-loves-me-not had come out in my favor. Similarly the phrase "Christ died for us on a cross" became so much a part of us during Holy Week that we kept on chanting it even after Resurrection. Again Aunt Theresa was obliged to come out and yell at us.

On Holy Thursday we dyed eggs. On Good Friday it was cloudy. On Black Saturday at exactly midnight Father Loukas said the "Come, partake of the light." The little church glowed. The saints' faces smiled down on the congregation. "Christ has risen." We lit each other's candles. Everyone felt close. "He has risen indeed."

David showed up on Easter Sunday when the lamb was roasting. We talked more than usual, and that, together with the wine and the scent of spring, made me forget everything we said. I only know that we laughed a lot and that I burst into tears that evening after he had left because I couldn't remember a thing we'd said. Even now I grow sad when I think that our only day together is lost without leaving any trace.

I must make him notice me. History says Alcibiades the statesman cut off his dog's tail so that the Athenians would notice him. I wouldn't do that though even if Mavroukos was still alive, first of all because his tail was already very short and then because I loved him too much.

I keep thinking about Mavroukos because recently I saw the tortoise he almost killed in the garden. He had been intrigued by the head and tail that hung out of the shell, and had started to bite. The tortoise of course retreated, infuriating Mavroukos and causing him to bark furiously. In a paroxysm of anger that sometimes seizes the strong when they realize they are impotent before the weak, he snatched up the shell with his teeth and threw it into the bushes. The tortoise ended up on its back with a crack down the middle, and that's the mark I noticed today on the tortoise that was plodding across the garden. And to think that Mavroukos is already dead. Certainly that tortoise will be here even after we are gone. They live for over a hundred years. Though to get around the property it takes them a whole year. I guess that's one hundred rounds a lifetime.

What if I ran away from home and everyone began looking for me and the whole neighborhood heard about it? David would certainly hear too. Perhaps he would go out looking for me in the forest at night with a lantern: "Katerina!... Katerina!" I would be curled up in a corner, wasting away. "Katerina!... Katerina!" Suddenly the lantern would light up my face, revealing the intense expression of a martyr, my eyes glowing supernaturally, my skin transparent from hunger. "Katerina, I love you," he would say. But perhaps by that time I would have grown used to the forest's solitude and would fancy instead the life of a nun seated by a window looking thoughtfully at a green meadow. "Life in a convent is pleasant," I would say, and then I would set out on a tour of the world because travel is even better. To places where it snows and people are fair-skinned, or to places where it's hot and people are dark-skinned. To places I where houses are one story high with small gardens, or to places where there are only skyscrapers. To places where women wear rings in their noses, and even to places where people eat fried frogs and lick their fingers.

So I would say to David, "You can love me as much as you like; I, however, am off on a tour of the world. I know Ruth's room quite well, Aunt Theresa's too; now, if you please, I'd like to try fried frogs."

What if I fell ill? They say sick women have a special charm. Before my glassy eyes flashes of fever would pass the way lightning breaks through clouds, and my hollow cheeks would have the pallor of a moonlit lily. And then as I drifted in and out of sleep I would hear him whispering, leaning over my forehead, "Katerina, you must get well fast, a life together awaits us."

Perhaps the best plan is to make him jealous. I'll take Petros's arm and walk back and forth in front of his house. It's a well-known fact that men need such prodding: if they think a woman is faithful they pay her no heed, but if they think they may lose her...

Petros was surprised when I asked him to go for a walk. I told him at the pavilion when Nikitas and Infanta had gone to the apricot trees.

"But Margarita is a friend of yours," he said with a certain irony.

We all knew they had been going out since the winter—since Lent when Nikitas had thrown a masquerade party. Margarita had dressed up as Spring. She was beautiful, but is there anything more stupid than dressing up as Spring?

"I don't see what my friendship to Margarita has to do with it. Anyhow if you don't want to come, I'll go alone."

"I'll come and fetch you at six, no, I'll wait for you in the woods across from Gekas's," he whispered hurriedly, because in the meantime Infanta and Nikitas had come back. "At six."

"At five-thirty," I had time to say.

"Okay, don't say a word to anyone. Margarita especially mustn't find out."

"Do you think I'm crazy?"

The first moments of the walk were sort of difficult. Petros had obviously come with different intentions.

"Should we go toward Helidonou?" I said at first. And then before he had time to say anything, "No—toward Louzis's. At this time of day it's better, more open."

Near David's I stepped on a thorn and I had to sit down. It was then that I noticed that in order to get to the observatory you had to climb an iron staircase, all rusted and funny-looking, and I began to laugh. But my foot was aching. I had stepped on the thorn with all my weight; when Petros leaned over to help me pull it out, he seemed particularly nice.

"How is Margarita doing?" I asked then.

"I haven't seen her for three days."

"How come?"

"She went to Athens to see her aunt."

"Will she stay long?"

"A week or so." And turning his head in the other direction, "I prefer you to her any day."

I found myself in a difficult position. Petros was really a nice boy. I didn't know what to do. I started to laugh, to pull myself up, though I hadn't intended to do so until David appeared at the window. My plan had been to take Petros's arm while David looked on and then stroll away like a pair of lovers.

We stayed until evening. No one came to the window. Only when it grew totally dark did a light go on in the house.

But finally on our fourth walk, as we were reading something Petros had written, David appeared standing above us with a smile on his lips, surprising us both.

"I see you like this place," he said.

So he had seen us the other times. The same disgust that I had felt that day at the pastry shop rose in me again, choking me. *It would be very satisfying to strangle David*, I thought, *to see how high his voice would get.*

"Yes, we love it here," I said. And then immediately afterwards, "Petros especially. The landscape inspires him. Petros is very talented, you know."

"What does he do?" David asked with an almost imperceptible irony, and without being invited he chose a rock, brushed off the dirt, and sat down.

"He's a writer," I said.

"Ah…"

David tried to stretch out his legs, but brought them in again. He couldn't get comfortable. He looked first at one of us and then at the other, as if we amused him. Facing the sun, his forehead had a pinkish tint, his hair and beard were red, his eyes seemed to sparkle with a gold dust, and his motionless hands had the wonderful transparency of an autumn leaf in the sun. You could make out the smallest veins.

Then, I don't know how it happened, but the two of them started talking together without paying any attention to me. The discussion became more and more heated. I looked up at the olive trees and wondered what I was doing there with them. David talked about his work in a way I would never have expected. Not once did I hear the word "star." For an astronomer this struck me as odd. It was more like geometry theorems. When Petros said something about "the poetry of math," David laughed. He was a cold man, but he talked of cold things with warmth.

In the meantime the sun had set and the sky had turned the color of anemones. In Ikaria, Rodia's island, there once lived a mad woman who planted trees and flowers from morning to night. Whatever she planted immediately took root, and grew with unprecedented success. The woman never did any other kind of work; some neighbor or other was always needing her, even the mayor sought her out when the main square was being built. One day, though, she took her little boy and tried planting him in the sand, thinking she would grow more children this way.

A strange calm came over me as I gave my hand to David to bid him good night. Petros and I didn't say much on the way back and as soon as I got home I ran to Rodia and asked her to tell me the story of the mad woman who liked to plant things.

Rodia was frying potatoes.

"Leave me to my work," she said. "I'll tell you another time."

Rodia had always exercised a certain tyranny around the house. Nobody dared cross her. Rodia's autocratic nature wouldn't have mattered much if she didn't also have a mania for asking questions, and if her authoritarian stance wasn't a cover-up for plain old-fashioned contrariness.

"Should I do the meat with tomatoes or lemon?" she would ask.

"Tomatoes," Mother happened to say.

"It's better with lemon, it's lighter," she would mutter. "I'll make it with lemon."

Rodia had her views. After she had decided something, no one could change her mind. But in order to decide she first asked a question, heard the other person out, and then with the utmost certainty took the opposite position.

"My dear Rodia, Rodoula, and Roditsa, I'd like so much to hear that story tonight," I pleaded again. My voice was sweet as honey and

I rubbed myself up against her the way cats rub up against a cook who's cleaning fish.

"The oil from the frying pan will spatter and burn you," she said, pushing me away.

I had to come up with a better trick.

"I too would prefer to hear it another time," I said, and then started to leave. "Only that poor child who ended up crippled..."

"Crippled, my dear? After she'd planted him in the ground like a seed, burying him alive, patting down the earth on top, after..."

Rodia began telling the story, "There once was a mad woman..." When she told stories from her island, which were usually about crazy people, her face, and even her soul changed completely. Her eyes took on the lost stare of a sleepwalker, and a smile of pure bliss played on her lips, even when the story was sad. Greek oracles and the ecstasies of India came to mind. Surely Rodia was in touch with the Divine.

When Mother came into the kitchen, the story was over and the potatoes were burned. She gave us a stern look.

"I don't want to see you in the kitchen at this hour again." And although she was speaking to me, she looked Rodia straight in the eyes.

III. THE FIRE

INFANTA also liked Rodia's stories, though she never admitted it. But then Infanta didn't even let on when she had a headache. The only signs were her pale lips and the taut skin around her forehead and temples that made her eyes slant like a Chinese princess. On the other hand, if Mother had the slightest headache, the whole house knew about it. She would complain that we didn't give her enough sympathy, she would close the shutters and lie down on her bed, letting out a moan every once in a while. Yet during the truly difficult times, she was very brave. If she had to have an operation she would go to the hospital smiling, and she seemed very calm the whole period of the divorce, though she must have been suffering. Father had hurt her. He had not been faithful to her. He spent his free time fixing radios rather than taking walks with her. And when he did say he'd come and pick her up, he'd forget and leave her waiting.

"I'd expect such behavior from a painter, an artist," Aunt Theresa would say. "But from a banker..."

Aunt Theresa wasn't remembering the way Father used to play the cello. Father too seemed to have forgotten. He would always bring it to Mesolonghi in the summer and accompany his sister Alkmioni, who played the piano. She died of appendicitis at sixteen.

Ah, the old house in Mesolonghi was a beautiful house, more beautiful than the Aristotelous house, and Grandmother would sometimes miss it. She consoled herself by wearing her three strings of pearls and visiting her brother, the general, or going to Syndagma Square. There she might meet Mrs. Montelandi and they would sit at the same table. It seems that Mrs. Montelandi viewed Grandmother as one of the few ladies with whom she should associate. She always greeted her first since she knew Grandmother couldn't see very well. The only thing that bothered her was that though the Montelandi name and Grandmother's maiden name were equally old and respected, the Montelandis had never served their country in any way. They were simply landowners, while Grandmother's family had produced great politicians and soldiers. "My brother, the general," she would say, or "My uncle, the prime minister," and Mrs. Montelandi would bite her lips, making sure, however, not to smudge her lipstick.

Mrs. Montelandi said that summer afternoons were the longest, and the most boring. For Grandmother, on the contrary, the hours she spent in Syndagma Square were her most pleasant; only then did she feel she had the right to rest. Grandmother had two children to look after, Miltos and Agisilaos. It didn't matter that the eldest was forty-eight and the other forty. They were still children. If you didn't take them something to eat before work, they would go off hungry, and if you left the serving plate in front of them during lunch they would eat until they got sick. She had to take care of their matters of heart as well, to smooth over things, especially when Agisilaos fell in love with married women and caused scandals. It was a good thing he hadn't married. She had gone through enough with Miltos's divorce. Anna was such a good woman, and rich . . . but it was her fault too. She was so proud and stubborn. Most men deceive their wives; the only difference was that Miltos did so openly. That's what Grandmother had told Anna, when advising her. She even talked about her deceased husband who, though an exceptional man, had cheated on her twice. "Miltos too is an exceptional man," she said. Mother agreed, but still insisted on the divorce. She showed such courage, though she complains and moans over the slightest headache.

Once she complained in front of Mr. Louzis and he looked so sad you would have thought he was the one in pain. Mr. Louzis seemed like a hypocrite to me. It was a good thing he didn't come over that often any more. He used to come every day, his heavy step scattering the pebbles, his cane rustling the branches of the pistachio trees overhead.

Although he did bring Mother and Aunt Theresa a pot of flowers recently, a polite gesture on his part. And whenever he hadn't been over for a while Grandfather would say, "You've forgotten us." "I never forget," said Mr. Louzis, and his voice was childlike and full of emotion. He looked off into the distance at the mountains of Parnitha and Pendeli. Imagine Mr. Louzis having a gentle soul—you never know. After all, there are books about murderers with tender souls.

It was hot. The day was colorless, and there was no wind. Since morning the pine cones had been cracking open. *Crack*—you'd lift your head, it must be a bird sharpening its beak, you'd say—*crack*—and if you looked quickly enough you'd see the pine cone break open all by itself.

Rodia teetered as she brought out the cherry drinks, and Mother's eyes had dark rings under them. Nevertheless she smiled when she saw Mr. Louzis. She was wearing a pretty dress, pale yellow like unripe corn. Her hair was black and shiny.

I liked the way Mother combed her hair, a part down the middle and then her hair flat against her head to the neck, where it was tucked under in a small bun, almost touching her back. When you looked at Mother's profile there was a mysterious balance between that low bun and her nose, which was kind of sharp. Similarly, when you looked at her from the front her clean part balanced with the uneven spaces between her white teeth.

"It's a wave. It will pass." Grandfather spoke into the silence.

We understood that he was talking about the heat. Conversation then turned to international affairs, only to end up discussing Mrs. Parigori.

"And the way she dresses . . ." continued Aunt Theresa. "She insists on being different from other women."

"I don't think she wears anything out of the ordinary," said Mother, who often came to the defense of someone to keep the discussion going.

"She might not wear showy things, but is there anything more eccentric than to adhere faithfully to a fashion that existed ten or twenty years ago, to dress in the styles of 1930 in 1945, and of 1910 in

1930?" Aunt Theresa spoke quickly and then stopped. Of course her own attire was slightly anachronistic, but it wasn't as if she consistently followed any one style. There was just a vague old-fashionedness about her. She might, for example, wear a yellowed lace collar on top of a smart, new dress.

And when she happened to give a similar lace collar to Infanta, Infanta made the same mistake, but somehow on her it looked charming, as if out of an English painting.

In the meantime Mr. Louzis had started to laugh.

"She's from Corfu, that's why."

Amidst his guffaws he explained that in Corfu everybody's a little eccentric.

"My family's also from the Ionian islands," he said as he burst into laughter again. His white linen suit tightened as his belly heaved up and down. Some of his hair had come out of place and stood on end. It was silver, but his skin was young-looking, pale rose, without a wrinkle.

The heat was unbearable.

Mother looked at him with surprise. Of course it was fine to laugh, but this just wasn't that funny.

"And do you think Ruth dresses appropriately for her age?" Aunt Theresa continued. "Short skirts, ribbons in her hair... She even goes shopping in Kifissia in her shorts."

"She's from England, that's why," explained Mr. Louzis, still laughing. Grandfather had to hold his stomach he was laughing so hard and Mother started too, even Aunt Theresa. I also began to laugh. We laughed and laughed...

... Then all of a sudden we saw the fire. It appeared first on one of the peaks of Parnitha, to the right of Aghia Triada, and progressed like a snake along the ridge. It must have begun during the day but we hadn't notice it then. The sky was red, you could see red flames and red smoke. I had heard that in such instances the forest animals run but can't escape, the deer, the rabbits. Sometimes even the birds forget to fly.

Mr. Louzis's laughter solidified and remained on his lips like a seal. Aunt Theresa's eyes shone with a strange voracity. If the mad woman had seen such a sight she would have died of sadness. Once she had almost killed Rodia for breaking the branch of a fig tree by mistake.

Why the glint in Aunt Theresa's eyes?

"Artists must experience strong emotions," she said suddenly. "Tomorrow I'll start a painting of the fire."

All night Infanta couldn't sleep. She stayed leaning out the window watching. For three days there had been no wind, not even a breeze, but now it would come. You could feel it like a hunch.

The sound of it first reached us from the distant woods; like the sound of waves breaking on a deserted beach, it crossed the meadow and came to the nearby woods sounding now like the splashing of the sea as it licks the pebbles and then pulls away. When it reached us at last it ruffled the branches of the willow and Infanta's hair.

Infanta was near me at that moment. She couldn't pull herself away. Her face was orange from the distant glow, her hair like the branches of the willow.

"Infanta," I said, "do you like the fire?"

She leaned her elbows on the window sill and lowered her head, getting comfortable as if she were in bed.

"Very much," she answered.

I expected that answer. I wanted to jump on her and beat her up. I was curled up in bed in the corner by the wall so that I wouldn't see anything.

"You were always like that!" I screamed. "Don't you care about the animals in the forest that are trying to escape? And the mad woman whose heart would stop, who would just die to see so many trees burning—"

"If anyone's mad, it's you," interrupted Infanta, turning her head calmly the other way without taking her eyes off the fire.

Well, that was too much. With one leap I came up behind her and I grabbed her by the shoulders. She didn't move or raise her hand to hit me. But as I pushed her back to the window I caught a slight look of fear in her eyes. At the same time I saw the fire. With the wind it had spread. The red snake was advancing at a frightening pace. The flames licked the sky, taking the shape of dancing demons. My hands, resting motionless on her shoulders, dug deeper and deeper into her flesh. It must hurt her. It must hurt a lot.

"I like the fire as well," I said, letting her go.

In return she made a little room for me at the window.

The fire lasted for three days and three nights. It almost made it to Bafi and burned people. Now the mountain looks like a wounded beast bearing its wounds to the sun. I'll never forget the fear I saw in Infanta's eyes the first night, nor her expression afterwards. One of these days my sister Infanta and I will get to know each other.

And to think that of the three of us she was the most fearless. Maria and I would shriek and kick our feet in the air if a bee came near, while Infanta would let it land right on her arm or her cheek. Sometimes we would dare each other to put our arms in the lavender up to the elbow after we heard lizards scuttling around in there. Only Infanta did. And one day when it turned out to be a snake instead of a lizard, Infanta took a stick and hit it on the head. Then she called us over—we had all fled—to show us how the tail was still moving even though it was dead. And if we happened to meet a herd of buffaloes in the meadow, she would go and dance in front of them, teasing them. On the other hand, she was afraid of the first day of school. And that fear never completely left her. When we returned from school in the afternoon, I remember, she would sigh with relief upon seeing the driveway. Anyhow she didn't make friends easily. Only once in high school did she get close to someone. A new girl named Miranda had arrived. She was always ready to laugh. Everyone wanted to be her friend, but she chose Infanta. They would sit at the same desk and look at the same things. They read the same books. There were times when they would both be struck by the same beautiful thing. They would look on in silence together. And when they saw the first chamomile at the edge of the schoolyard, they wondered how winter could be over so quickly and have passed so happily.

The next year Lina was the new girl in class and everything changed. Miranda switched places so she could be near Lina. She looked out her window now and avoided Infanta. The magic had disappeared. And for Infanta the fear of school and people started all over again. My God, how bitter she became . . .

It had been a long time since Nikitas had come over.

He thought of Infanta at night before he went to sleep and in the morning just after he woke. He never dreamt of her, though, and all day he tried to forget her. When he thought of her, the pain was so sharp that he wished he could be indifferent. *I don't love her.* And when he was indifferent, he insisted on rekindling the pain by imagining her in front of him. *I love her.* Neither statement was the whole truth.

He would set off with Victoria early in the morning, making her gallop, totally consumed with getting there, as if seeing Infanta one minute earlier would make a difference, and then suddenly he would stop at the turn. He would say he was stopping so that he and his horse could catch their breath. But to tell the truth, it was because he was about to turn around and head back.

The perfection of her face amazed him. Yes, the first time that he noticed her was at Marios's. She was walking down the steps of the veranda wearing a white dress. Her hair was up. He remembered the white roses and how when he was a child he would go out into the garden after a rain and shake them.

He lacked courage. He didn't have experience like Stefanos and Emilios. If he wanted to dance with a girl he would wait until she put her hand on his shoulder. He would say to himself, "Next time I'll put my arm around her waist, next time I'll do it first."

With Infanta there was a moment when they both were standing still amidst the other dancing couples. They were even getting pushed around. They blushed. He didn't put his arm around her waist. She didn't put her hand on his shoulder. Their eyes, though, happened to meet and they both began to laugh. They started dancing. It was their own moment that no one else knew about.

And when they lay next to each other in the woods, they talked like friends.

On that particular day he got it in his head to break off a twig of thyme and place it on her breast. They had just arrived in the woods. Their horses were grazing a little ways away.

He tried to put it in the last buttonhole of her blouse. She leaned down, embarrassed, and helped him. When, a little later, she raised her head, she saw for the first time his eyes: dark, heavy, strange as if someone drunk were dancing there. *I won't look away*, she said to herself, though she felt as if she were falling into a deep, dark abyss and that she was sure to get lost. She heard her heart beating, once, twice, three, four times, and then the moment had passed. She turned her head away and took a deep breath.

"We rode a lot today," she said. "I'm exhausted."

"Me too."

There was a faint sound of anger in his voice.

"You know," said Nikitas after a while, "the others say that we are in love . . . the gang that is, Emilios, Eleni . . . Petros is sure."

"Let them say whatever they like. I don't care."

Her hair wasn't combed. The wind was blowing. A whole strand kept falling in front of her nose over one eye. She would lift it with her hand and throw it back, her fingers revealing a growing impatience. You could almost imagine a moment in which she would grab it and pull it out of her head altogether.

"Since we know we're only friends, what does it matter?"

Love for her was the sight of the rabbit giving birth, which she couldn't bear. And one day she had seen two dogs . . . It was disgusting. And Maria with her belly out to there, getting larger each day— my God!

"What are you thinking?" asked Nikitas slowly.

"About my sister Maria."

Sometimes when she touched his hand or when her skirt tickled his leg in the wind he felt a tightening in his heart, in his stomach; he wasn't sure exactly where, and he hated her. Then he would tell her something mean to hurt her. She would turn and look at him with her eyes slanted like when she had a headache, her lips a pale, straight line. Ah, she would never forgive him. She would pay him back. But for now she wouldn't say a word. The more she restrained herself, the more angry he grew. He wanted to beat her. If only he dared. He would rush off and not be seen for days, even weeks. Infanta would wait. She knew he would come back.

She would go out to meet him smiling. The bitterness that was left over from last time would be already almost gone.

"Where have you been?" she would ask.

In her voice and manner there would be a sweet submissiveness.

Then crazy Katerina would come out of the house singing "Every woman's life is a search for a master. Ah, the thirst for submission, the thirst for submission..." And then she would begin again, "Every woman's life..."

"Oh, Nikitas, you're here?"

She'd pretend to be surprised. Infanta would throw her a nasty look.

"So, what happened? Did you forget about us?"

Infanta threw her an even nastier look.

Nikitas liked to watch the three girls walking in front of him hand in hand wearing their big straw hats.

"Maria! Infanta! Katerina!"

They'd all turn at once.

Maria's eyes were black, Infanta's green, and Katerina's brown. They would laugh. Still children. And Maria in the midst of them, her belly large and heavy, was somehow shocking.

Mother would come out shouting, "Katerina, go upstairs and tidy your room."

"Later, Mother, later..."

"Your clothes are all over the place. Go up immediately."

"I can't now."

A door slammed. Mother was angry. Katerina would curl up in a corner, sad.

"Well, Nikitas," she would say after a while.

It was time for him to read them his most recent poem. Two minutes of silence passed. They moved toward the pavilion and chose their places. Nikitas sat by the table so he could spread out his papers. Another two minutes passed without anyone saying anything. All you could hear were the cicadas and the shuffling of paper as Nikitas tried to find the first page.

He began.

"Under the windows of the drowned men a peacock cries because its feet are ugly. And little Helen has left us."

A strange anxiousness is in the air. Nikitas's voice changes when he reads poetry. The day has become cloudy. "What's the title, Nikitas?"

"The Shipwreck."

Infanta looks him in the eyes. A few days ago he offered her water in his hands.

Aunt Theresa pops her head out of the window of her atelier.

"I'm sending down your embroidery so you don't sit around with idle hands."

Infanta takes it and arranges the colored yarns in a row on her knee. She pays attention to nothing else now.

The peacocks, Infanta, Nikitas's poem . . .

"Look, here are the peacocks!" says Nikitas, pointing to her embroidery. He laughs and everyone joins in.

IV. MOTHER'S SECRET

BY ALL accounts last summer was a very different kind of summer. For a start there was the weather. Each day was like the next, the same heat and goldish tint, except for that one day with all the rain when Marios and Maria stayed shut up in the kitchen and then later came in holding hands and announced their engagement. And we were only expecting pudding. A shock, I remember, but a pleasant one. Infanta, her eyes moist and shining, did not stop laughing all evening. I even thought to myself that I must have been wrong to think that she was interested in Marios. Then it flashed through my mind that in novels and movies it is exactly such moments that sad people laugh the most. But then what followed and Infanta's behavior made me quickly drop this idea as pure fancy.

I have a tendency to make things up, to fabricate them and then later to think they're true. When I was small I would describe dreams I hadn't had, and when other people believed me I would end up convincing myself as well. I once told my school friends of a trip to Egypt, a place I had only seen in photographs. Another time I came home panting and told Grandfather and Mother how as I passed through the woods I saw two people cutting down trees and heard them say, "Choose the straight ones because they make good masts." "I think one of them might have been Gekas," I added, without thinking what I was saying. Grandfather dressed hurriedly to go to the police and I was obliged, after fifteen minutes of extreme agony and embarrassment, to explain that I had made it all up. As for why I chose Gekas, he had a habit of roaming about the woods, his eyes bulging, his head cleanly shaven. Who knows how long I had been secretly harboring a dislike for him.

I then went through what they call a big moral crisis. I doubted myself. I, who tried to be worthy, had been proven worthless. I, who admired great deeds, had now done something so base. I would loiter outside of Gekas's taverna just the way Raskolnikov did outside the old lady's house, and when I happened to see him pull up three chairs to stretch out on, I made myself stare at his bulging eyes and his shaven head, just for punishment.

This year, however, the weather is different. No day is like the next, and the changes in temperature are like none we've experienced before. The week of the fire we could barely breathe. There was no wind and it was as if the oxygen had left the earth for another planet. Many people even said that the fire had started by itself from the heat. Now today it's cold. The wind is blowing. The trees bend down to the ground and you feel like running and never stopping. But our property is too small, and I'm afraid of the meadow. Yesterday when I went out walking there, though it was midday, it got dark all of a sudden. The sky clouded over and hung low. Pendeli, across the way, became an old hag, while the meadow stayed golden, lit up, making you wonder where the sun was coming from.

Now my sisters and I no longer lie around in the hay talking. We aren't all in the same place the way we were last year and other years. And when we happen to be together it's as if there is a new awkwardness, as if we had betrayed one another by doing our own thing.

Certainly some day the awkwardness will pass, though time will never undo the betrayal. And perhaps when it does pass we will long for the time when we all lay around in the hay and our desires were so fluid and uncertain that they were no longer our own. They became the air we breathed; a thought of Maria's became mine and mine Infanta's—a kind of unearthly communion. When one of us sighed it was as if we had all sighed. And when there was a laugh, we all felt its reverberation deep inside, as well as a joyful trembling.

So I thought that we should all get together to talk. It was necessary since I had something very important to announce. And even though we saw each other every day at every hour I gave each a written note separately: "Tonight, after dinner, I await you at the pavilion. Make sure no one follows you—not even Marios. Don't tell a soul. We need to talk. Katerina."

This is what had happened. Yesterday I had been in my room reading. It was afternoon. The sun was hiding behind the mountain. By the sea it would have been half under the waves and half floating. Mother was playing piano. I couldn't hear well because the wind kept sweeping away the notes. Mother plays differently when no one is around, as if she is expecting something to happen. How would she react if I went down and gave her a kiss? It would be a way to make up. I'd been rude to her for some time now and she had begun to treat me coldly.

When I came down the stairs the piano stopped. And from the balcony door I could see that she was no longer at the piano but bent over her desk as if she was reading something.

The moment I entered, she got up, turned around, grabbed the desk with both hands as if to steady herself and looked me straight in the eye without saying anything.

I stayed where I was, motionless. If I took a step, said something, everything would be the way it always was. But I couldn't, nor could she. I could only stare. My eyes wandered down from her face to her hands and got stuck there. Her pale nails contrasted with the dark wood and between her fingers you could just make out a crumpled piece of paper.

Like a magnet I couldn't take my eyes off that piece of paper. Besides I wanted Mother to know that I had seen it. So there it was: she and Mr. Louzis exchanged letters. It wasn't enough that he came over for visits.

Suddenly she said, "Run upstairs and bring me an aspirin. It's in the top drawer of my bureau."

I threw one last determined look at the paper and scurried off. When I returned Mother was sitting in the armchair in front of the balcony door rubbing her forehead with her palms.

"Do you have a headache, Mother?"

"Yes."

I was standing there, undecided. I wanted to kiss her, but it was difficult.

"Do you have a headache, Mother?" I asked again.

"Yes."

Standing behind her I could see the top of her head, the straight, white part separating her black hair in two. It was so smooth it made you want to touch it. Sometimes as a child the softness of her skin would make me shiver, while the perfume she wore back then would get me all mixed up. I would want to cry. She no longer wears perfume, but still...Why couldn't I run up to her and say, "Mama, I don't want you to have a headache, nor to be sad about anything. As for the letter, it's your business." She lowers her head and rubs her forehead, then looks far away, toward the garden. She is thoughtful. I can tell from the line of her neck as I stand behind her and from the curve of her shoulders.

It is difficult for people to get close to each other. There is a kind of embarrassment, I don't know...

"Never mind, it's nothing. You'll feel better after the aspirin."

My voice was cold, icy. It surprised me.

I walked slowly down to the garden. The idea that the piece of paper was a letter from Mr. Louzis began to dissolve like a white cloud.

"That's what I wanted to tell you..."

Infanta and Maria were silent. Perhaps they were distracted and they hadn't heard a word. As the moon rose, the pavilion became a game of light and shadow.

"So?"

"And?"

I started to get annoyed. Neither of them moved or talked. I got up and paced back and forth in front of them, almost stepping on their feet. On purpose, of course.

"Like a general on the eve of a great battle," said Maria giggling.

"Tell me, if Mother is in love with Mr. Louzis and Mr. Louzis with Mother, what do you want us to do about it?"

She let a moment pass and then, emphasizing each word, "Anyway it wouldn't be bad if they got married. Mr. Louzis is a good man and he's rich. He would take Mother on wonderful trips..."

The idea that Mother would travel was unbearable. Even if I were to travel, I wanted her at home waiting for me. Maria could be so wrong, and so annoying.

Then Infanta's voice was heard, in a monotone, as if she were speaking to herself.

"She always keeps her desk locked. And one day when she couldn't find the key she was beside herself..."

"There, you see?" I cried.

An owl hooted. And another farther away. A bat emerged from a pipe and others followed. They passed in a line in front of the moon and then disappeared.

"Something even more mysterious was going on," I said seriously. "The crumpled piece of paper wasn't a letter from Mr. Louzis."

But on the night of the full moon something happened that made me reconsider the whole affair. When Mr. Louzis was leaving, right at the door, while the moon lit up the meadow, I heard him whisper to Mother, "Did you receive what I sent you?"

And she answered, "Yes, I did...You shouldn't have done that, Mr. Louzis..."

I was confused. A few minutes passed. Mr. Louzis left. The others went in. I stood outside the house before the open meadow. It was silver. The train passed and blew its whistle. I don't know how it happened, but I started to run and soon found myself behind Mr. Louzis.

"What did you do to Mother?" I shouted.

He turned and looked at me. His rosy complexion was pale and his white suit, almost blue. His eyes revealed his great amazement. For a minute. But then they began to sparkle. He was a clever man, everyone knew that. He passed his cane to his left hand and patted me on my shoulder with his right in a friendly way, never losing eye contact with me.

"What's up, Katerina?" he said in a cool, calm voice.

Then he started to laugh, and the farther away he got the louder his laughter grew. He must have arrived home out of breath from laughing.

I was so concerned with Mother that I forgot about David for a while. When he came over the other day I looked at him blankly. And he had the audacity not only to notice, but to mention it.

"Usually you look at me differently, Katerina," he said.

"I've never looked at you differently."

As the others had work, we sat alone on the veranda.

It was very embarrassing; we didn't say a word. Once or twice I tried to start a conversation, but David answered with yes or no and the discussion got no further.

"I'm bored," I told him.

"Me too. I'm always bored except when I'm working."

And saying this he stretched out his legs and leaned his head back. His beard was shorter than the last time. He must have decided to cut it, but because he doesn't like sudden changes, he snipped it off little by little. It's strange to see yourself suddenly changed. It makes you think of death and all sorts of other things.

"Yes, work..." I said. "It's the only thing that matters."

"But you don't do anything. You've finished school, right?"

"I'm writing a novel," I said absentmindedly.

David's laughter brought me back to earth. I heard myself repeating in a serious tone, "Yes, I am writing a novel."

David laughed again. He never laughed heartily like Mr. Louzis. Instead he had a reluctant laugh, reluctant but sharp.

"And what's it about?"

What's it about, what's it about? ... He mustn't catch me telling lies. Why did I say such a thing? Why on earth? It was like those dreams I had never seen and my trip to Egypt. It was not my fault, though. First I heard the words and then I realized what I'd said. Perhaps there are people who kill first and then realize they have killed.

"It's about...hmm...it's a story about a letter. No, it's a story about three girls. Yes, like Maria, Infanta, and myself. Like us, not that it's about us."

"No, yes, the story of a letter, of three girls. You don't sound very sure, Katerina."

"And aren't you confused sometimes by what you see in the sky?"

"Nothing is confusing in the sky," said David. "Each star has its own place and orbit. And everything can be calculated."

Silence.

"You know, I don't think hanging about with Petros is doing you any good."

He was suddenly very serious. I looked at him. He stood straight and tall and brought his hands close together as if he were knitting.

"I'm saying this for your own sake. I've also heard that Petros is superficial. With girls, I mean."

A joy rose, flooding me, covering me like a wave. I wanted to get up and run, to climb a tree. David was jealous, it was clear. He was jealous.

"Ah, Petros is a charming guy," I said.

"It's not enough for a man to have beautiful eyes and a pleasing walk."

"But Petros also has a heart of gold. He's not like the others—how can I explain it? He isn't bad-tempered the way they are."

David smiled a bit, just slightly.

"I don't like bad-tempered people either," he said slowly, rhythmically.

"How can you say that when you ..."

I stopped myself just in time and raised my eyes. David was staring at me.

"What would you say to a walk?" he said, taking me by the hand.

I felt a vague fear. Not exactly fear—more like the feeling you have when you are about to take an exam or when you're going on a trip and you're waiting for the train at the station.

"At this hour I don't go to the woods," I said. "It gives me the creeps. I'm kind of a nervous type..."

It's nice going for a walk. You breathe deeply, the wind blows through your hair... For a moment my hair seemed to have copper highlights, David said. As for my eyes, he thought it was strange that one was a little darker than the other.

"I used to be a little cross-eyed," I said. "That is until the age of two..."

David laughed.

"Anyhow, Rodia says it's the sign of a lucky person to have one eye darker than the other."

He stopped laughing.

"All I know," he said, "is that it suits you."

And taking me by the shoulders he turned me toward the sun and looked at me. He had witch's eyes. I lowered mine.

"Maybe you're embarrassed by me?" he said.

I laughed.

"Embarrassed by you? Why should I be embarrassed by you?"

We were walking.

"Tell me," I said suddenly, "is it very unethical to open a locked drawer, to look inside a locked drawer that doesn't belong to you?"

"The questions you come up with!"

"Answer me seriously. I'm not joking around."

"But it depends."

"What do you mean, it depends?"

"If by opening the drawer you might save a life or something like that..."

"No, I'm not talking about saving lives."

"Just curiosity?"

"Yes, just curiosity."

"Then it is very unethical."

And after a bit, "What are you worrying about anyway? Is your heroine about to break into a drawer full of terrible secrets?"

"Yes, that's it. And you see, she is a curious person, but not unethical."

"Well then, she shouldn't open it."

"But if she doesn't open it, the novel will have to end right there."

"Hmm."

David was thinking. He had bent down his head and with his smooth hands he was stroking his beard. There was something devilish about him. I wanted to run away.

Suddenly he said, "So is it a detective story?"

I started to laugh. I had to sit down I was laughing so hard. David sat down next to me. We were in something like a ditch, and across the way in front of the sun there were three solitary reeds. It looked as if they had been designed to fit in the sun's circle, and sitting close to them and down low they seemed to surpass Parnitha in height. No, it was not funny. Life was very serious, and very beautiful.

"When you look into your telescope are you scared?"

"Of what?"

"I don't know exactly. The sky...the grandness of the universe... the seriousness of life."

"I see things scientifically," David responded.

"The blackberry bushes outside your door have bloomed," I said.

I knew he wouldn't have noticed them. Had he seen the reeds then?

"Look, they're higher than Parnitha."

"That's because we're near them, and Parnitha is far away."

"Of course that's why."

"And if you lie down they'll seem even taller. Put your head here."

He lay down and I put my head on his chest. We lay like perpendicular roads.

"Your hair smells good..."

"It is full of static and scares me with its clicking sound when I comb it, especially when the weather changes."

I was about to say that my body does the same thing when I take off my clothes at night, especially when the weather changes. But I didn't. It seemed somehow indecent since I was lying on him.

"We must go," I said.

I saw him standing in front of me, politely offering me his hand.

It had grown dark. The wind was blowing. The reeds had become sound. And I wondered as we walked back if David would ever love me. Certainly I would love him for the rest of my life.

I had a lump in my throat and couldn't bear the thought that we would part ways soon. Only a tremendous desire to hold his hand for a minute—for a second—to squeeze it in mine and let it drop; because David never put his hand down the way other people did, instead he let it fall; and this habit of his concealed an invisible, tender hopelessness.

"Shall we go for a walk again some time?"

"Yes, let's."

"When?"

"I don't know. Whenever it happens."

We had arrived.

"At your orders, my lady," David said, and before I knew what he was doing, he had bent down and kissed my hand, bowing like a knight from olden times.

In jest, of course.

That night I couldn't sleep a wink. I twisted and turned in my bed like a worm. Not only because I was thinking of him but also because I got it into my head that if I slept, the wave of sand that used to blind me in my dreams as a child would return. I even saw Miss Gost, alive again, spreading white sheets across the mirrors, warding off the devil. That memory made me want to peek in the mirror in my room—one peek. In the beginning this desire wasn't strong. I told myself, *Better not to look*. But then the good sense of that phrase began to torture me. Was it really better not to look? And what would happen if I did, anyway?

A late, pale moon rose—it was some days after the full moon. I turned my eyes in that direction abruptly. It must be the shadow of the furniture or the clothes hanging... It couldn't be anything else. Miss Gost couldn't be right. Something stirred, just the wind blowing the clothes. It couldn't be anything else...

The tension was horrible.

Finally I reached out my hand, lifted myself up, and turned on the light. The room lit up. I was no longer afraid, and to prove it to myself I jumped out of bed, walked around the room, and went and stood provocatively in front of the mirror. I greeted my own gaze, the eyes I knew so well. And I realized they were to blame. They had something foreign in them, something strange like David's eyes. And as I stared at my body it was as if David were the one looking at me. "So that's what they mean when they talk about the devil," I said. And although I could still see the devil I was no longer afraid. I even had the courage to pull down the nightgown I was wearing on my shoulders so that I could see the line of my neck that always pleased me, the one that was the same as my Polish grandmother's. I smiled. I had an urge to dance in front of the mirror, so I did. The nightgown had slipped off my shoulders and fallen to the ground. I was stepping on it. I almost lifted it with my foot and tossed it out the window for the fun of it.

I danced until my cheeks were burning and my eyes shining. Later I curled up in a corner of my bed and began sobbing. It was as satisfying as dancing. I wrapped myself up in the sheet and cried. When I felt a bit better I tried to sleep. I turned off the light, faced the wall, and it was then that I wanted David more than anything. I remembered the afternoon, each word, each of his gestures—and when I reached the scene of separation I would begin all over again. He was jealous of Petros. And Margarita was jealous of Petros. Lately she has been looking at me suspiciously. It wasn't my fault if Petros preferred me. But it had been a while since he'd come over. I wonder why. "At your order, my lady," David had said. When he does things like that I want to slap him. Is he thinking about me now? How can you know if others are thinking about you? I must ask someone. I must get advice. Maria is the most appropriate, but in her condition . . . And besides, I must find out tonight.

I jumped out of bed and turned on the light, picked up my nightgown, slipped it on, and went out into the hallway. Infanta's room was right across from mine. I knocked on the door. I knocked again.

"Who is it? What's up?"

"It's me, Katerina."

"What do you want at this hour?"

"I have to tell you something. It's urgent."

I heard her get up and unlock the door. She always locked her door. I don't know why.

When she opened the door I fell into her arms.

"Oh, Infanta," I said, "I am madly in love. I just want to die."

At first she went pale, but then she smiled.

"A dream?" she asked me tenderly and stroked my cheek.

"I just want to die, I tell you. I'm too in love. It's as if something is leaping up and down inside me, cutting off my air supply. The time will come when I will want to breathe and I won't be able to. That's how my life is sure to end."

I cried a bit.

"Sit down," Infanta said. "You're all worked up. Or better yet, lie down on my bed."

She was being nice to me. I couldn't complain.

"How long have you been in this state?"

"Since this evening."

"Hmm..."

She smiled again.

"No—you don't understand. I've been in love since last summer, or rather since last fall. But this wanting to die only started tonight."

"What do you mean?"

"Up until now I wanted to see him and when I saw him I got all confused... But today..."

"What?"

"I don't know... It feels different."

"So who is he?"

I hesitated a moment. It had been almost a year that I had kept this secret. Was I going to give it away now?

"David," I said.

"David?... David?..."

She thought this was strange. She said his name again and again, her eyes wide with astonishment.

"David?..."

"Yes, David."

For a second she looked dreamy.

"So?" she said.

"What? You don't like him?"

"His eyes scare me. He seems wicked."

She was scared of his eyes too. It couldn't be that...

"So, you don't like him?" I insisted.

"No, I don't."

I went over and kissed her.

"I, on the other hand, like him very much," I said with a sigh. "And I want to know if he likes me. That's what I came to ask you. How do you tell?"

"How should *I* know?" said Infanta, and went and stood in front of the window the way she had the day of the fire.

"How did you know Nikitas was in love with you?"

She turned abruptly toward me, her eyes flashing.

"I forbid you to say such things!" she screamed.

Her hair was up, but when she shook her head a hairpin fell out and it came undone on one side. She was wearing a white nightgown with lots of pleats. You couldn't tell the shape of her body inside.

"Ah, so you are also in love..." I said. "And I am... All of us are. We're all in love."

Her anger seemed to vanish.

"Come, talk to me, Infanta."

A sweetness spread across her face. She leaned over and picked up the hairpin with her delicate hands, and again with those delicate hands put her hair up again. Her gestures were like waves after a storm, but before the sea has completely calmed down.

"Come on, Infanta..."

At that same moment a cry was heard. Then footsteps, and voices. We stayed where we were, motionless. Only that Infanta's hairpin fell out, and once again her hair came undone on one side. Someone was coming down the stairs. It sounded like Aunt Theresa.

I opened the door and rushed out.

"Aunt Theresa, what's going on?"

"Maria's gone into labor."

I stayed at the top of the stairs and watched her go down. My heart had stopped. My feet refused to go forwards or backwards. Of course I knew that Maria was going to give birth, but I hadn't been able to imagine this exact moment.

Meanwhile Infanta had come over.

"Maria..." I began to say.

"I heard," she said.

We clasped hands and started down the stairs. We hadn't walked that way for years. Though now it was as if the two entangled hands between us were Maria. Oh, we loved Maria, we loved her very much. And now she was about to bring a child into the world. Maria, bringing a child into the world. We heard another cry. That couldn't be Maria. She didn't shout like that... My God! We squeezed hands. Maria, Maria... You must know how much Infanta and I love you. Another scream and then silence. Infanta was trembling. Me too.

"Go put something on," Mother said when she saw us. "And calm down. All women give birth. And all people on earth are born of women."

I guess she's right. There's no denying that all people are born of women.

"Besides she isn't in pain right now," continued Mother. "In the beginning that's the way it is. The pain comes and goes."

It must've been one o'clock. We got dressed quickly and came downstairs again.

"You can still go see her," said Mother. "Go keep her company."

Mother was sitting in the dining room at the table as if about to eat. She seemed peaceful.

"I'll come over later. I'm waiting for the doctor now."

We left the house shivering. The truth is, it was cold.

Maria's house was all lit up. Marios was at the door. When he saw us he smiled and his jaw trembled. Maria was standing up straight and tall in the middle of the room.

"Good evening, Maria," we said.

"Good evening, Infanta, good evening, Katerina."

It was stupid to say good evening at this time of night.

"How are you, Maria?"

"Fine."

We were worlds apart at that moment, but we loved her and she loved us.

We sat down.

"Won't you sit down too, Maria?"

"I can't."

She was standing up straight and tall in the middle of the room wearing a cherry-colored robe. Her hair had grown during the pregnancy. It now reached her shoulders. It had a healthy and vibrant sheen. Nothing could happen to Maria. Her skin was bursting with health. It was soft and pink, even now. Only her eyes had circles under them, and her palms were sweaty. She kept wiping them with a handkerchief. Her forehead was sweaty, too. As for her belly, I had never seen anything so huge in all my life. It took up all the space in the room, pointing upward provocatively.

"How was your walk?" she asked. "I saw you go off with David."

She tried to tease as usual, but at that moment her face went tense and her eyes grew wide with pain. She grabbed the chair in front of her with both hands and squeezed hard.

"Does it hurt, Maria?" whispered Infanta.

"If only we could . . ." I said.

She wiped her forehead and smiled.

"See, it's over," she said.

"Do you remember when we hid outside of Tasia's?"

They heard a car pull up.

"The doctor," she said with relief.

She had been waiting anxiously for him though she hadn't said anything.

"Now you go on inside," said Mother, who soon showed up with Mr. Parigori and another doctor. "Take Marios with you."

Until then Marios hadn't moved from the door—not in or out. He wore a silly, distracted expression, and his jaw trembled.

We recrossed the garden and went into the dining room. Aunt Theresa was pacing about with that uneven gait of hers. Grandfather was sitting, his stillness concealing his uncertainty. They were like each other, Aunt Theresa and Grandfather. Only that in the one case the uncertainty and lack of resolution came out in nervous futile gestures, whereas in the other it was concealed by silence and stillness. Grandfather rarely spoke, almost as if he wasn't taking part in our lives; Aunt Theresa had an opinion on everything. But deep down they were the same.

"I kept telling you she should go to a hospital," Aunt Theresa was shouting as we came in. "But that Maria is a stubborn one."

Not a word from Grandfather.

"In the hospital everything is easier, the disinfectants and all that."

The phone rang. It was Mrs. Parigori wanting news. Before twenty minutes had gone by the phone rang again: Mrs. Parigori. Father, even though he knew, didn't call.

"Perhaps he's already forgotten his daughter is in labor," Aunt Theresa whispered loudly, but I shut her up with a look.

We saw Marios running around in the garden. He couldn't bear standing in the door any longer with that silly smile on his face.

The clock struck three, three-thirty, four.

"A difficult birth," said Mother when she came over to get something from the house. "Everything will be fine, though."

Rodia came and went, crossing herself every so often.

The clock struck four-thirty, five.

And again Mrs. Parigori was on the phone.

Five-thirty.

We heard some screaming, some horrible screaming. The child was born. It was a boy. Dawn broke and the sky was a whitish, uncertain color.

When Father came the next morning with a bouquet of half-wilted flowers Maria was still asleep.

The house was unusually calm.

"It's a boy," Mother cried out, about to run to him. But then she must have remembered they were divorced.

Father sat near the table and rested the bouquet in front of him. They were white roses. Some had only the stems left and others fell apart the minute you touched them.

Nobody spoke. Everybody knew that Father wouldn't ask questions, and instead of making it easier for him they made it more difficult. It was as if there was a secret agreement between Mother and Aunt Theresa: "If he wants to learn he can ask. We're not going to tell him anything." So Father waited.

He looked out at the garden from a slit that was left between the drawn shutters. In a minute Yangoulas, Mother Kapatos's black sheepdog, ran by.

"Whose dog is that?" he asked.

"Mother Kapatos's," I said. "She's a woman who lives near here."

Father lived in Athens. He of course didn't know of Mother Kapatos, or her children, or Amalia who read Russian books. I wanted to tell him so that he would know something about our life. We didn't know much about his either. He never spoke of his friends to us, nor of the blond woman.

"Shall we take a walk in the garden?" I asked.

And before he could answer I took him by the arm and pulled him outside.

"Mother Kapatos," I began, "is a poor woman. Her husband spends most of the time in jail, and when he's out he does odd jobs around here. At David's, for example. David is a young man, an astronomer. His house looks like a Mickey Mouse tower. Amalia is the daughter of Mother Kapatos and she plans to be a teacher."

But all that was rather stupid since Father was really waiting for me to tell him about Maria. He looked absentmindedly ahead, longing to hear about her. Finally I squeezed his arm a bit and began narrating the events of last night down to the smallest detail. The only thing I left out was Aunt Theresa's phrase, "Perhaps he's already forgotten his daughter is in labor," because it might have hurt him. He listened attentively. He bowed his head slightly. His eyes were like deer eyes.

I always felt there was something removed about Father. And perhaps this will seem strange, but this was related in some way in my mind to Rodia. In the same way that Rodia's soul was related to Mavroukos's eyes at those times when his bulldog face was flooded with kindness and melancholy.

Father tried not to show any interest in anyone. And in front of Mother and Aunt Theresa, just out of childish stubbornness, he wouldn't ask about Maria.

But with me things were different.

"Was she in much pain?" he asked.

"Yes, a great deal..."

"Like how much?"

"Well, in that final moment she let out such a scream you'd have thought the house would crumble. Up until then, though, she was very brave."

"And the child?"

"The child is a monster," I said without thinking.

And after I had thought a minute, "It's because he's a little baby. Not even a day old..."

Maria woke up around midday. I have never seen her more beautiful. Her face had a radiance that I will never forget. Her black hair was all over the pillow, and she lay with her head to one side, and her eyes, oh her eyes, had both a brightness and a mistiness about them, an extreme expression of submission and pride.

Father leaned down awkwardly and kissed her.

"He brought you some beautiful flowers too," I said softly.

Then it seems Father remembered to look in his pocket. He took out a small package and unwrapped it.

"An icon," he said with a certain embarrassment. "If you like, put it in the cradle with the child."

He didn't say anything else. Grandmother, though, had once shown it to me and told me that when she herself had been born, her uncle, the prime minister, had hung it in her cradle as a gift, and the same icon had hung in her father's cradle, too. It was the Panaghia with Christ. Maria looked at it carefully.

"I will certainly put it in the baby's cradle. I really like it."

She sent me off to fetch a ribbon.

"A pale blue one," she called after me.

By the time I had brought her the ribbon, we had hung the icon and looked at the baby for a minute, Father wanted to go. He said goodbye in an extraordinary hurry and didn't even want me to accompany him to the door.

"Miltos, if you like, come and see the baby again," Mother had time to say.

And oddly enough, the same afternoon when I went to open the door of the living room where I had just heard Mother playing the piano, I found it locked. And when I went out into the garden to calm my nerves after the excitement, I saw her leave all dressed up, although it was certainly her duty on such a day to stay at home with Maria.

V. MARIA, LAURA, RUTH

MARIA wakes up at dawn every morning to nurse the child and to start working. Now her days are full.

Every once in a while she remembers when she was first married, how she and Marios would wake up at noon just in time for a walk in the woods. Then night would fall and the day would be over. Time slipped away, leaving only the faint scent of cyclamen and heather and the oncoming rain.

And even before that there were long, empty hours spent with Nikos and Stephanos. As for that afternoon in Kritikos's hut, it was because the lavender had bloomed and Stephanos was being such an idiot. It didn't come out of nowhere. It had been maturing inside her for a while, torturing her. Ever since, she had lain on her back in the hay, or strained her ear to hear a cry in the night. It was the continuation of the moment when at thirteen a boy first kissed her, and even before that, when the letters of her school books danced before her eyes and she shivered to hear her own laugh.

The odd thing is that she had started to think about Marios just after leaving Kritikos's son when she started up the hill on Elia Avenue. That's who she had in mind when she said "I want to get married" in the midday silence of the dining room. The next day when she met Stephanos she let him know that they would no longer be seeing each other. "There's no room for why," she added. And it was true. There was no why. It's just the way things happened, no need for an explanation. It was the natural turn of events.

And look how it had all brought her to this, a child. Something real. You could touch him, grab both his feet in one hand, even nurse him.

The breast-feeding hurt in the beginning. Her milk hadn't come in fully yet and the baby pulled on her nipple with an unexpected harshness, almost as if he wanted to hurt her. But after a few days there was plenty and it no longer was painful. What an indescribable sweetness to feel him there sucking away, his eyes closed. She liked to call him "my little kitten," "my little bird," and other animal names, but Marios got angry and said it wasn't right. "Since we know we're going to baptize him Yannis, we should start calling him that now." But Maria couldn't call him Yannis, he was too little. When she talked to him she would string various syllables together, creating new words like "my *koukouki*." It was silly, but it pleased her and she had the sense that the little one sort of understood her. She spoke softly and in secret. It was their language—hers and the baby's. No one else needed to hear.

Spyridoula, one of Kalomoira's daughters, came to help her with the housekeeping. But Maria tended to all the child's needs. She insisted on washing his clothes herself and hanging them out to dry. This was the task she liked best of all. To hang the white clothes on the line, the wind blowing, and every once in a while to feel a drop of water. She would sing the "little white boat" and many other songs. It was odd, but the older she got, the more she returned to the songs of her childhood. Her voice would get swept up by the wind. She would lean down, take a piece of clothing, and hang it up. It would fill with air, making the sound of a sail when you untie it and move it from one oarlock to another. The boat would come about, how nice . . . the sea would grow rougher . . .

And turning her head Maria would see the pines and the house and in front of her the laundry hanging. Here there was no "who knows what lies around the next bend" like the song, here you knew exactly what was coming.

What a lot of pain there is in giving birth, my God, what a lot of pain. She sweats when she thinks of it and her heart beats faster. She kept repeating to herself during the contractions, "Don't scream, Maria, be brave, tomorrow it will all be over." She clenched her teeth and didn't scream. And the next day it was over, true enough. The child had been born, and she herself was lying peacefully in her bed. The memory of the pain, though, did not go away. That's why she would sweat and her heart would beat faster whenever she thought of that night. And she knew there were other nights like that to come.

She wouldn't stop singing. The baby was asleep inside. Spyridoula would listen, transfixed, from the kitchen. Marios was not home. He left every morning at seven to pick up his father and then they'd both go to Athens. Maria and he just had time to have breakfast together and exchange a few words. Besides, Marios wasn't very talkative in the morning. He seemed distracted and in a hurry to leave. He even scolded Spyridoula if the milk wasn't ready on time.

He would give Maria a quick kiss, just brushing her lips, and then set off at a brisk pace without looking back.

Marios would come home in the evening. That's when he'd want to talk. He'd describe everything that happened during the day. And when it was something particularly pleasant he would leap up from his chair and rush over to kiss her, warmly, not like in the morning. She would laugh.

"And you, what did you do?" he would ask.

What had she done? What could she say? She hadn't done anything in particular the way Marios had.

"Well, the baby…"

"You should go for walks," Marios would say then. "Why don't you go with Katerina, who likes walks."

"But Katerina is in love. She will only want to go on walks with him or alone…"

She'd laugh again.

"Do you know I haven't been to Athens for over a year?"

"A year?"

He looked at her with surprise. He looked her in the eyes.

"A year?" he repeated.

He went every day.

And so they decided to go to Athens, to the theater.

They left hand in hand. Though she began to regret it as soon as they were out the gate and walking across the meadow. And throughout the performance all she could think of was that little *koukouki* whose tiny hands could grab with such strength, making such beautiful fists.

Often in the afternoon Mrs. Parigori would come for a visit, either alone or with Mrs. Montelandi. They would drink something refreshing and talk until evening. All about Athens—mostly gossip.

There were times when Maria couldn't stand it any longer. She would light a cigarette and go out in the garden. She didn't know why, but she would often feel as if she were a girl of fifteen waiting to go for her first walk with a boy; in her mind she was wearing a dress with a floral print and looking expectantly at the gate. And who should be there? Why, Marios.

"Oh, Marios," she would say, and run toward him.

What happiness, my God!

"I missed you so all day long," she would say. "This very moment I was thinking of you . . ."

She would stop.

"So tell me, what did you do today in Athens?"

She would take him by the arm and they'd go into the house. Her dress didn't have a floral print; it was a solid color, but a warm, soft one.

"That dress really suits you, Maria!" Marios would say.

"Do you think so?"

He looked at her again and took her in his arms.

"Yes, yes, it really does."

"You don't think a floral print would suit me better?"

"Nope, I don't. Do I hear Mother's voice?"

"Yes, she's here. So is your grandmother."

Marios would then take part in the conversation. It was pretty tedious. Maria would grow silent listening to him talk. But soon she would be adding her two bits as well, discussing A who got married and B who got divorced and whether A and B had done the right thing or not. Time passed and soon it was evening.

"What are you doing tonight, Mother?" Mrs. Parigori would say to Mrs. Montelandi a few moments before leaving.

"I'm going over to so-and-so's."

Not an evening would pass without her doing something.

"Me? But, don't you know? I seldom go out. Yannis will already be waiting for me at home. We'll eat and then I'll go to bed and read a little."

She would sigh, say good night to everyone, and then both of them, Mrs. Parigori and Mrs. Montelandi, would descend the stairs of the veranda and vanish into the darkness at the end of the garden.

Although recently Laura Parigori's eyes shone more than usual.

I must have noticed it, the way I noticed that she had a new drawl when she spoke, because these things came to mind when I saw her walking in the meadow on David's arm.

Somehow I managed not to scream. Instead I fell to the ground like soldiers do when they see the enemy.

They passed by only twenty feet away. It was dusk, almost dark. They had their heads bent together and were talking. At first I couldn't make out what they were saying. But then I heard, "So you'll be leaving in the fall?"

I held my breath.

"Nothing's certain yet."

"Ruth told me."

"Yes, we got a letter from my father asking me to go. He might change his mind tomorrow and write again. Even if I go, I won't stay long."

"So what is it that keeps you here, David?"

At this point Mrs. Parigori must have turned toward him and smiled provocatively. I guessed this from the tone of her voice, not that I could see her. I couldn't breathe at all now. What would David answer? "You?" or "Katerina?" The die was being cast.

"The climate," answered David in his usual, slightly ironic way.

They had already passed. I couldn't hear anymore. I stayed there on the ground, wiggling around like a worm, wondering why I wasn't crying. I tried. I really tried, but no tears came. I don't know how long I stayed there. I wasn't thinking about anything, just gnawing on a piece of hay, already yellow and brittle. The summer was almost over.

What was going on between them?

I've never had such a horrible night. I couldn't sleep, and the mere idea that another day would soon dawn drove me crazy. I heard the clock toll each hour. He was certainly sleeping soundly. As for her... perhaps she was awake like me. Mrs. Parigori, why did you go fall in love with David? Can't you see that he has witch's eyes and an annoying voice.

That was the night when my love for David reached its peak. It couldn't reach any higher. I was suffering, and this pleased me. There was no getting over this kind of love.

So I began observing Mrs. Parigori, how she ate, how she talked, how she walked, how she lifted her skirt when she got out of the carriage as if it were long, the way she fixed her hair when the wind mussed it up.

One evening I decided to walk by the Parigoris' house. I had a plan. I found Leda in the garden. She was trying to make a swing.

"I love to stay at home when everyone else is gone," she said. "I can do whatever I like. What? You don't believe me? Come on, let's go into the kitchen and I'll break a plate for you, or two, or three. Who's going to stop me? Yesterday I broke four."

"That's why you like to stay alone? So you can break plates?"

"No, you don't understand..."

She had a faraway look in her eyes.

"It's just that I wanted to test myself, to see whether I am strong enough to break them." She laughed.

"They smashed into smithereens. And what a noise they made!"

While she spoke she puckered up her lips, wiggled her eyebrows, flared her nostrils. Then she took a little walk, more like a dance, and went back to the swing. One rope was already tied to the high branch of a pine tree. Now she just had to tie the other.

"If you want to help me with this," she said, "that's fine. But I don't have time to sit around and keep you company. The swing must be finished today."

She took the second rope and began to climb up the tree. I followed her.

"Grab that branch—no, not that one, the other. Like that..."

The task accomplished, we climbed down.

"Do you want to try it first?" Leda shouted.

Before I could answer yes or no she had already climbed on and was swinging, standing up.

"Give me a push," she said.

She went higher and higher.

"I'm going to reach the very top."

She pointed to the tree across the way. With each swing she got to a higher branch, and back, and forth, higher still, and back and forth. She was drunk. She shouted and laughed.

When she reached the top, she let the swing slow down. From the standing position she found herself sitting. She dragged her feet on the ground, coming to a sudden stop.

"Your turn," she said.

When I was a child I hated swings. They made me dizzy and gave me headaches. "Higher, higher, higher," everything would swirl around me and on the way home I would stumble.

"I don't like swings," I found the courage to say.

But then I regretted having said it. Not just because of the disappointment I saw written all over Leda's face, but also because in order to say something like that I must have changed and this change puzzled me.

"Well, I like them a lot," I heard her say a moment later.

All serious, she sat down on the bench.

"And do you know why? It helps me think about my idea."

I looked at her.

"Yes, I have this idea. And when I swing and go high..."

Perhaps we would become friends, Leda and I. I moved closer to her on the bench.

"And what is this idea of yours?" I asked, pretending to look elsewhere.

"I still don't know exactly," she answered, without looking at me. "It's just that I want to do something with my life..."

She was fourteen years old.

"What?" I insisted.

"That's what I'm not sure of yet," she said.

Silence.

"You also want to do something with your life, right?"

I could hear my heart beating.

"Yes," I said.

"But you don't like to swing? Funny..."

"I like walking in the meadow," I said.

"Ah ha!..."

We were already friends.

She dropped a hint about Petros and we laughed. We talked a little about the others as well; about Emilios, Stephanos, Eleni...It was time to go ahead with my plan. I mentioned David's name as if by chance.

"Sure, sometimes he accompanies Mother home," said Leda. "Recently she seems obsessed with Ruth. I don't know why."

When two women love the same man they fight over him to see who wins. I guess I will have to fight with Mrs. Parigori. I will have to start going to Ruth's just like she does. And then we'll see whom David accompanied home.

Ruth had a famous stamp collection as well as a catalog with a picture of each stamp, its history, and value. I would take a small collection of Infanta's and pretend to do research in Ruth's catalog. I liked this idea.

Ruth was very pleased to see me: "I'm so desperate for company," she said. "I want to talk to someone, to talk, discuss. I'm very lonely here...till Laura comes..."

"Oh, does Mrs. Parigori come often?" I asked.

"Almost every afternoon, especially recently."

I told her about the stamps and how I wanted to look at her catalog. She got all excited and started clapping her hands.

"What a great idea!" she exclaimed. "What a great idea! I'll also start collecting again."

She got up and walked around opening drawers, closets, full of enthusiasm for the new project.

"Let's go to the dining room and spread everything out on the big table there."

I didn't dare say that the dining room had no windows and that it would be suffocating to sit in there with the lights on when the sun was shining brightly outside.

"We'll turn on all the lights," she said happily.

All lit up like that, the dining room looked as if it were ready for guests, as if it were night. I sat with Ruth under the lights amidst the papers and books. We had a magnifying glass that we looked through every once in a while.

"What have we here? Two old wise men sacrificing their lives for the sake of knowledge," said David, chuckling as he came down the stairs.

He didn't offer to walk me home. It was midday, so maybe that's why. But still, it was as though we had never gone for a walk together, never looked at the reeds. "Oh, I'll pay you back, David," I murmured.

But in the meantime I would go to Ruth's and look at stamps with her. It was very boring. I hated it. As Ruth talked I'd get distracted and walk around touching the furniture. I would feel the wall, looking for a window. And when I thought about how there were no windows, I'd see in my mind those lit up red letters spelling "Emergency Exit," which instead of a door conceal a solid wall.

All this had an effect on my love. I spoke to David coldly as if he were my enemy. He was the one preventing me from the morning sun. I would never forgive him. "Please come tomorrow, please come tomorrow," Ruth would say. And I would go in order to see David. I would throw him nasty looks, though, and he, in order to get back at me, acted reserved, almost formal.

At home I was also difficult. I fought with my sisters over the smallest thing, and also with Mother. I was rude to Aunt Theresa—I had a history of hurting her anyway—I tormented Rodia. No one dared talk to me. "Just look at the evil in her eyes," Rodia would say. "Look at that stubbornness." One day when I was bickering with Infanta—I don't know how I let myself do it—I pinched her arm. I was sorry immediately, very sorry. I asked her to forgive me and she did.

All of this was of course David's fault, the approaching autumn, my voluntary imprisonment in that sunless dining room morning after morning.

I don't know why, but one day Ruth showed me a photograph of her father. He looked exactly like David. Except that his nose was crooked, whereas David's was Greek. Fortunately.

"Their voices are also very similar," said Ruth, "and the way they move, particularly the way they move their hands. Ah, and when Father spoke of the history of our people, only to hear his voice and see his hands made you cry."

Ruth was serious now.

"He was a Zionist," she said dreamily.

I looked at her.

"That is, he believed that the Jews should all go to Palestine to found their nation and live there. To cultivate its soil and build it up from nothing stone by stone ..."

Silence.

"And he wanted to go himself to dig in Palestine with the young people, even though he was sixty then. He left the store he ran in England ... But then he died."

Life is strange.

"I'm a Zionist too," said Ruth.

The stamp catalog was still open in front of us.

"Except that I'm not made for digging and such . . . I miss Stavros a lot," she said. "Stavros is David's father—I often dream of him."

I'm not sure why, but after that I wanted to give Ruth a small present. I thought she would like a little animal to place on her bureau next to the others. But since we had some darling new ducklings, I took one of them instead in a basket. She was as pleased as a child.

"I never realized how much more beautiful real animals are than glass and porcelain ones," she said.

She called him Donald like in the comics and built him a little pond. Donald gave David's house new life.

VI. IN THE OBSERVATORY

THE CLOUDS wander across the meadow. Sometimes across the mountains. They make patches of shade as they pass, while everything else stays golden, as long as the sun is out. And when it disappears, all the color goes out of the earth.

Then I think of the birds who travel to warmer climates. And I am envious. For them the whole world is their home. They fly across the ocean, the little ones resting on the backs of the bigger ones.

It's strange to be a Zionist, but I guess it happens sometimes. Perhaps it's just as strange to be Mrs. Parigori and thinking about David. Especially when you have my sister Maria as your daughter-in-law and a grandson who is named Yannis after your husband.

Everything is strange and new, and the weather changes every day. Yesterday it was raining. Today the sun has the color and sweetness of honey, and there's a donkey braying sadly in the distance. Is there such a thing as a happy donkey? Now there's a challenge, something to do with your life. Take a donkey and make him happy. I should run and tell Leda. You'd have to comb him every morning, give him as much as he liked to eat, take him for walks whenever he wanted without loading him up. And maybe then he'd sound happier.

Father is waiting for the blond lady to get a divorce because—what a coincidence—it will be her second marriage, too. Although, according to Aunt Theresa, many things could happen before then.

Maybe I'll go over to Leda's this afternoon and tell her my idea about the donkey. Then I'll hang around on the way back just in case David and Mrs. Parigori pass by. I'll see if I can hear something and find out what is going on. I am sure that when I met Mrs. Parigori at Ruth's she looked at me differently. She kept stealing glances at me whenever I turned my head away. She must suspect something; maybe she found out that David and I had been spending time together, who knows? I kept looking at her as well, though only once straight in the eyes and then only to say, "You look just fine, Mrs. Parigori. You've gained weight, but you still look wonderful." She was terribly worried about gaining weight. And David was between us talking first to one then to the other with his shrill voice and his laugh. He would clasp his hands and then spread them out so they filled up the whole table—two times I caught her looking at his hands.

But then something odd happened; he ran after me when I was leaving and just at the point where the potato fields end and the road with the blackberry bushes begins he told me that if I wanted to see the sky with a telescope I could come Sunday night. He didn't accompany me home the way he accompanied Mrs. Parigori though.

And it was only Monday.

On Tuesday morning clouds gathered, in the afternoon they cleared; on Wednesday they gathered again and it rained; on Thursday it was sunny. These were difficult days. I wandered around indecisive, feeling lost. When I passed the kitchen to go down to the garden I would stand and absentmindedly watch Rodia's hands peeling potatoes. I would sit down in a chair, get up, go over and cut a branch of vervain, come back... "The wandering Jew," said Rodia, and I shivered all over. David was exactly like his grandfather, the Zionist, except for his nose. And one other thing, he wasn't about to go dig in Palestine. Since he was Christian he would never set out on a new crusade.

Last year at this time I felt so free. I ran around hitting the bushes with my stick, and my friends were the heroes of the books I had read. Now even if I called his name, Alyosha wouldn't come. In front of me and wherever I looked I saw David's eyes, black and shiny witch eyes. I saw them in the meadow, on the surrounding mountains, even in my plate when I ate. And if on Sunday night he looked me straight in the eyes and said "jump out of the window," I'd have no other choice. I was very scared that Sunday would be my last day alive. I waited with secret longing though. And with the awe appropriate for someone about to die.

That's why I washed my hair and wore a white dress and started on my way calmly after such an anxious week. Without letting anyone know, of course. At home everyone had gone to sleep. Aunt Theresa snored a bit when I peeked in her door to listen. From the garden I could see the light on at Maria's house. The baby must've woken up.

The night was beautiful and so calm it made your heart ache. I felt a dog licking my legs. "Shhh ... Yangoulas," I whispered, "shhh. Down boy, go home." And I don't know why, but instead of thinking of Mavroukos, my mind turned to Dick, even though all I could remember about him was that he had one black ear and one white one. I wondered about how calm I felt. Maybe I had fallen asleep and was dreaming. I must wake up, go to David's, and look at the sky with the telescope.

There was no moon, and the sky was full of stars. Each star was a world. It made me crazy thinking about it, thinking about all that motion around the sun, and that human beings had seen it all and studied it. Amalia would of course say that all that was nonsense since we hadn't yet managed to make life on our own planet bearable for everyone. Some day I'll have to sit down and think about what Amalia says.

And what if David had forgotten what he'd said? Or what if he'd said it as a joke?

How I wanted to go back, take off my clothes, and fall into bed. In my room I knew how the light slipped through the shutters and played on the opposite wall each morning and how high the ceiling was and what cracks there were, cracks that looked like faces and a thousand other things.

But I had already reached the road with the blackberry bushes. A small light shone in the observatory window. The rest of the house was dark. David was waiting for me at the end of the field. He was smoking. I smiled sort of stupidly. I had thrown a light yellow jacket over my shoulders, covering my white dress. I didn't know whether I should leave it on or take it off. He also smiled sort of stupidly, and he didn't know whether he should let me wear it or help me take it off. He acted awkwardly.

"I'll leave it on."

Then we greeted each other and he asked me to sit next to him at the edge of the field.

"We've got plenty of time," he said, pointing vaguely in the direction of the light that was shining in the observatory.

And right afterwards he let his hand fall with that familiar gesture that concealed such a tender hopelessness.

"David," I started to say.

Oh, how I loved him at that moment.

"What's been going on with you recently?" he asked, turning abruptly toward me.

"What do you think is going on with me?"

"How should I know? You're the one who should know."

I grew silent.

"You're not going to tell me, Katerina?"

I wanted to speak, to tell him about Mrs. Parigori, the sunless dining room, to tell him everything. Though, what right, David could then say, what right did I have telling him not to go for walks with Mrs. Parigori? So I clenched my teeth shut and said nothing. I stretched my neck taller and lifted my eyes, staring far away.

"You are so stubborn," David whispered, and after one more puff he threw his cigarette on the road.

It stayed lit for a minute or two and then went out. That's when I said, "And you, what's the matter with you, David?"

It seemed as if he were trying to find my eyes in the dark. As if he touched my hand, a little, just slightly.

"How old are you?" he asked.

"I'm almost eighteen."

"I'm twenty-six," he said.

"Is Ruth asleep?" I suddenly asked.

"No, she's in Athens since yesterday."

"Ah..."

I was alone with David. In this deserted field, by a deserted house, in a deserted world. David and I. It frightened me a bit. What if he really did ask me to jump from the window of the observatory?

"It's time," I heard him say.

I got up. He took my hand to help me over the rough spots. My jacket slipped from my shoulders. How annoying.

"You are indecisive," said David, and he laughed a little.

"Why? How can you tell?"

"You can't decide whether or not to leave your jacket on."

He laughed again.

It was true. That is, it was always hard for me to make a decision. But when I did . . .

"Yes, I'm indecisive," I agreed. "And do you want to know something else?"

We had arrived at the bottom of the spiral staircase.

"I don't like these kind of stairs. They make me dizzy. I don't like swings either."

I lifted up my head to look. The spiral staircase wound round and round.

"You'll see how nice it is up there," said David.

It was a round room, without any corners. It had four rectangular windows that faced east, west, north, and south. Instead of a roof it had a heavy metal dome. When we came in it smelled a bit stuffy. Under the lamp a book was open to page four hundred and twenty. Farther off there were other books piled up. I also saw the telescope and other instruments that seemed related to the telescope.

"So this is my own house," said David, and his voice seemed to be hiding some emotion.

I then thought of my secret hiding spot and all the time I had spent there. But I couldn't say anything about it. How could I talk about the shade and the sound of the leaves and how the birds were not afraid to come near me? Some had red and blue feathers, others were black with white bellies. How did anyone decide to travel around the world? I am already so nostalgic for the places and things that I see every day. I sighed. David said, "You'll get hot. Let me open the ceiling."

And before I understood what he was saying, he turned off the light and I heard a noise like thunder, and in a single motion the metal dome slid open. I lifted my eyes and saw the sky. And around me the walls, smooth and round, so there was no beginning or end. It was something I couldn't have expected. Nor could I have known that at the exact same moment David would embrace me and kiss me. On the lips. A sweet anxiousness made it impossible to talk. I was sure I'd never speak again. I thought I'd never walk again, think again. But it didn't matter. The only thing that mattered was that that sweet anxiousness shouldn't go away, shouldn't ever go away. I felt again for David's lips. And when he held me tightly in his arms like in a cage, I thought, *The hour of death has come, Katerina. The death that you waited for with such secret longing.* Instead he decided to show me the sky with the telescope.

And when we had seen how amazing the universe was and how much grander it was than the earth, David asked me whether or not I wanted to wear my jacket. We went down the stairs though it was still early.

"I'd like to walk home alone," I said when we got to the road with the blackberries and he had started to accompany me—like he did with Mrs. Parigori. "I'll come again, though. I really liked it, David."

I wanted to laugh, to sing, to cry, to shout—I don't know. The wind was blowing. It took me and swayed me this way and that like a reed. In the dark I could make out the darker shapes of the trees. And I was one of those dark shapes, too, and the trees were looking at me. Dark blood was running in my veins, I could feel it, the taste of David's kiss was still on my lips, the sweet anxiousness was a part of me forever. *Whirr... Whirr...* how the wind blew. My God, I could almost fly. I untied the ribbon in my hair so that it blew freely. It hummed like the pines. I was ready to dance with the wood fairies.

They were waiting for me at the clearing, and when I felt the rhythm it was difficult for me to separate myself from them.

I woke up just before dawn, and was surprised to find that I had fallen asleep in the woods. I still remembered though. I touched my lips with my fingertips, I touched them thoughtfully... My face was still misty like everything around me.

I think I fell asleep again for a minute or two or half an hour. When I opened my eyes again I got up abruptly; around me the ground was covered in lavender. The sun was just coming up. The marble of Pendeli and the lavender were the same color.

In the woods everything was waking up and trembling. I stretched my arms and took a deep breath. And everywhere there was lavender. I leapt carefully so I wouldn't step on it. In the olive grove everything was different. There was a stillness, a calm, a uniformity that deserved respect. The ground was bare and red and there was hardly any shade.

And now, the uphill part of Elia Avenue. I took big steps. For me uphill was a game. There were times when I preferred it to the level road. Maria had told me this part tired her out.

The more I walked, the faster I went. It was late. They mustn't know I was out. I was hungry. The goats were already grazing here and there, and the hens were pecking for worms. I heard Kalomoira's pig scream as if it were drowning. It was hungry, too. Water was running in the big stream, and the smell of mint was everywhere. The reeds near there had shot up, and recently at their tips silver-golden puffballs had blossomed. When the wind blew, the puffballs made a raspy, pleasant sound, which accompanied the sad sound reeds make when they sway. What color would the sea be now? Right now the shutters of the island houses would be opening, letting the sea breeze in, the pebbles would be shining, the gulls would be fishing in little groups.

I would have to climb over the fence and slip inside. And just as I was passing furtively by the kitchen, in that final moment, I saw Rodia suddenly appear, and I blushed, and turned green.

"And what are you doing up so early?" Rodia asked.

"I heard Mother Kapatos calling her children."

I ran up the stairs and finally got to my room. And when I saw my bed all neat and tidy, I felt very strange. As if my bed were a person whom I had betrayed. I put my forehead on the white sheets. "David only kissed me," I whispered. And as I was looking out at the meadow it suddenly struck me that he hadn't said "I love you," as one would expect under such circumstances.

In the garden I met Infanta.

"Where were you last night?" she asked without looking at me.

Silence.

"I knocked on your door and when you didn't answer I opened it and found your room empty."

"What time?" I said provocatively.

"After midnight."

Silence.

"I wanted to ask you something…"

She looked into the distance.

"And it was as if I had asked you and you were giving me your answer. By not being there, you gave me your answer, you see? Perhaps…"

She stood up straight and her eyes became slits.

"I don't know though, I still don't know."

And after a while, "Did David kiss you?"

"Yes, he kissed me."

We were in the pavilion. I was lying on the bench and my eyes were half-closed. I was annoyed. I got up and looked at her.

"So what if he did?" I shouted. "Why shouldn't he kiss me? I'm almost eighteen years old."

"I'm nineteen," she said distractedly.

She leaned her head on the pine.

"It's as if something stops me, Katerina," she said.

I felt a lump in my throat. I got up laughing.

"Let's go to the fig trees," I said.

At the very top there were still some figs. They were very sweet. I broke some off for Rodia as well. I knew that she liked them even if she was always saying how little taste they had: "Now figs in Ikaria!"

When I spilled them onto the kitchen table, Rodia looked at me suspiciously.

"Something's up with you," she whispered. "Your eyes are sparkling."

"Oh Rodia, my dear Rodoula," I said, "I was up all night dancing with the wood fairies."

I grabbed her by the waist and made her dance around with me.

"Now you leave me alone," she said sternly. "I see you've begun telling stories again like you did when you were small."

THE THIRD SUMMER

I. MAY AND JUNE

FATHER and Uncle Agisilaos can now do whatever they please. Forget to eat or eat too much. Go out with a jacket that is missing all its buttons. They no longer have anyone to look after them. Grandmother died this winter. I remember it was raining hard on the day of the funeral and I was cold to the bone. Father was very sad but he didn't cry or say anything; neither did Uncle Agisilaos. At one point they exchanged a look; it was full of the uncertainty and hopelessness of children who have been left orphans.

It was morning when I learned. I burst into tears. Infanta and Maria arrived and we all cried together until the afternoon.

The funny thing is that Marios lost his grandmother around the same time. Poor Mrs. Montelandi suffered, it appears, for years from a disease that slowly ate away at her. Mrs. Parigori wore black, which, as everyone said, suited her.

But David was not there to see. He was in England. He left two Sundays after he kissed me. As for Nikitas, he was in Athens where he was studying hard in his first year at the Polytechnic. He wanted to become an engineer. But he would be back soon now that winter was over.

Infanta wanted a new dress. We went together to Athens to shop. She chose a blue-green one to match her eyes and I, a bright red one with flecks of white that looked exactly like the strewn seeds of a pomegranate in the sun.

That day, though, I had a plan. I had thought of it the night before, and then I couldn't sleep.

I told it to Infanta after we bought our dresses.

"Shall we go see Father?"

"Where? At the bank?"

"Yes. At the bank."

In the meantime the plan had lost some of its magic. I hesitated to talk about it. It all seemed kind of silly now. But I couldn't change my mind now. And since it would only get more difficult if I let time pass, as soon as we had greeted Father and sat down, I said very seriously, "Listen, Father, you should get married. We don't have any objections."

He looked at me, and his look had an ineffable sweetness about it. I looked at him, too. Surely we would never forget this moment.

"A signature, please."

An employee was standing in front of his desk. Father took the piece of paper, read it carefully, stamped it, and then signed. Infanta was surprised by this, and she looked uncomfortable in her seat.

The employee left, but the magical moment had passed. We couldn't think of anything to say. I took some blotting paper and began to cut it into tiny pieces.

"We wanted you to know that it's fine with us. That's why we came. Isn't that right, Infanta?"

"Yes, of course," she whispered

"Maria doesn't have any objections either."

Father seemed to smile.

"Not objections—what I mean is that we don't mind. Of course we're in no position to have objections."

He seemed pleased.

"I had wanted to tell you, but this makes it easier. Katerina and I are planning to get married this summer."

Her name was Katerina. Now there was something I couldn't have imagined.

"You both have the same name," said Father, and he pretended to read another piece of paper.

I left relieved. I whistled softly as I walked down the street. Of course, as with every plan that materializes, what actually happened bore little resemblance to what I had planned. I had imagined something grander, I'm not exactly sure what. But Father looked pleased, that was the main thing.

And each of us returned with our packet. Mother said, though, that as we'd only just taken off our mourning clothes for Grandmother we could at least have chosen slightly less bright colors. She didn't understand how blue the sky was after the winter, how red the earth, how green the trees.

The countryside was covered in wildflowers. There were times when I looked at them and thought of David and other times when I looked at them and didn't. His face—the way it would sometimes vanish completely from my memory, and I would desperately try to recall it—made me anxious. I would run over to Ruth's and beg her to show me the photograph of her father. But his crooked nose spoiled the effect. David's was so straight. He hadn't written me all winter. He said he didn't know how to write letters, and besides he was totally consumed with his Ph.D. Only his father in the letters he sent Ruth would say, "David sends greetings to everyone," and once or twice, "David sends greetings to everyone and Katerina."

There were hours when I was filled with his absence. His absence was something different from him, but it was also like him. It stood by me those moments when I was sitting at Ruth's table and kept me company on my afternoon winter walks. I loved his absence.

It's just that everything was so unknown, hidden by a curtain of rain. It was only possible to guess at what lay beyond. Finally when Aniksi Avenue overflowed with water and became a stream, then there was finally something certain, the steady sound of water running.

And although the winter days passed in a haze, my memory of them is now very clear. And damp, like the earth that hasn't yet had time to dry.

Infanta saw the first poppy. Then the meadows were full of them. Daisies also sprang up, especially along the fences. Everywhere there was the smell of chamomile. The kid goats were acting crazy. They would bend down their heads and run to one side for a bit, then arch their bodies and run to the other. Bending and twisting, their stomachs and their legs going in all different directions, they would leap in the air once, twice, and then stop abruptly, their eyes transfixed, as if they had suddenly heard something, and then they'd go back to their leaping again.

Sometimes I would play with them, and without meaning to I'd also stop and stare into the distance trying to hear a sound. Something wasn't enough in life, and something was too much, overflowing.

"You'd like to live two lives," Maria once told me. "Your face gives you away."

"Not just two, but thousands, Maria, or one which could be a thousand."

In spring everyone acts crazy like the kid goats.

So Infanta ran toward me to show me the first poppy. But as she ran the poppy faded and its petals fell off, and the only thing that was left in her hand was the stem and its black center.

"See, you can't pick poppies. It serves you right."

She turned away as if angry. Deep down, though, it was to hide her sadness; perhaps she was thinking that it wasn't possible to do such a bold thing, like picking a poppy. I went and put my hand on her shoulder.

"You forget," I said, "how you killed a poisonous snake here in the lavender."

"That was easy," she answered. "All you have to do is lift up a stick and hit its head, holding your breath."

"Everything is easy," I then said.

She seemed to think about this a bit.

"Perhaps. But someone has to make me feel that it's easy."

And it was as if someone else's voice was speaking from inside me when I began quickly, "Yes, and to make you feel it before you have time to think. Something like lightning, right, Infanta? Something which you see first and only later realize was lightning."

"Yes, like lightning," she whispered.

Then we thought of Nikitas.

He came back to Kifissia after exams. He was skinnier than last year and paler. Perhaps he had also grown a bit taller.

He had done well in his first year. Even though it was his father's idea that he go to the Polytechnic, now he liked it. He never missed a class, studied systematically, patiently. He would make a good engineer. He didn't write poems anymore, not one the whole winter. His last was "The Shipwreck," which he had read to them in the pavilion one day near the end of summer when it was threatening to rain. He still remembers Infanta's trembling fingers when she spread her needlework of peacocks on her knees and their strange stillness when she began to embroider. Her hands were like doll hands when she embroidered, the ones that wind up and then make the same motion again and again. The memory tortured him.

He also thought that her friendship was not enough for him. He wanted to take her and squeeze her in his arms, to squeeze her hard and to kiss her. That's what he wanted. And that head of hers that she carried so high . . . He must break her, make her lower it. Yes, he wanted to see her head bent and her hair loose, hanging helplessly on both sides of her face. He would then take it and braid it for her carefully. His heart melted thinking of this. Ah, he would act differently this summer. Not like when he got nervous because she touched him, and spoke brusquely to her, disappearing then for days. He would behave like Emilios did with Eleni, and all the other boys who went to the woods with their girls. Slowly, of course, so as not to shock her, not like lightning. First he would have to change the tone of their friendship. He wouldn't take Vicky down to go for a ride as usual, but he would send her a note saying that he would like to see her alone, how he would be waiting impatiently at such and such an hour at the deserted well where they often used to stop to quench their thirst and water the horses.

It was afternoon and the sun was setting when Infanta got the note.

Romeo seemed to fly the next morning. She squeezed her knees against his belly and left the reins loose. Her hair blew freely. She was drunk. When she rode life was all hers. She could conquer anything.

She felt the beating pulse of the animal beneath her and something inside her leapt.

"Bravo, Romeo! Run, Romeo!"

Desire. And her look would get lost in the distance, insistent, as if it could pierce a darkness that didn't exist. Life is worth living when you can conquer it, when you conquer it without fear, freely, like now, in a gallop. The wind hit her in the face. She wanted to arrive a little before he did and wait for him. She would lie in the thyme.

But he was already there, sitting on the ledge of the well, bent over. Behind him his blue shirt billowed in the wind. He had folded his hands and was staring at the ground. His posture suggested an immense solitude. He did not hear the horse's hooves. This irritated her a bit.

"Nikitas!" she cried.

And he was surprised that her voice was so harsh.

Something had already separated them. They started to talk about their usual topics. Except they decided he would no longer come and fetch her from the house. They would meet here secretly instead. She would have something to hide, he too.

"Do you want it this way?" he asked.

"Yes, I do."

"Why?"

He looked at her. She averted her eyes. It is difficult to keep the free feeling you have when you are galloping. She grew silent.

"Why?" Nikitas asked again.

"I don't know. There isn't a reason."

Her voice was cold now, and his look sad. Oh, if only she could wrap her hands around Nikitas's neck and say, "Nikitas, I don't want you to have that sad look. I never want to see that sad look again."

"There's no reason," she continued. "What are you trying to say? I don't understand."

And Katerina, who had said it was all so simple . . .

Sometimes when she was with Nikitas she would go over and caress Romeo. Her hand would pet his ears, his mouth, then his eyes, gently. And when Romeo neighed, she would lean on him, touching his nose to hers, sinking her eyes into his.

Nikitas would get annoyed.

"You certainly love that horse," he would say bitterly.

"He helps me to overcome things," she would answer, laughing.

"Overcome what?"

"Overcome life, the trees, the distance, I don't know. When I run with him I can overcome anything." She laughed.

She told him about the day when, against her will, Romeo had started to gallop up the mountain and how nothing could stop him.

"That's why I love him," she said.

And when Maria saw her racing across the meadow, alone and free, she would say in a loud, preoccupied voice which sounded strange to her own ears, "How could anyone be so pure as Infanta?"

She sighed. Maria was expecting her second child. She was already beginning to feel heavy. Little Yannis had started to talk and crawl. She couldn't call him "my *koukouki*" anymore. She'd save that for the new baby. She was looking forward to another child, especially the nursing.

As for me, thousands of things consumed me: David's homecoming, the heroes of the books I was reading, and Mother, who although seemingly calm for a while, her only concern the jam of the season, would then suddenly lock herself up in the living room in front of her desk, for one or two days straight, and then leave for hours on end.

I must say that before June 21st, which was for me the most amazing day of my life, a lot of things happened. First David came back. My heart almost burst when I found out. I jumped down the stairs two at a time and then ran back up them. I didn't know what to do. I changed my dress, combed my hair, started to speak, to shout, but couldn't. For one moment, though, I guess I did—a scream rose up from inside me so strong, both Mother and Rodia came running up to see what had happened to me.

"What's going on? . . . What's going on?" they cried when they saw me standing in front of the mirror with my new dress on, shocked by my own voice.

"What's going on? Nothing," I answered calmly. "I was just testing my vocal chords."

Mother threw me a stern look, and Rodia left, murmuring how it would do me good to remember every once in a while the story of the boy who cried wolf.

David had returned. For a moment I was so absorbed with looking into the mirror that I forgot who I was, who David was, and my face went misty. My lips turned white. I wanted to see him, to see him at once. I went down the stairs again, I ran past the garden and out onto the plain. It was morning and a Sunday. I didn't notice that it was a beautiful day, but I felt the sun on my shoulders and the top of my head and I smelled the thyme. I heard the bells of the church. The second service had just begun.

Everyone knew that at this hour Mrs. Parigori was leaning out the window of her house in her nightgown and robe watching people go by. Ah, I'd prefer that David hadn't returned just so that she wouldn't see him again. It was ridiculous to lean out a window and look at people, not to mention indiscreet. After all they weren't actors, just people passing by after church.

One day I will be straight with David. Choose one or the other: me or her. I might even say it today, and perhaps since I'll be seeing him first he'll choose me.

But who should be the first person I saw at David's? Mrs. Parigori. I was confused. She should be leaning out her window. I was so confused that I saw her double, leaning out her window and standing in front of me under the electric light smiling, leaning on the little organ.

"Why Katerina, what's this?" she said, and pretending not to take any more notice of me, she went to get something from her bag.

I stayed, staring at the deer antlers. I counted the various branches. Then I went over to her.

"I came to see David," I said.

"He just got in last night," she responded. "Quite suddenly. I happened to be here. The three of us had dinner together. It was very pleasant."

At that moment I heard David coming down the stairs. I felt extremely calm and appeared even more so. He smiled when he saw me and squeezed my hand. It was an extremely warm greeting.

"Why so early, Laura?" he said, turning toward Mrs. Parigori.

He now called her Laura.

"I didn't sleep well and woke at dawn. And then there are those church bells. Besides I promised Ruth I would come over and help unpack your bags."

"Ah, thank you," David said then, "but I don't want you tiring yourself out."

And saying that, he fidgeted nervously, searching for his lighter, and then ran over to light the cigarette she had just brought to her lips. She had lifted her head toward him, imploring him with her eyes to light it.

"Have a nice day," I said then, looking at them sharply and leaving.

At the end of Aniksi Avenue just before Elia Avenue groups of people had gathered and were talking. This is what I heard when I passed. "Playing marbles this morning," they said, "one of Kapatos's sons and the Kouvelis boy fought, and Kouvelis shot the other dead."

I started to run to Mother Kapatos's house. I was out of breath. Michalis, the tall boy who wore a cape over his shoulders and walked around all day grazing their three goats and the sheep, was dead. I had come upon him many a time sitting on a rock watching the clouds, whistling, or singing a tune.

From a distance I could see the boat and the pile of old metal scraps. The door was open and the house was deserted. Only Yangoulas, lying in a corner with his snout between his front paws, opened one eye halfway and looked at me. They had probably all gone off to see the place where it had happened.

The next day I didn't dare go again. After a week, when I finally ran into Mrs. Kapatos, she told me in a thoughtful, submissive tone that perhaps someone in the family had to die so the rest could live.

"We'll get a lot of insurance money," she explained.

I thought then of a shipwreck, when the boat fills with water and the weight is too much and someone has to jump overboard into the sea, and also of a song about a ship short of food where the lot fell to the youngest—it was his first trip at sea—and they ate him to save the others.

II. NEW FACES

ONE DAY I heard a cicada singing. Just for a moment. Then it started up again, its voice getting stronger and stronger. Now its song is so continuous it sounds the same as complete silence.

It was really hot on that 21st of June. David and I were climbing up Aniksi Avenue, walking toward Kifissia. He had kissed me twice since he had returned, once in the olive grove and the other time in the woods. He buried his hand in my long, curly hair and mussed it up as if he were caressing me to sleep. I liked it, and he seemed to like it too, even though he was distracted. When he took his hand away for a moment I don't know what came over me but I screamed. He put his hand down abruptly and looked at me in surprise.

When we arrived in Kifissia, David went into the stationery store to buy something and I stood outside looking in the store window. Suddenly out of the corner of my eye I saw Mother, who, after hurriedly crossing the main street without even glancing at the people who were sitting at the pastry shop, began climbing Othonos Street, her step young and sprightly. On either side of the road water was running in the irrigation ditches and her dress swirled this way and that, keeping time with her stride.

I had never seen her so absorbed. She looked straight ahead. Her hair shone, drawn tightly together in a bun. Her skin, too, seemed stretched across her brow.

I saw her climbing, getting farther and farther away; my heart beat faster. David wouldn't come out of the store. He always took a long time when he shopped, especially at stationery stores. He'd test the weight of the paper a hundred times, passing it from one hand to the other, and he'd check the pens carefully to make sure they didn't have bent or rusted nibs.

Mother had arrived at the top of Othonos Street and was about to turn right. I started to walk, almost running, my heart beating. She turned right and then disappeared. Which road did she take? I chose one, guessing. My heart was really beating. And there she was in front of me on the road with the poplars that goes to Kefalari. I slowed down my step and kept stopping behind the poplars. If she turned her head she would see me. But she didn't seem to be paying attention to anything. Only just before turning, she stopped and looked carefully around, quickening her pace. I hid for a minute at the corner. The road was open here. I couldn't follow her. But before I had time to think what I should do, I saw her stop in front of an iron gate on the left and, opening the latch as if well acquainted with it, go in. She didn't ring a bell or call for anybody to open the door.

I sat on the sidewalk. The sun was burning. It must be almost midday. A thousand thoughts were whirling around in my head, the one stranger than the next.

Three quarters of an hour or more must have passed with me sitting there, when I saw her lift the latch again and come out, taking the road home a little more slowly now. I didn't have time to run ahead—she would have seen me—nor to turn off onto another road. I clung to the poplar like a cicada to a pine tree, taking tiny steps to the right so I would be at the other side of the tree by the time Mother passed. She passed right in front of me. I could hear her breath. I was holding mine. It was a good thing no car came by, because if she had stepped any farther to the left we would have been face to face.

I sat down again on the sidewalk for about a quarter of an hour. And when at last I walked back to Kifissia I found Mother, Mr. Louzis, and David sitting together at the pastry shop. David threw me an angry look, though he said very courteously, "What will you have?"

Mother and David were drinking lemonade and Mr. Louzis, ouzo.

"A cherry soda," I said. "Phew! I'm so hot."

"Where were you?" Mother asked, turning toward me.

I looked her in the eyes.

"Oh, I had a wonderful walk, high above the cemetery."

She looked slightly confused.

"What business did you have up there?"

Her voice shook a bit.

"Katerina, you are a dreamer," Mr. Louzis added out of the blue.

I'm sure I blushed. But I managed to say with a smile full of dignity, "Why do you say that, Mr. Louzis?" He began to laugh.

"I was remembering one night with a full moon... Ha, ha, ha! A night with a full moon down on the meadow, ha, ha, ha! But of course the moon was to blame.... Because when there's a full moon..."

He couldn't go on; he was choking from laughter. His face had turned bright red, and he looked like he was going to burst.

David started to talk about the influence of the moon on animals and people. He gave various examples.

"Perhaps you were going to talk about that," he said, turning calmly and politely to Mr. Louzis.

"You, my friend, are interested in scientific explanations. I only know that when there's a full moon the wise go mad and the mad get madder."

It was as if the sound of "full moon" pleased him. He said it louder and clearer, pausing after "full" and prolonging the "oo" in "moon." He had begun to laugh again, and people from the surrounding tables turned to look at us.

"I have noticed dogs react," said Mother in a slow and measured voice so as to balance out the overly excited Mr. Louzis. "They bark strangely those nights and—"

"And they howl. Yes, why not just say the word 'howl'?"

It was me who had spoken in such an unjustifiably self-righteous way.

"You didn't let me finish my sentence, Katerina. Please don't interrupt next time."

I was embarrassed that she had spoken to me disapprovingly in front of David. Of course I could have gotten back at her by saying where I'd seen her only an hour before. Instead I said in a tone that could be read as concealing either great respect or great impudence, "You wouldn't have finished the sentence, Mother."

David turned and looked at me. At the same moment Mr. Louzis and Mother exchanged a glance.

"It's time to go," they said.

They got up. David and I got up, too. I pulled on his sleeve, letting him know I wanted him to stay behind a bit.

"Tell me something," I said, "when exactly did Mr. Louzis arrive at the pastry shop?"

"Twelve, twelve-thirty, I don't know..."

"Please try to remember. It is very important."

"About ten minutes before you did. Yes, that's right."

So perhaps he had been "up there." He could have left afterwards, when I was sitting on the sidewalk deep in thought. And when he saw me? Perhaps that is why he said "Katerina, you are a dreamer."

"And Mother?"

"She arrived a little before him."

He wouldn't say anything more. He hung his head, his brow furrowed. That's why, out of stubbornness, I didn't explain my abrupt disappearance from the stationery store. Only at the end of Aniksi Avenue, before Mother and I turned right and Mr. Louzis and David, left, did he give me his hand—he was obliged to—and instead of saying "bye," he said very softly without changing the expression on his face at all, "You're impossible."

In the short distance I walked alone with Mother we didn't say much. I wanted to annoy her, to get her angry. I would have liked to see her lips tremble and her eyes flash. On the other hand I loved her more than ever.

Perhaps she also felt something similar, since I heard her say abruptly that I should pay more attention to the way I dress when I go to Kifissia, not to wear faded dresses and muddy sandals. But then she said, "David's a very nice boy, isn't he?"

"Not in the least," I said.

At the table she found another reason to reprimand me. I, though, totally absorbed with the thought of going to that house in the afternoon, an idea that was fast becoming a decision, didn't notice her. I said nothing, and that made her even angrier.

"Your impudence knows no limits," she cried, and leaving her food unfinished, she left the table.

When someone gets angry because you've screamed at them it's a bit depressing, but when it's because of your silence . . . I felt a drunkenness, a sense of triumph. I looked straight ahead with a fixed stare. Everyone's attention was focused on me.

"The truth is that Katerina hasn't done anything wrong," Infanta bravely said.

Grandfather of course didn't participate in the conversation. Each day he grows more and more distant. It's as if he has already begun to die.

"Yes, but it's her attitude . . ." shouted Aunt Theresa. "Just look at her."

Mother was standing out on the veranda. I was still looking straight ahead. Except that my cheeks were bright red.

"It's as if she were out to provoke the whole world."

Aunt Theresa, in support of Mother, was also angry.

Infanta and I then happened to exchange a glance, and I'm not sure how it happened but we started to laugh. We laughed so hard tears were running down our faces. We had forgotten Grandfather, who had calmly lit his pipe and was watching us as he smoked. His face, serious to begin with, became cheerful and then serious again. Grandfather was like that. His mood would swing from deep melancholy to extreme happiness and then back again, all of a sudden, for no obvious reason. Perhaps, though, it is just his eyebrows that give this impression. They are so thick that when he frowns, all sorts of wrinkles appear between his eyes, and then when he stops, they smooth out and lift, leaving his forehead open and giving his face a totally different expression. Grandfather's face has something undecided about it, unfinished, vague. In this way Aunt Theresa resembles him.

I couldn't stand it any longer and, taking Infanta by the hand, I ran out into the garden to the back of the house so that they wouldn't hear us laughing. Every time we looked at each other we began laughing all over again.

"Don't look at me! Don't look at me!" Infanta would cry.

"But you're looking at me," I would say, and then look at her.

And we'd keep laughing. We loved each other most when we were laughing. It's as if there was an understanding between us, illogical, but intense. The same thing happened with Maria. In any case we always ended up saying the most important things to each other after we'd been laughing, in the sudden silence that would follow.

But our laughing bothered Mother. Perhaps it was because she felt excluded even though she was the one who had brought us into this world. We did love her, just in a different way. She ought to understand.

It was late afternoon when I found myself in the cool silence of my room. I fell asleep immediately and dreamt that I was sailing. Perhaps this was because a few hours later, climbing up the hill, I would turn my head and see for the first time a bit of sea in the distance. All these years and I hadn't known that at exactly that spot of the meadow you could see the sea. Life was so unpredictable!

I put my hand between the iron railings and lift the latch. My legs are shaking as I walk toward the veranda. The elderly man and the woman, who were bent over the table before they heard the gate creak, stare at me. I have an excuse, though. I'll pretend I have a message from Mother.

"Good evening."

The elderly man shows no sign of surprise. As for the woman, she gets up immediately to give me her chair and, going into the house, says to him, "Play a little with the girl and I'll be right back."

All of this was certainly strange.

"Sit down," the elderly man says.

"I only wanted to tell you ..."

"Please sit down. What number do you want?"

His tone of voice is courteous yet authoritative. The woman has gone. I look at the table. It is covered with a green cloth with numbers on it, and in one corner there is a small roulette.

"What number do you want?" he asks again, this time impatiently.

"The five," I say, slightly uncomfortable.

"I'll put my money on the twenty-eight."

He says this phrase slowly, weighing each syllable, keeping his eye fixed on the wheel. At the same moment he picks up a bunch of multicolored chips that are in front of him and lets them drop one by one onto the table, thoughtfully holding the last one a little longer than the rest, and finally placing it on the twenty-eight. He gets up and throws the ball. We wait.

"Five," he shouts suddenly.

He turns and looks at me. I become as small as I can in my chair. But his look is friendly and full of admiration.

"I once broke the bank with the five," he says. "It came up three times in a row."

"He's crazy," the woman whispers, appearing again.

His look is impassive, his limbs lifeless. He absentmindedly strokes his pajama buttons, perhaps because they look like chips, and every once in a while he takes a deep sigh. He is wearing huge slippers. His heels don't reach the ends. And the way his feet are, one next to the other, they seem vulnerable, touching.

Suddenly he becomes lively again. "It's your turn to bet," he says with authority.

I take a chip and put it on the five. Mechanically, of course. I then turn toward the woman. It's time to find out. I pronounce my mother's name with trembling lips and begin to explain her made-up request, when . . .

"Five!" shouts the elderly man.

He's very upset. For a moment I also get a bit upset and forget my reason for being there. "One chance in thirty-six that that number would come up," he was saying with a tremor in his voice, "and here it is twice."

The woman had shown nothing at the mention of my mother's

name. I say it again slower, just in case she didn't hear me, and try again to explain the request. I wait for something to happen, for the elderly man to start screaming, for the woman to faint—something. One or two seconds pass.

"We don't know that lady," she says.

She seems to be lying.

"She comes here often," I insist. "I've seen her come here with my own eyes."

"Well, if we say we don't know her," she says again in a high voice, annoyed now.

"How can that be, why even this morning..."

"Oh, it must be the lady who goes to the little house around back," she cries.

She becomes nice again.

"Is she your mother? Go past the vineyard and take the little road down..."

But I'm not listening. I'm already far away. And I see the little house around back blurring into an image of the elderly man whose feet seem so vulnerable in their huge slippers. The five has come up twice, the wheel turns, everything is spinning in my head: David, Mother, Mrs. Parigori, my sister Maria who is expecting her second child, I'm almost running, then I lift my head, I'm not sure why, and see standing before me, tall and thin like a cypress, an old man with thick white hair. His face has an immeasurable calm and wisdom about it, as if he has been born and died twice.

"A warm welcome to Anna's daughter," he says.

He gives me his hand and we climb the steps together. I find myself in a well-lit room full of books. The sun has set.

"You're the youngest, right? Katerina?"

My lip trembles. Everything that has been gathering inside me today is now going to burst. My legs feel weak but I also have a nervous energy. I try to lift my head. I stretch my neck...But at the same moment I meet his eyes, deep and sky blue, peeking out from beneath his thick, untidy eyebrows.

"I wanted to spy on Mother," I said slowly.

He smiles.

"Never mind," he says, "it's no big sin. It's just that you love life so much."

Silence.

"Sometimes one feels the need to broaden one's horizons, eh?"

"Do you mean to make a single life like a thousand lives?"

"Perhaps ... Yes, something like that. It's why some people travel, others read, and others spy."

His voice has no trace of irony. He gives the word "spy" the same value as the others.

"And you, what do you do?" I ask slowly.

I watch him flip through some papers in front of him. He turns one page and then another, and another.

"It's the journal of Andreas, my son," he says absentmindedly. "He travels."

And as if he's forgotten that I'm there, he begins turning pages and reading a line here, a line there, then stopping, going back again ...

"*Algeria, June 25th*. Today Algeria is celebrating the return of the pilgrims from Mecca. Life is good. We are going to hold a ball. The heat is insufferable; the dry, hot wind won't let up. Tomorrow we leave for Gibraltar.

"*Sailing toward Gibraltar, June 28th*. I am on duty ten hours a day. On July 3rd we'll be on the Atlantic and then back to the Mediterranean on August 27th.

"*Madeira, July 7th*. This is the most beautiful island, the prize of the Atlantic, even more beautiful than Skiathos. Only there is no harbor and so we are anchored in a little bay where the ocean waves toss us about. From here we'll set off for the Azores. St. Miguel in particular. Everything is green in Madeira. How about our little garden? I am missing Kifissia.

"*Sailing toward the Azores, July 9th*. It's two in the morning and I am manning the sails. But as it is raining hard I've left my post for a bit and come down to the control room to write you. These days the sea's the devil. I'll be home around the end of September, and I hope to find the house with the carpets already laid down.

"*St. Miguel, July 13th*. Now as I write you it is eleven o'clock in the evening, four in the morning your time. The landscape here is strange, grand, with lots of volcanoes and gardens full of pineapples. From here we set out for Portsmouth.

"*Portsmouth, August 9th*. Yesterday we arrived at the most northern stop of this summer's trip. But let me start at the beginning. We first went to Le Havre where we anchored for five days because the sea was very rough and when that's the case there's no joking around. We also needed fuel. I even got to Paris. I saw the Eiffel Tower, the Louvre, Versailles, and in the evening I snuck into a cabaret. When I left that night I felt horribly sad. London is only three hours from here by car. We were invited by the ambassador and so we went. I saw Buckingham Palace, St. Paul's, the Albert Hall, the zoo, the British Museum. We left a wreath on the tomb of the unknown soldier. We happened to be there during Navy Week. Nelson's ship has its own tank of water. We have really been suffering with the cold and rain that doesn't stop. Horrible food. The people are extremely polite, but it's strange—they don't drink water. Their streets are as clean as the floors of their houses. When I get home I would like to find the carpets already laid down. It creates such a nice atmosphere. British girls seem so serious, as if they didn't want you to look them in the eyes.

"*Lisbon, August 17th*. The journey from Portsmouth to here would be impossible to describe. We passed the Bay of Biscay, the ship's graveyard, as it is often called. We suffered some damage, tore a sail. Not one good day of weather, all rough sea, cold, rain, and storms. Lisbon is very beautiful. Tonight I'm going to a bullfight. When we leave here we only have two more stops, either Bizerte or Oran and then Palermo or Naples.

"*Gibraltar, August 27th*. We left the Atlantic behind an hour ago and are now in the sweet Mediterranean. We've anchored to get fuel, at six we depart for Bizerte. We leave Bizerte on September 9th, and on the 11th we will be in Naples. On the 22nd we'll arrive in Poros and on the 23rd I'll come to Kifissia. I would very much like to find the house with the carpets laid down. We'll return by way of Malea, not Isthmos."

Silence. Two minutes pass, maybe more. The light goes dim as if it was about to go out, but then gets strong again. Something's not quite right with the electricity.

"That was from his first voyage on the training ship *Aris*," I hear him saying. "Since then he's gone to so many places... Of course all voyages are really one—*the voyage*. And in this way Andreas, by leaving some days from his life in Barcelona, some in Le Havre, some in Athens, carves a single, unique line. That's the line I want to find and express, the line that represents the essence of his life and that perhaps even he doesn't know about. I want to be like the artist who, in a moment of inspiration, captures a resemblance, expressing the whole person, the person at all times in one painting. I once saw a painting like that. It was of a woman. But you could also say it was about submission. Submission was characteristic of that woman, but in her life it wasn't obvious, it didn't reveal itself all at once, instead it spread itself among her various gestures, each one quite distinct from the next. It wasn't condensed the way it was in the portrait, which managed to combine a submissive look from one day with the submissive movement of a hand from another day, and so on."

He looks at me carefully as if for the first time. His expression changes. He smiles, even laughs a little. His laughter has the unconscious cunning of a child.

"You should know that I won't tell you your mother's secret."

"I'll figure it out on my own."

"All secrets are simple, and all simple things are secrets. If you really want to figure it out... Anna... But what were we talking about? Oh yes, about the painting of the submissive woman, and about the single, unique line in each person's life. Those who travel, like Andreas, deceive themselves. I, on the other hand, who for forty years have looked out of this small window at this same bit of garden lit up in the day and dark at night, know about this. The difference is that some become slaves to this uniformity, while others see its harmony. It's always a circle, a line making a circle. A little earlier you asked what I do to broaden my horizons. Well, I create people, make them up. I write about lives that are connected to each other. But now I am writing about someone like my son; this character will resemble him the way the painting of the submissive woman resembled the submissive woman; that is, it will be more real than he is himself. On paper his extraordinary indifference must turn into harmony and force, the same with the irresponsibility in his eyes that makes life seem like a wide sea. There are no limits for Andreas. He is truly free; he feels no responsibility, no obstacles. He doesn't know what thinking means. Isn't that cruel, but also beautiful? If on returning from a journey he doesn't feel like seeing me, he doesn't come to visit. He goes off for another year or two. But then he writes to me every day. He sends me his journal, and there are times when his words are so tender and childish. He tells me when he is cold or hungry or if he has had a strange dream. And when he writes about the places he travels to he is like the bird who turns, scraping the ground with its wings as it changes directions because it is about to rain, noticing in a new place only the volcanoes and gardens full of pineapples and whether the people who walk the streets are black or white. This wouldn't have been enough for me. All sorts of other questions would have plagued me. I would have wanted to know what was hiding behind these appearances. But now I'm sick of searching. Now I'm only concerned with forms. Forms are so beautiful, like those branches in the tree where the one breaks into two and the two into four ... Everything starts with one, no one should forget that, because forgetting that is like forgetting God. The one branch becomes two and two, four, or if you like you can go the other way and start from the many branches until you get back to one ... "

I met Nina a few days later. Her eyes, which are set apart, much further than most people's, impressed me, and her big mouth, red with lipstick, like a seal on a letter, the only showy thing about her. Her skin was the same color as her eyes and hair, a pale brown, sort of earth-colored. She always wore dresses that color too.

As soon as she arrived, she sat down, crossed her legs, and, opening her handbag slowly, got out a wooden cigarette case, took a cigarette, and lit it. Then she looked at the case as if for the first time. There were two heads carved on the top, two women, or a woman and a man, it was hard to tell. All you could see in their faces was the tragic, sensual timelessness of the African people, and a sense of melancholy.

Nina, though, was very lively. She talked about a million different things, leaping from one topic to the next and drawing from everything a conclusion, almost like a philosophical truth, which at first intrigued me, but then started to get on my nerves. She kept on using the word "intensity." The old man listened to her silently. I did, too.

She was saying that the most intense moment of her life was when Andreas had thrown her a love letter from an airplane. It was when he had left the navy for the air force. Of course he didn't stay there long either. He was such a rebel, always the first and best fighter in every uprising. Once they put him in jail for a year at Oropos. Then he went back to the navy, the merchant marine this time, and became a captain. That day, though, she had gone out into her garden. She was living in Faliron then, not by the sea, but inland a bit, in a beautiful house with a windmill and pistachio trees, when she saw the airplane circling above her, going as far as the sea and then back again, dipping so low she thought it would touch her hair. The letter fell and landed in the tree. It was only one week after she and Andreas had met. Later they got married, and then a child, then the divorce. She herself couldn't remember dates. Everything happened so quickly and suddenly. One never knew what to expect with Andreas. For days, weeks, he would forget that he even had a home. Only every once in a while would he bring presents. He'd bring Nina the largest size dress, though he knew she was tiny, and the toys he bought were never appropriate: a two-wheel bicycle when the child wasn't even a year old and only later a rag doll that cried when you pressed its chest.

"It's best not to marry," concluded Nina. "Besides, marriage doesn't suit our age, isn't that so?"

She had risen and was pacing back and forth. Every now and then she'd stop for a minute in front of a photograph or a book in the bookcase, which she would pull out just enough so that she could read the title. For one moment she bent down to smell a rose and her breathing was loud, exaggeratedly loud. Similarly, she took big steps as if to hide the fact that she didn't have long legs. All of her movements, even the smallest, showed a studied naiveté, an affected simplicity. Her hair, straight and shiny, quite thin, wrapped around her face making a circle. Only at the temples was it thick, making her forehead appear narrower there.

"I've been dancing a lot recently," she said out of the blue. "But it bores me. The *Vita Nuova*," she said, pulling a book off the shelf. "I don't understand why Dante wrote such a thing. How he meets his beloved and what he feels each time he sees her, over and over again from beginning to end. The only original thing about it is that fatal number in Beatrice's life, the number nine. Nine . . ."

Nina looked into the distance for a moment.

"Nine is three times three," said the old man.

"And it's not that I want to go dancing," continued Nina after she had put the book back in its place. "Different friends are always dragging me off. At times I feel as if I was destined for something more serious."

"But dance can be something very serious," said the old man, laughing. "When I was studying medicine in Vienna I was in love with a woman. The most serious moments of my life were the moments I spent dancing with her."

He paused for a bit and then continued, always laughing. "She was beautiful, very pale with deep green eyes. One night, I remember, I was on call at the hospital, and she sent me an invitation to the opera, saying that she would be sitting next to me. I thought I was dreaming; she had always refused to go out with me. I got dressed and went to the opera and waited and waited . . . She must be inside, I thought. I went and sat in my seat. The first act finished without her coming, then the second . . . I got up and left, searched all over the city on foot; it was dawn when I reached the hospital. The next day she wrote, 'I came for the third act. You should have waited.'"

I heard his words the way one hears sounds just before falling asleep. The same sweet vagueness. And perhaps because I didn't try to understand their meaning I will always remember the feeling they gave me, in the same way that I won't forget Nina's or the old man's posture, the way they moved, pronounced their words, their looks, their tone of voice.

My curiosity and interest in Nina grew out of the uneasy feeling she gave me. She was acting. That was clear. She was even acting when she opened and closed her eyelids or breathed. And she wasn't beautiful, with such a big mouth and eyes so far apart. Her chatter, which on the surface seemed varied, was really quite insipid. In the middle of talking her voice would suddenly slow down and take on a plaintive tone. That was when you wanted to hit her. And I would wonder how it was that she seemed so charming if her legs were short, her body, bony, her face, ugly, and her voice, so plaintive. Because the fact remained, Nina was an attractive woman. Even if I tried to convince myself that she wasn't, that it was all in my imagination, I still couldn't take my eyes off the way she brushed her hair back, or touched various things with that affected freedom of hers, nor could I stop listening to that unpleasant voice of hers. The only thing I wasn't sure about was whether that charm would have existed if she hadn't met Andreas. I wondered whether the way he looked at her, the things he told her, and his touch hadn't somehow been incorporated into her being and that her charm was now a reflection of his treatment of her.

I would imagine him standing tall on the deck of his ship giving orders, while all around him waves rose like mountains and the wind blew fiercely. He would be looking straight ahead, his collar turned up of course, and his arms folded across his chest. He would stand with his legs wide apart so he wouldn't lose his balance, like a mast immovable in its base that nonetheless follows the rhythm of the waves, tossing this way and that, he would sway without changing positions, an inseparable part of the ship.

I also thought of him fighting enemy planes, the flames dancing across the deck. That had happened, it really had; the old man had read it to me from the journal. It was when Andreas was transporting ammunition from Bordeaux to Barcelona during the Spanish war. "Hell couldn't be worse," he wrote of the Spanish harbor. "Poverty and misery know no bounds here. People dressed in rags, hungry.

Women, babies in their arms, waiting at the docks to give themselves to the sailors in exchange for a bit of bread. I told my men all hell would let loose if they took advantage of these women. Some gave the women bread anyway." And further on he wrote, "I met Pillar. She has the blackest eyes and the most beautiful legs, but no shoes. I promised to bring her some back from France on my next trip."

It was on the next trip that they were bombed. Five planes attacked the ship *Ilona*, a hard battle. The ship was cut in half. The bow went down with the steering wheel. Andreas was acting drunk, so was the crew. They rushed around like demons amidst the flames, their voices wild. They called the enemy planes mosquitoes. Thus with their crazed courage they were able to chase away the planes; they even shot one down, and with a makeshift steering wheel and motor they got back to the Spanish harbor with half a boat. Everyone was very excited, the wounded *Ilona* became a legend, and Andreas was decorated with the highest medals.

"Even Pillar's shoes were saved," he wrote in his journal. "But unfortunately she can no longer wear them since her legs were cut off in the air raid. What a shame, such beautiful legs. When I saw her in the hospital . . ." At that point he started writing about something else, totally unrelated, about a new way of disembarking, if I remember correctly.

During those same days I said to David, "Would you fly a plane over my house and toss me love letters?" He laughed a lot. "Would you sail a ship across the seas, and when it was cut in two continue on?" He laughed even harder. "What fairy tales are these?" he cried out. I was serious though. It often happens now that I am serious and he is laughing, or I laugh when he is serious. This is a change from last year. David wants to see me all the time. He comes over often— and to think that I went on those silly walks last year with Petros just to make him jealous! There are times when I want to see him so badly that I have to cry. I don't think Nina is right that love passes quickly. "It only lasts until you know each other well," she says. "When you can wait for him without being anxious, without your heart beating faster, then it's over, the mystery's gone."

On the other hand I see Marios and Maria. They have known each other since they were children and when they see each other their hearts don't beat faster. But surely they are in love, in a different sort of way, perhaps in a dangerous way, since the strength of their tie depends on their testing it, fighting against it, and someone is always getting hurt, and they both suffer. But it is love, and then they have little Yannis.

I tried to tell this to Nina, but she insisted that love only exists when your heart beats faster and you tremble like a leaf.

"What do you think of Nikitas?" she asked then. And when I looked at her inquisitively, "Yes, I met him last summer, and I know you and your sisters have known him for a long time. He seems like an interesting type, eh? Or, to be more forthright, he's at an interesting age, the age when boys become men. You see," she added, turning to the old man with a smile that hid a certain bitterness, "I've begun robbing babes from the cradle. It's just that I'm so worn-out...these past few years... Andreas..." Here her voice took on that plaintive quality. It became distant and melancholy. I almost felt sorry for her. The old man was smiling.

iii. THE FEAST DAY OF PROFITIS ELIAS

"COME on in, ladies and gentlemen, come see the wondrous sight, the greatest scientific experiment, the amputated head that will answer all your questions."

"The mad woman's hair, the mad woman's hair..."

"Come on in, ladies and gentlemen, you'll also see the goat with two heads and four—no, not four but nine—legs, ladies and gentlemen, nine legs, not one less."

"Young girls, widows, and married women, here we have Kostaki, the bird from Australia who will tell your fortune..."

Is David going to come?

The air is full of fireworks, noisemakers, voices; it's always this way on the feast day of Profitis Elias. And in the church the priest recites the liturgy. The crowd extends all the way into the courtyard, and when it moves slightly from the door of the church you can smell incense, human breath, and melted candles.

Ruth finds Christian holidays very picturesque, so she's always here for them. She never goes into the church, but she brings with her fireworks that turn the night into day, and all the kids go crazy. It gives her a rest from her own religion she says—only last week she had to climb Mount Parnitha. She stayed for twenty-four hours without eating or drinking. And besides, you have to be constantly thinking of the religious meaning of the day, to concentrate and be respectful, otherwise it doesn't count. Mrs. Parigori never comes to feast days. Our goat Felaha is sick and lies around all day on the hay and sighs. And there's Amalia waving from afar. She's almost done with teacher's college. As for Koula, she has chosen to become a dressmaker and already bends her waist as she walks, differently though than Mrs. Gekas, whose hips tremble as if she were a mare before an open meadow on a spring day. Every once in a while Felaha lets out a cry, a sad cry as if she were asking for help.

Petros pulls on my hand, "Come, let's go to the raffle."

And since I see David arriving with Mrs. Parigori leaning on his arm so that the uphill won't tire her, "Margarita will hate me," I say laughing, and I let him take my hand.

"It's because she's in love with me," Petros says.

Really, all these things are very funny: the priest chanting, the smell of incense, and the venders who insist that you buy their plastic bracelets and pins and rings with red and green stones, and Amalia who looks at it all with longing even if she reads those books. Can you imagine if the trees started dancing imitating all the people turning this way and that as they chat? But those kind of things never happen. Too bad.

"Come on over, Kostaki, ladies and gentlemen, the bird from Australia will now tell the English lady's future."

"Laura, Laura, come and let the bird from Australia tell your fortune. I've been told I don't have many more years to live," Ruth shouts. "Isn't it amusing?"

Mrs. Parigori, over at the café on the corner, refuses with a nod of her head. She's probably worried Kostaki will give away her secrets. She has in front of her an ouzo that she drinks sip by sip, looking sometimes at David and sometimes into space so that she avoids looking at the festivities.

"What's the matter, Laura? Are you day dreaming again?" David says, smiling.

He looks at her attentively while his hands play with an empty glass.

"David, won't you come with us to the Great Monster Show?" I yell as we pass by.

Petros and Nikitas giggle.

"Katerina always acts as if she's drunk," says Mrs. Parigori.

Petros and I buy a noisemaker and drive everybody crazy. I like life a lot. Margarita comes over.

"You certainly don't have any manners," she says.

David sneaks looks in our direction. He smiles when I turn toward him, but I know how dark his eyes really are. The other day in the olive grove he scared me, and then afterward I kept thinking of him, more than ever before. Perhaps we'll go again to the olive grove after lunch when everyone else is sleeping.

"What do you mean no manners?" I ask Margarita, and laugh. Oh God, do I laugh.

Here comes Infanta. It's as if a path opens before her. She looks at everyone with indifference. She is wearing the blue dress we bought in Athens. Her eyes are unusually bright. Nikitas seems troubled. She comes up to him, though, and greets him.

Maria is sitting on the stone bench outside the church. Nikos and Stephanos come up to her.

"How are you doing, Maria?"

They tell a few jokes and then ask about the child.

"We've certainly changed a lot," says Stephanos.

"Yeah, we've changed," says Maria.

"Have you heard about Emilios and Eleni getting married?" Nikos asks.

"Ah..."

"Your eyes, Maria, are more beautiful than ever," Stephanos says.

She smiles. It is really lucky that the little one, Yannis, has her eyes and not Marios's.

Why is Nikitas avoiding Infanta?

"Do you want to go to the shooting gallery?" she asks him.

He turns and looks at her surprised. It's as if a lump has gotten stuck in his throat and he can't say a word.

The truth is that the same morning strange things had happened. First of all, between the two stones of the well, there, where they always met, a flower had bloomed, a flower that looked like the sun and had many thorns. As they leaned down to look at it, their hair got all mixed up and they felt dizzy, as if they were losing blood. Infanta took a step backwards. Nikitas teased her—perhaps about her hair, which she had begun to wear tied back with a white ribbon. This look made her neck seem even freer, her profile even prouder; it was very annoying, more than when she jumped ditches without his help, or scampered over fences, or when she made Romeo leap over puddles by pressing slightly on his belly and they both seemed to be laughing in the air—yes, even the horse was laughing.

Afterward, immediately afterward, Nikitas took a step forward and they came face to face. He put his hand on the back of her neck where the ribbon was tied, in a strange way, heavily, as if he wanted to make her kneel down in front of him; his eyes were shining, and his lips drew near hers, so near that they touched and . . .

Then Infanta, with the unruly gesture that horses make when you pull too hard on the reins, leaned down and abruptly turned her neck away. He was left with the white ribbon in his hand, unable to move. She was already running, her feet jumping over the thorny underbrush, her heart dancing, her lips pale, and the skin by her forehead and temples tight, making her eyes slant. For a moment she disappeared behind a tree, then she appeared again, then disappeared, and each time she was farther away.

When she felt that she was alone and that no one was watching her, there where the meadow begins and the trees stop, she collapsed on the ground beneath a pine with big branches and dense shade. Ever since she was a child she had especially loved this tree. If she happened to pass by there with her mother or sisters she would hang behind in order to touch its rough, dark brown trunk. In the summer she would search for cicadas in its branches.

Once she had an amazing dream as she lay there. She could never remember what it was about, whether it was about people, things, or clouds, only that when she woke up—she remembered this clearly— Jacob's dream came to mind with the ladder resting on earth, ascending into the heavens, the angels climbing up and down. Her breath was unusually sweet. There was a wind, and the birds were singing, and she had thought that surely God was somewhere nearby.

In this way the tree became her secret. When she had first talked of it to Miranda, she trembled a bit—it was springtime and a slight breeze came through the window of their classroom. When they stopped being friends, the next spring, and she saw her sitting at Lina's desk, she grew bitter and wished she could take back her words and everything she had said about the tree.

She hadn't said anything to Nikitas yet. She hadn't even shown it to him, saying "Look, what a nice tree." But tomorrow, yes, tomorrow... She closed her eyes and felt the tears beneath her lashes wetting her cheeks. Tomorrow... Now she knew that she wanted him the way she wanted to fall into the cistern on hot days or drink water when she was thirsty after a walk and heard the sound of the crank pulling up the bucket. She would lean back her head and close her eyes. He would kiss her then on her lips, on her hair, but mostly on her lips. How she wanted him to kiss her on the lips. But she would never tell that to Aunt Theresa...

"Shall we go together to the shooting gallery?"

For the first time Infanta's voice was sweet and patient. They got lost among all the people.

I go up to Maria. She is alone now. I'm also alone. I don't love David, or anyone else. I only love Maria. I sit next to her pretending to be indifferent. "So, are all these people making you dizzy?"

"No, I like it," she says, "I like it."

"And the walk didn't tire you out?"

"Not at all. My body doesn't feel as heavy when I'm walking."

Her eyes are slightly swollen, so are her cheeks.

"Are you thinking about the birth?" I ask, putting my arm around her shoulder.

"I think about it," she says looking away, "but I can't explain it, you won't understand. I am kind of looking forward to that pain again, what can I say, that moment..."

Her eyes are shining now, people are coming out of the church, the fireworks have started up.

"I'm happy," she whispers.

Her voice has a slight tinge of melancholy.

In the spring when you see the grass come up, you don't think about how long it has been growing under the earth, or the earth's agony. I say this to Maria.

"When you're pregnant, isn't it a bit like that?"

"Yes, something like that," she says seriously and then laughs.

Her laugh is rich, jolting, like old times when we used to lie on our backs in the hay and she would tell us that storks didn't bring children. But it has a different warmth.

"I must go. Marios will have returned from Athens."

I look over at the café.

"Why don't you ask Mrs. Parigori if she wants to go with you? Marios always walks back with his father."

"I don't think she will want to"—she turns her gaze toward the café—"she's an odd woman."

"What do you mean?"

"Well, sometimes she seems to me like a girl of sixteen who still hasn't decided what she wants to do with her life, and who always seems to be on the verge of something, uneasy, waiting. Doesn't she seem that way to you? Her eyes…"

I feel like saying everything, letting it all out in a burst of anger. But that wouldn't do. Mrs. Parigori is Maria's mother-in-law.

"I don't know whether her behavior is like that of a sixteen-year-old, but she is certainly quite old when it comes to looks."

Maria smiles.

"I must go," she says. "Marios is sure to be back."

The church gets dark inside; a woman dressed in black makes the rounds collecting candles and blowing them out. The venders turn on their gas lamps; the plastic bracelets catch the light nicely. When we all lived in the same house with Father, Dick would scratch at the door in the morning and wake him up by licking his cheek. "Look who's here. It's our Dickie," Father would say. And Mother would get annoyed because Father seemed more interested in the dog and in his walk than in her. Father loved Mother more than Dick, of course, but it's easier to say sweet things to dogs. You can show your affection without being embarrassed. And Dick all the while would be jumping on Father pretending to bite him as soon as he got out of bed and ran down the hall. Dick would follow him, with Father saying one nice thing after the other—he had never said such things to us. Once Mother wanted to give Dick away because he was a nuisance in the house, and Father without saying anything picked him up and took him in the train to friends in Kiourka. Not even a week had passed when Dick came back on his own. People say they saw him boarding the train like a regular passenger. After that Mother agreed to keep him. I know that part from Maria, but I myself remember quite well how Dick would jump up on Father and how Father would say "Dick, Dickie, my dear dog Dickie."

"Perhaps you are thinking about the locked drawer, that mysterious locked drawer?"

David snuck up on me silently, slyly, as always. I jumped.

"You have such an unpleasant way of creeping up on people," I said loudly.

I would like to be alone in the world, all alone, and to think about Father and Dick. But David moves in close to me as I sit there on the stone bench. He touches my hand, tentatively at first, like the wind or a leaf. Then he squeezes it until it hurts; later he loosens his fingers again and they play with each other like a leaf in the wind. I want David to be near me like this forever, to be even closer to me than he is now.

"I can't remember if I've ever told you that I love you, Katerina."

"No, it's the first time."

"Well, I love you."

"Me, too."

Then he takes my hand and kisses each finger one by one on the tip where they are most sensitive.

"You know I don't like that."

"I'm trying to teach you to like it," he says, and laughs softly.

I've got pins and needles in my legs, I don't know why. I shake them. I kick them up and down, I begin to chatter about this and that. David is still laughing, the lights playing on his face. I pull back slightly.

"There's no need for people to see us."

And then, "How did you manage to get away from Mrs. Parigori?"

"Ruth came by and took her for a walk." He had gotten used to calling his mother Ruth, a practice that struck me as stupid and unnatural.

"Do you find her attractive?"

"I like women who seem distracted. You also seem distracted . . ."

He comes over close again and takes my hand.

"I'm going to the shooting gallery."

I get up. He gets up, too. He won't leave me alone tonight, not until he kisses me. When he touches my hand he always wants to kiss me afterward. In the olive grove that day he scared me. The gaslight makes it impossible to see the stars, only the moon. Everyone is shoving each other trying to get into the Great Monster Show, a green tent with red crocodiles on it.

"What's your name?"

"Gorilla."

"Where were you born?"

"In Africa."

"What do you eat?"

"Everything."

The cut-off head can say all that.

Infanta beats everyone in the shooting gallery. She puts the gun on her shoulder, closes one eye, and the bullet, steady, goes right to the bull's-eye. The target happens to be the heart of a cardboard doll, which shakes its arms and legs when you hit it. Infanta starts to laugh. Her eyes glow. Why did she run away like a frightened deer in the morning? She should tell Nikitas that she didn't mean to, that her feet had just taken off on their own. She aims again and shoots.

"Bravo, bravo!" everyone shouts.

It's nice to win. Nikitas smokes silently.

"Bravo, bravo!"

A shrill female voice cries. Nina's voice. I turn my head.

"Good evening, everyone."

She takes a step and gives me her hand, then she looks over at

Nikitas. Nikitas doesn't know what to do, how to behave. Nina laughs. Her mouth is redder than ever and everything else about her is earth-colored, even her dress.

"Do you know each other?" Nikitas says for the sake of saying something.

"Yes . . . that is . . . we met at the pastry shop, if I'm not mistaken."

"You're not at all mistaken," says Nina. She's a good actor.

"And your sister?" she continues with a polite, questioning tone, almost protective.

Infanta is standing aloof watching the whole scene. She still has the rifle in her hand. Nikitas introduces everyone. Infanta's smile is cold, Nina's is overly warm, as for David he has on his ironic, unpleasant look.

"You are a wonder," Nina says, taking a step toward Infanta. "And I've heard you're also good at riding . . . You even beat Nikitas once, isn't that right?"

And without waiting for an answer, "You know, Nikitas, the Swedish professor is here, the one I talked to about you. I read him some of your poems. He's at the café waiting for us. Good night, everyone."

She turns to David and Infanta. "Nice to meet you."

With her usual affected naiveté she takes Nikitas's arm, and before we know what's happening they are lost in the crowd.

"Don't wait for me," I tell David. "I'll go home with Infanta."

His face darkens. He won't get to kiss me, that's good revenge for him having sat all afternoon with Mrs. Parigori.

I find Infanta's hand and we walk down the hill together. The celebration is in full swing. The ouzos are being ordered two rounds at a time. The songs and the nostalgia for songs rise into the night air.

When Nikitas started home it was already late. The moon, though, hadn't gone down yet. The poplars played with their shadows. He could still hear Nina's drawl echoing in his ears, and her laughter: "You believed all that about the Swedish professor? I just wanted to be alone with you, silly child . . ."

So he had offered her a cigarette because he didn't know what else to do, and she had started to laugh and she kept on laughing all evening. On the dark road back, though, when she came up close to him, he put his arm around her waist. "I see that you're braver in the dark," she said. And she began choosing the darkest roads, the ones where the moonlight hadn't found its way through the trees.

He kissed her by a fence. It was totally mad. His lips refused to let go. He wrapped his hands around her throat so that she couldn't get away. "I thought you were going to strangle me," she said slowly and seriously, with a different voice, as soon as she could catch her breath. "Your eyes are like a weasel's," he responded, wanting to kiss her again. But she pulled back. "In the morning I usually take a walk," she said. "Come by tomorrow to pick me up."

Nina was a woman, a real woman. Her waist bent, her slight body changed shape in your hands, and her mouth tasted like carnations and smoke, bittersweet and dangerous.

He thought of Infanta and felt a pain inside. He had dreamt of her so often and now look ... How did she get away from him this morning ... Just when he had finally touched her lips. She was a strange girl, wild. Yes, but they couldn't go on being just friends forever. They were grown up now, he couldn't bear it any longer, this going with the horses and sitting on the grass at a distance from each other. Infanta with such beautiful eyes and such beautiful lips.

The pain grew stronger. "I must forget her," he whispered. Her face made him anxious, a strange, worthwhile kind of anxiousness. The same way he felt when he wrote a poem or when upon waking abruptly just before dawn, dressing half-asleep, he would find himself hungry, running across the meadow. A bird must have woken him, and he liked to think that of all the sleeping people he alone had heard it, that he and the bird shared something sacred, a secret. And it wasn't only in the morning. Sometimes his heart would beat faster because he had seen something beautiful and he would feel like shouting. Hot tears would come to his eyes, as if someone had touched a secret part of him.

Now that part of him was harder and harder to find. In the same way that he no longer woke early and wrote poems. There were his studies now. He gave himself to his studies systematically and patiently. Nina, after all, was a very charming woman. Tomorrow morning he wouldn't go to the well. He'd go by Nina's and pick her up and they'd go for a walk, perhaps to Ekali or Kokinara. In Kokinara there was a gorge with a thick canopy of leaves overhead. That would be very pleasant.

When he arrived home the garden was all lit up. Two or three tables were set up on the grass and people were playing cards. His mother, young and beautiful still, wore a pastel dress and moved easily among the guests. "Welcome, my boy," she said when she saw him. And when she leaned down to kiss him, "You must be more careful the next time," she whispered, laughing. "Your lips are covered in lipstick." Nikitas laughed. He was glad to find the people there. He even asked his mother if he could take her place in the game for a round.

The sky grew pale in the east when he climbed up to his room. He looked out the window, closed the shutters, and, falling onto his bed, cried. It wasn't long, though, before he was asleep.

IV. THE COUPLE

THE MEADOW has the color and the power of buffalo with their curly horns just after a rain.

A large herd passed by recently. They stretched across the whole plain. Some were beautiful, cinnamon-colored or white with brown patches and shiny coats, while others were old and weak, their bony hindquarters sticking out a foot above the rest of their body, sharp enough to slice the sky. The udders of the old cows hung down. They were going to the slaughter house. They say they plunge a knife right between the eyes and then it's over. It doesn't last a minute; they don't even know they're dying. Only the pig suffers when you kill it because you have to cut into its heart.

Felaha got better, thank God. The swelling went down, she got back up on her feet and went out to the meadow to graze. She also saw the herd go by. She watched it until it disappeared. This year she has the company of a kid. In the beginning all it wanted to do was suckle. It would run away only to come back and jump up on her or butt against her. Now, though, if the grass is tasty it stays away longer.

Little Yannis likes crawling around in the grass and has struck up a friendship with the kid. As soon as he sees it, he opens his eyes wide, smiles, and begins to laugh just like when Maria dresses him and tickles his feet.

Maria also laughs then . . . It's a funny sight to see that little naked body so pink and round, his fingers so tiny, the nails as small as the head of a pin. And when he wants to speak and he can't . . . He pronounces a syllable, says it again, and again, loudly, even angrily. Maria laughs . . . Sometimes out of habit the child tries to reach through the opening of her blouse for her breast. When she first weaned him she couldn't hold him without his hand going there. Maria worried, "Perhaps he thinks he's lost his mother," and she would lean down and whisper in his ear that she couldn't give him any more milk because soon they would have another baby. When she stopped nursing him it was their first separation. They'd never be so close again. She thought about how there would be a time when she wouldn't even be able to hold him in her arms, and then not even on her knees. And if he traveled when he was grown up? "God, don't let him go away," she would say and then laugh. Wasn't she being silly, little Yannis wasn't even a year old.

Now that she was pregnant for the second time, in the evening sometimes when she had finished with the housework and little Yannis was breathing the even breaths of sleep in the next room, she would go out on the veranda and cry softly for no reason. Then she would be filled with a sweet calm, something like apathy, and she would dream, but as if it were someone else dreaming, not her, not Maria.

One New Year's her father had brought her a beautiful doll for a present, one of those dolls that opens and closes its eyes and cries "Mama" when you rock it. She held her breath and wrung her hands in excitement, and then taking the doll in her arms, she sang to her. Suddenly, though, she shut her back up in the cardboard box and ran to get her old doll, the one with no color left in its cheeks and no hair, and she clasped her firmly to her breast to show her that she would always love her, even if the other doll was so beautiful and new.

On Sundays when they used to go to the sea and she would swim and then get out and lie on the beach, her body would become a little pebble. She would watch Katerina and Ellie sitting cross-legged eating pears, Infanta with her changed expression telling stupid jokes and flinging her arms around excessively, Uncle Agisilaos going on and on with his stories. How had she come to know these people and how can you eat pears if you're only a little pebble?

Last winter, sometimes, before the sun had risen, the church bells would wake her. *There are women*, she thought then, *who get up at this hour, wear their black scarves, and go to church for confession. Their knees must freeze on the stone floor.* One morning when it was still dark she got up from her warm bed, crossed the damp meadow, and found herself in church, kneeling with women in their black scarves. She didn't know if she was praying, nor did she understand the words of the priest, she simply bowed her head down, all the way to the floor. And when she was walking home she remembered her little garden where she had planted all sorts of vegetables, Mr. Louzis sitting on the veranda, Marios who would come over on Mondays to tell them what had happened on Sundays, and that day when they played castles for the last time, and then Mavroukos's death and Katerina's cry, "Mavroukos, Mavroukos, Mavroukos is dead." And then she remembered unfamiliar faces, people she had happened to meet on the same day, the taste of peas—"a little dill would make them even tastier," Aunt Theresa said before she had even brought the fork to her mouth—and Mr. Louzis's look when he turned and saw Mother embarrassed by Infanta's insistence over the horse; Katerina had hid under the table she was so embarrassed. And the day of her wedding, "I will now become as pure as a lily. It's nice to be pure, eh Katerina?" And the dressmaker who was as dark as a gypsy and liked to tell everyone about her unhappy love affairs, but as soon as dusk fell you would hear whistling and a young man with a tipped hat would be seen waiting outside the garden; he looked like the ticket taker at the cinema, also a bit like the waiter at the pastry shop. How many faces does one see in a lifetime? . . . Impossible to count them. You begin with one and then another comes to mind, a third, a fourth, a chain of them. It is strange the way things from the past come back to haunt you, things you didn't really notice when you were living them.

When she arrived at the wooden gate, before she opened it, she stood for a moment to catch her breath. Her face was sweaty even though it was cold. *I think I'm pregnant again*, she had thought then, even though Yannis was only four months old.

She also thought that no one should know that she had gone to church, that it should stay a secret the way the strange dreams she had as a child were secret, the ones that made her blush and shiver. All of that was mysterious, and the bowing down in church that made one feel so strange.

How nice it is to have a baby sleeping in the next room ... Only every once in a while does he cry in the night. Perhaps a bad dream. Marios says she's to blame when he cries out like that because she talks to him too much during the day. "Children get nervous from too much talk," he says.

Marios has become very serious. His words are measured and he doesn't hang out with Nikitas, Emilios, or the others anymore. He doesn't have any time; he's at the hospital all day, leaving early in the morning with his father and then returning late at night. In the car Mr. Parigori told Marios about his past life, his professional struggles, his love for Laura. Marios would then tell him of his ambitions and how he had fallen in love with Maria when he was only a child. "Perhaps she loved me back then, too, but she didn't show it." And he thought about how he had suffered, the way she had acted with Nikos, with Stephanos and the other boys. He had seen her kissing Stephanos.

Life was different now, very different, now her devotion seemed excessive and weighed on him. It was as if since she had denied herself the rest and put up such boundaries, she wanted what was left all to herself, like the child she had borne and the others she would bear— hers, all hers. As he was dressing in the morning her gaze annoyed him. He thought about the thin, blond nurse who would say to him in a high voice, "Mr. Parigori, you will be even greater than your father." Maria never said things like that, she just looked after him, his food, his clothes, as if he were a baby like Yannis. She wanted to have her way in those matters. But she still had a habit of asking how his day went at the hospital. What did he do? Whom did he meet? In particular about the women. Were there any beautiful patients, any extremely beautiful patients? He couldn't describe how it was at the hospital, it was something very different from this life here, she wouldn't understand. He couldn't tell her that the lady with appendicitis chose him of all the doctors the day she had pain in her kidney. She took his hand and brought it to her heart, just above her breast, and squeezed it, saying, "My doctor, I'm in pain, in pain, in pain." Nor could he tell her about the blond nurse. So what was there left to say? Nothing. There was nothing to say.

The first few months of Maria's pregnancy were tiring, strange. She was anxious. Even her voice changed. She remembered the outing to Parnitha last February with a group of doctors and their wives. The car had to stop because the road was blocked by snow and they were obliged to go on foot. Marios happened to go ahead with one of the other wives and she was left behind walking slowly, feeling heavy, especially on the uphill parts. On the way down she fell behind again. Marios stopped to help her so she wouldn't slip on the slope. He put out his hand to hold her arm and she broke into tears, for no reason, there in the middle of the snow. "What's the matter? What's the matter?" he asked. "Is anything wrong?" She said that she had once been hit by a snowball in the eye, a really hard one, and that she had just remembered it; that she had pulled a muscle getting out of the car, just a little, nothing serious, but she felt so heavy, she didn't know what was wrong; and why couldn't she keep up with the rest of them on the uphill parts, like him and then that woman who seemed to have such a light step. She didn't know what was the matter, the snowball had been hard, and now that she thought about it, it had been painful—very painful. And she cried in the middle of the snow and Marios didn't know what to do, how to behave.

Later she would have bouts of melancholy where she would sit around silently, and when you tried to say anything to comfort her she would answer, "But I am happy." *The agony of happiness*, Marios would think, and he would remember the great joys of his life: the day he graduated, his wedding, the birth of his first child. "Then why such a face?" he would ask brusquely. He wanted to escape, but from what? He wasn't sure. "Why are you just sitting there?" Maria turned and gave him a long, thoughtful look. His words must have hurt. Well, so much the better. "Don't you understand that your expression annoys me, your mood?" He raised his voice. She tried to smile, her lips trembling.

In the morning before he left for work he was nervous. He was always sure that he was late and that it was everyone else's fault. He would get cross with Spyridoula because the milk didn't boil fast enough. This bothered Maria and she would raise her voice, saying something to hurt him. Marios would then respond in the same way, and so on. These scenes always left her feeling slightly sad, a drop of bitterness in her day; and drops accumulate over time, the way salt from the sea settles grain by grain and forms a layer.

Then evening would come. Oh, in the evening he was happy and calm as if the stillness that reigned in the garden at that hour had taken over him as well. The day was over. He would go take a peek at little Yannis, who was sleeping. He laughed, told jokes, and made Maria very happy. And at night when he felt her sleeping in the next bed, his love for her would grow and overflow and he would want to wake her and caress her face, her body and her feet—out of gentleness of course, not the passion he'd once felt. He especially wanted to caress her belly, which was large for the second time, and if it was possible to feel with his palm the heartbeat of his second child, the way she said she could.

EXCERPTS FROM MRS. PARIGORI'S DIARY:

September 2nd. My dressmaker told me that if I was just a little thinner from my waist down, I'd look twenty. I went on a very strict diet, but my build is to blame. Even though I've lost weight, my waist and thighs are still heavy. My skin, though, is very nice now. Yannis says it's in its second bloom. Probably because I eat a great deal of fruit and tomatoes, and avoid salty things. The little bit of lipstick I use is becoming.

Last night I had insomnia and I read a whole book. I read until the sun came up. The book said that woman has two different and contradictory desires, on the one hand to be free and on the other to submit. In Maria, obviously the second has won out. As for me, I'm not sure. It's as if the two sides are still fighting it out and that in the end neither one will win. That must be why I am never content.

Perhaps this is the last time I will fall in love. I am almost forty-five. When our eyes meet, mine grow dark. "What's the matter, Laura, are you dreaming again?" he asked at the feast day of Profitis Elias, and his look was deep, so deep, and I said ... As for his hands, his hands, ah, what can I say? I can never get enough of looking at his hands. I adore them.

Mrs. Parigori once said, "There is nothing as exasperating as conjugal bliss."

V. DAVID'S PROPOSAL

MARIA sleeps calmly now. As soon as she falls into bed she sleeps a sweet, dreamless sleep. She remembers with a certain nostalgia those sleepless nights when she was a girl and when she was first married.

"These days I don't sleep a wink," I told her the other day. She said it was normal for my age.

Maria has no inkling of my worries, which at times reach such a level. The day before yesterday I saw Andreas's ghost right in my very own room. He was wearing his naval uniform, and as he passed he leaned down to look at a jar of grape jam that was on the bureau. But I shouldn't be seeing ghosts. Only children, they say, see ghosts. Their soul is not yet completely tied to their body, so they can communicate with that other world. Besides, Andreas is not dead, and only dead people can be ghosts. But I'm sure he leaned over to look at the jam, and he was wearing his uniform.

I also hear strange cries at night and see lights going on and off. One of them must be the light in David's observatory because at night he writes his book, which is already a thousand pages. As for the cries, lately there's a lot of quarreling over at Kapatos's because Koula has been flirting with a young man after sewing class and comes home late, and since she is still young, who knows what could happen, she could even end up with a child and not know what's hit her.

All these things are linked together and I want to know how. That's why I'm so anxious. Also, I want to be able to describe the brilliance of the world just before the sun sets, when it falls on the grass, and how green the grass looks, and all the other beautiful things I've seen, for it's a shame for them to last only as long as I am looking at them.

"To be able to feel the essence of things and to be able to express it in words. To express their shape, their color and their sound." The old man had written that in one of his books. He writes about lives that are intertwined, and his main hero now is his son Andreas. "He has lied ever since he was little." That's how one chapter begins, and then it goes on to tell of how Andreas, because of his cunning, was able to lead a group of Jews to Palestine. The British weren't allowing any Jews to enter Palestine, and there were captains who collected huge sums from the poor Jews with promises that they would take them there, and then after sailing for days and months they would let them off somewhere else. They even said that one captain drowned a thousand and pretended it was a shipwreck. So Andreas, as soon as he arrived in Palestinian waters, knowing that no ship had managed to disembark in the harbor, unloaded all the rescue boats and ordered everyone into them; then signaling for help, he took the ship and fled. This left the British in a difficult position. They couldn't leave the people in the boats, nor could they send them back, nor could they drown them. So the Jews landed safely.

Certainly the way the old man writes about these things is quite different. It sends shivers down your spine to hear him read, something like awe, and you can only think of the world and all its brilliance. His heroes come to life before your eyes. As if you had opened a door and there they were each with their own particular walk and smile. You're almost scared one will come too near and touch your hand or try to caress your hair. This is also the way they appear to him at night before he sleeps, whether he likes it or not, and they insist on keeping him company, never giving him any peace. Each one with his own ideas and expectations, one accusing him that he didn't do a good enough job creating him, the other that he gave him too small a role, always leaving the old man feeling guilty. The happiest heroes are the ones that die, he says; it's that final experience that their soul thirsts for. The dead man is wise in the eyes of the living and perfect, like a precious stone worked to the point where no chisel could improve it.

"I also feel a thirst for death when I see that bright red rose bush in the sunlight." Listening to the old man speak like this I think of

Grandfather, who is scared of death. He can't bear to hear of animals dying or plants wilting. The strange thing is that the vagueness Grandfather used to have in his face and in all his gestures has started to fade. Also his gait is unstable. He seems uncertain. His features are changing, finishing themselves off. His hair, which was not exactly white or black, has suddenly become all white, the wrinkles on his forehead, on his cheeks, and around his mouth have grown deeper, final. Before, when he looked around and his cool, absentminded gaze would fix on a plate or a piece of furniture, it was as if he were asking where these things came from and what they wanted. Aunt Theresa would also do this. Now, though, his gaze doesn't wander. Yes, his face was taking its final form, and that scared me because when it had taken that form, Grandfather would die.

Maria can't see such things, nor would she bother about them if she could. It's as if she has forgotten about all of us. Just as you see her coming toward the house, she disappears. It's been such a long time since we sat together at the pavilion amidst the jasmine. The other day I tried nonetheless to get her to listen to me, her and Infanta. I told them how I had seen Mother going up Othonos Street, and how I had followed her, and how I had seen her lift the latch of that house. Infanta got up and left before I had finished my story—they say Nikitas is with Nina for good. Everyone has seen them together. As for Maria, after she had heard my story to the end, she smiled. "I don't see anything mysterious," she said. "That man must be an acquaintance of Mother's and she went to visit him. It's very simple." Then I got angry. I yelled down to Infanta, who was strolling a little ways away. I told them neither of them were worthy of such secrets, that even a person of normal intelligence, not as smart as us, would understand that something was going on, that there was a connection between the crumpled piece of paper that Mother had clasped in her palm and the old man. Didn't they want to know why she shut herself up in the living room for hours, why she never spoke to us of the old man. "You certainly don't deserve to hear such things," I told them, "and I'll never speak to you again of these matters."

The funny thing was that now I was the one hiding from Mother.

I would go up the hill as if I had business in Kifissia, and then head up there, taking all sorts of precautions. When I lifted the latch I would look around carefully. I went to visit the old man often. I liked listening to him talk, read. I even liked to look at the papers scattered on his desk and the straight row of books on his book shelf. All these things, though, increased my anxiety. This man had found the link I was looking for.

He also wrote about a well eighty meters deep that Andreas used to leap across when he was a child just to see if he could make it. And how he never studied in school but would beat up all the kids until he was finally expelled. And the same thing happened at cadet training camp—he was forever laying into someone—so he was dismissed and his future was in danger, when he happened to save the daughter of the commander-in-chief, whom he found drowning in the sea, and they forgave him. And then later as captain—his achievements, his bravery, his recklessness. "You struggled and put up with a great deal on my behalf," he wrote in his journal to his father. "Now I hope you can take satisfaction in my achievements: by the grace of God, I command a ship."

And then there's David, who's always walking up and down in the meadow, and I have to hide from him as well. And if he doesn't find me at home he interrogates me later:

"Where were you yesterday afternoon?"

"On a walk."

"Where?"

"A walk. I don't remember where."

Then he looks worried and tries to light a cigarette, but he can't find his lighter in his pocket...

"If you were an astrologist you would know where I'd been," I told him one afternoon, laughing, and I ran off and he ran after me and we ended up hand in hand under a pine. It was very nice—I love David, I love him very much.

Andreas is the freest of men, and that's because he has no idea what "tied-down" means. He doesn't even feel bound to his father—

only in his journal does he show him any tenderness—nor to his child. Unfeeling and unscrupulous, says Nina.

After we had been sitting under the tree for quite a while and we were very close to each other David said, "Katerina, I'm going to make some serious decisions."

"I hate serious decisions," I told him, and left abruptly.

Andreas is both the freest of men and the craziest. He does not know what life is, but he is life itself. He has no imagination, but everything he does exceeds one's wildest dreams. He may never have thought about how wide the world is, but he measures it every time he travels the sea, he measures it with his body and soul. The waves break across the deck, the foam rolls in, while he, unmoved, sways this way and that like the mast. *The Sea Captain*. That's the title the old man has given his book. He very much doubts Andreas will ever read it.

All these things are linked together, and I must find out how. The way Kapatos spits twice on the floor when he gets excited, the way I laugh loudly and sometimes for no reason feel so sad, the way Mrs. Gekas's hips wobble when she comes down the hill on Aniksi Avenue, and Grandfather's face changes shape, and Nikitas doesn't wear blue shirts anymore, and Mr. Louzis is hopelessly in love with Mother.

Mr. Louzis has been coming over in the afternoons again. The pebbles in the garden grind under his heavy step and Grandfather was obliged to trim the branches of the pistachio trees along the path because they were suffering so from Mr. Louzis's abrupt movements every time he changed his walking stick from one hand to the other, paying no attention to whether he hit the branches or not.

Anyhow, I will think about all this when I lock myself up in my room for a week. Things have reached such a pitch, my life has come to such a difficult place, that it is the only thing left for me to do in order to calm down and make the necessary decisions. If I could I would go to the desert like the hermits; there, they say, a person can concentrate better, find himself, the way a diver finds the bottom of the sea. But let me put things down in the order they happened.

Yesterday afternoon when the old man was reading me a chapter of *The Sea Captain* I suddenly saw Mother's green dress and her shoes coming right toward me the way a train in the movies gets bigger and bigger, filling up the whole screen. With one leap I found myself in the next room. She was already knocking at the door.

I heard my mother greeting the old man in such a friendly and polite way: "I brought you a jar of grape jam." And I waited. The moment had come for me to learn everything.

I heard her talking about the apricot trees, which bore a lot of fruit this year, and about the tomatoes, which caught some disease. About the rabbits that died and nobody knew why—did the cat drown them? Was it the male rabbit? And about Felaha, who got better, from all the care, of course. About little Yannis, who has started to stand and puts everything in his mouth, even stones, and about Maria, who would soon give birth to her second. "If it's a girl she'll have my name," she said. "If it's a boy they'll call him Miltos. Not that Miltos has shown any interest. He would never let on, but in any case it's the proper thing to do." About Infanta, who has been so moody recently, and about me and how anxious I've been and how I have a difficult personality. "Luckily she doesn't lie anymore," Mother said. "She used to spin such tales as a child . . ."

The old man coughed then and began to talk. *Now I'll finally learn*, I said to myself, *now I'll learn*. And I waited. Time passed. "I must go," I finally heard Mother saying, "in order to get home before dark. Father was a bit dizzy this morning. It had me worried."

"Any news?" she added a little later. "No," answered the old man in a barely audible voice. Then they whispered something I couldn't hear at all.

The door opened and closed. I was terribly disappointed. I had lost my one chance. I was very distracted as I listened to the end of the chapter from *The Sea Captain*, and when I arrived home, late, I was in a foul mood.

Everyone ran to welcome me, which was unusual for us. "Katerina, Katerina," they shouted back and forth, embracing and kissing me. "Congratulations, congratulations." Mother then took me by the arm and in a formal way told me, "Let's go into the living room." Her voice was emotional. "Turn on all the lights," she continued, "even the little light over the piano." She had sat down in an armchair, and as I stood there in front of her she clasped my two hands. Grandfather, Aunt Theresa, Infanta, and Maria were waiting in a circle. Marios was sitting a little farther back. Rodia came running in.

"My child," said Mother, "I wish you every happiness. We all love you very much. David is a fine boy."

I turned and looked at them all.

"I don't understand what's going on," I whispered.

"He asked for your hand, silly girl, just an hour ago," Maria said, and her voice reminded me of her voice as a girl. "Don't pretend you didn't know."

I don't understand what's going on," I said again, somewhat stubbornly.

"How could you not know what is going on," said Aunt Theresa, "if we know—"

"That you like him," added Mother, trying to keep up appearances.

"And that you go for walks together," Aunt Theresa went on. "And how…"

"Oh my little bride, my little bride," Rodia began to sing.

I felt my body tightening, tightening…Blood rushed to my head.

"But have you all gone mad?" I shouted.

Mother then changed her tone.

"How dare you speak that way?" she said coldly. "What do you mean you don't understand? David came and asked for your hand in marriage. And we all know that you love each other, that you love him, that he loves you."

"So you want to force me to marry him?" I shouted again.

Aunt Theresa raised her hands to the heavens as if to ask for help. Rodia still hadn't caught on and was singing away, "My little bride, my little bride," and wringing the end of her apron.

"So you're going to force me to marry him?"

Mother then got really angry.

"You are impossible, and crazy. No one can get on with you."

And saying that, she dropped my hands, got up from the armchair, and began pacing back and forth.

"But all parents are like that," I continued. "They never want true happiness for their children."

Everyone looked aghast. Aunt Theresa almost fainted. Maria lowered her head, perhaps she was thinking that she would some day hear the same from her children. As for Mother, her eyes got red, a tear was just visible in the corner, but before it could run down her cheek, it disappeared.

Then I began to sob, such sobs . . .

"I don't know what I want, I don't know what I have," I shouted. "Punish me, Mother, do whatever you want to me."

"Calm down, child," Mother said.

And after she had managed to hide her trembling hands, she lifted her head and said, "You are free to decide as you wish."

That's when I realized I had to shut myself up in my room for a week to calm down, and if it was possible, to find my soul like the hermits in the desert because there are times now when my own self so shocks and horrifies me.

VI. MOTHER'S SECRET
(THE SEQUEL)

FROM UP here where I am I can see the sun come up from behind Pendeli a little later each day, and go down behind Elikona a little earlier each afternoon. Summer is almost over. Like a day when it's almost over, the late afternoon just before dusk. The shadows in the garden have changed, even the shadow of the house is different, more beautiful this season, longer and thinner.

I picked up a book forgetting that I was only supposed to be thinking about David and everything he had said. About the movements of the stars, which have been calculated so precisely that we can tell the exact moment when a comet will appear a thousand years before it happens. About the constellations, which we also know a lot about, even those farthest away. About the theory of male and female constellations. Oh my God, how strange that even in the sky there are male and female domains.

From one of my windows the sky is milky white; from another, pale blue. I see the dust rising from the airplanes over at the airport. I am sorry I have cut myself off like this. But now that I told everyone I would, there's no getting out of it. Besides I'll gain some respect from them this way and I like that. Especially from Rodia. I know that because yesterday she came and told me various stories about real saints who go for years without seeing the light of day. Of course, God also gave us the sun, but it's saintly to live alone away from other people, Rodia said.

I reminded her then of the bird that the neighborhood kids had chased with a hose and wounded on the wing which I had brought to my room so the cats wouldn't get it—last spring it must have been—

and then it had committed suicide. It went and banged its head against the wall once, twice, three times, over and over, till it fell dead.

"I'm talking to you about saints and you go on about birds," Rodia said, somewhat hurt. Then she added that she would certainly go to Ikaria this year. For twenty years she had been threatening us all that she would up and leave for Ikaria. She liked to hear us beg, "Don't leave Rodia, my dear Rodoula, my Roditsa. How could we live without you?"

The switches from the osier bushes and the reeds grow soft in the stream, how could he not notice this, how could he only care about his thousand-page book. "He's the intellectual type," said Ruth. But he also knows how to kiss, and he gets all confused when he strokes my hair and looks into my eyes. I love him very much at those moments. If I married him we'd have all the time in the world for looking into each other's eyes.

I can't sleep, it must be past midnight. Grandfather's over his dizziness, but it scared him. I can't sleep. My eyes are wide open, distracted, fixed on the top of the eucalyptus tree that fills my window. The tree is dark, darker than night.

And suddenly it is all lit up. Someone has turned on the light on the first floor. I leap out of bed, lean out the window. The light is on in the living room. Just as I am, in my nightgown, like a sleepwalker, I put on my sandals, throw something over my shoulders, go out into the corridor and down the stairs. Perhaps Mother is entertaining Mr. Louzis at this hour, and perhaps . . . I better watch out for the last few steps, they creak horribly, and across the way is the living room. I must slip by like a shadow, like a ghost.

My nightgown gets caught between my legs. I almost tumble down the stairs. I catch myself and go outside. It is cool and the birds are flying low. Not that they scare me, the whiteness of my nightgown is more frightening.

Mother is alone. She is sitting at the desk. Before her a pile of letters lies scattered. She writes for a few moments. Then her left hand rests on the envelopes, fingering them thoughtfully, while her right holds her head; her elbow resting on the desk.

She must be crying. I can see her rubbing her eyes with her fists the way children do, hunting for her handkerchief. Yes, she's crying, a sob shakes her shoulders, she cries freely, as I have never seen her cry before. And she can't find her handkerchief. Every now and then she looks again for it in her pocket, hoping that she didn't search well enough the last time. She wants to blow her nose now; the tears fall on the desk, on the letters, the ink must have run on some of them. She looks again in her pockets and finds nothing. She gets up and goes out of the living room. It's the first time her face looks so naked to me.

Who knows how I ended up over by the desk, how my trembling fingers opened up one of the envelopes, the letters dancing before my eyes: "My dear child, I would very much like you to send me, along with the photographs of little Yannis that you promised, a picture of the house and cistern and the meadow. If I remember correctly there are three pines by the gate and they are the tallest on the property. Because as the years go by, my memory of that part fades. Each day that passes I forget something and this is so painful to me…"

The Polish grandmother!…The Polish grandmother!…I can't breathe. I want to shout but I can't. I feel as if I had a knot in my chest, in my heart, in my throat. The Polish grandmother!…Oh my God…So that was my mother's secret—they were writing each other all these years, maybe even since Mother was a child. What a passionate soul Mother has, and here she never shows it, instead she pretends that her only interest in life is setting the table with the utmost care, and making jam, orange marmalade in the winter, apricot in the spring, and cherry in the summer…

My eye falls on the lines she wrote just a minute ago. She is writing about me: how I behaved, and how I hurt her. Oh, Mother, will you ever forgive me? Why must you hide, Mother, why must you hide your whole life long, like Infanta, like me, like all of us? We are all hiding from each other, I from David, David from Ruth and Mrs. Parigori, Mrs. Parigori from Mr. Parigori, all of us, all of us are hiding from each other.

I open two or three more envelopes and cast a glance quickly across the pages. So that is it, she poured all the passion that gathered and settled in her when her marriage failed and she had to live alone without a man into these letters. Whatever sorrows and joys she had experienced and even those she hadn't but wished she could have. And I didn't know what to look at first, the letters of the Polish grandmother or Mother's.

I am about to open another envelope when I hear Mother's footsteps, regular and calm. I vanish through the balcony door like lightning and run into the garden. I am very cold and my cheeks are burning.

Mother sits down again at the desk. Her eyes are dry now. She is holding her white handkerchief crumpled in her hand. She throws a glance around the room somewhat nervously as if she feels the atmosphere has changed. She then puts her handkerchief back in her pocket and continues what she was doing; she puts each letter in its envelope, piling them one on top of the other and then tying them up...

Oh, Mother, if you only knew, oh, Polish Grandmother, if you only knew, how much I love you both, how much...

And I still know nothing about your life, Polish Grandmother, only that you are anxious to remember this place here. Rodia used to say that you left no part unexplored, by foot or horse, and that as soon as the sun had risen you were out in the meadow in your robe, which used to get torn by the underbrush and thyme, and you needed a new robe every year, and Grandfather would complain. And I, who have never traveled and know only this place, I could tell you where each stone is, each tree, the colors that the water turns in the cistern with each change of weather. You should see, Polish Grandmother, on really hot days, when you lie out on the ledge of the cistern and close your eyes, and then open them a little later, how a thousand little suns leap up and down before your eyes and all around water is reflected on the trunks of the pines, trembling and golden, like little waves, and everything glows, everything, and it makes you want to laugh...You should see the trees in my hiding place: how they've grown, their branches linked together, the shade so dense, so dense and refreshing in there. It is a good place for thinking, for philosophizing, as Rodia says.... You should see the color of the newly plowed field, fresh and virginal. Whatever you plant grows so quickly, doubling, tripling in no time; you'd think the mad woman had a hand in it...You should see, Polish Grandmother, you should see...

I have not gone to Lisbon or Algeria, nor to Madeira, nor any other place. I only know them from the map. You, my Polish grandmother, have gone all over the world, you and Andreas. That's why places fade from your memory and you confuse one with another...Yes, the three pines are in front of the gate and they are the tallest on the property. We cut a lot of branches from one to lighten it. Also, because we needed wood for the stove.

And I will not stay here forever, Polish Grandmother, sometime I'll set out for a tour of the world. And I might even marry, and shut myself up in that gray house of David's with the red bricks around the windows and the fields that produce thousands of pounds of potatoes each year and so many onions. Not that David needs to cultivate potatoes. His father is a shipowner, but it's just what's done around here, everyone competes to see whose fields yield the most. And of course Mr. Louzis always wins because he has more land than anyone. Even his gardener, Kostas the cripple, has become rich, and all the other gardeners are jealous. And his daughter is not at all surprised when Mr. Louzis leans over and kisses her on the neck as she prunes the roses.

I'll go on a tour of the world and I will meet all those people that the old man describes in his books, you and Andreas and all the others. How lives intertwine—Infanta's with Nikitas's, Nikitas's with Nina's, Nina's with Andreas's, Andreas's with...

I will marry David, I love him and I will marry him. Then I will tell him to muss up my hair, all day long I will tell him to muss up my hair, that's how we will pass our days. And we'll stare into each other's eyes for hours on end. And when he gets into that strange confused state of his and wants to kiss me, I will let him because, after all, he will be my husband. And then I'll ask him to muss up my hair some more and that's how we will pass our days.

My God, how low the birds are flying...they must be owls. The tragic sound of their voice tortures the soul but somehow one needs this song, and not the nightingale's. Especially on such a dark night. Now, with the wind whistling in the pines, the bats come out in groups, making circles that are in such harmony with one another that you could swear they had plotted their arcs ahead of time, and then they turn and fly one behind the other in a row. The whistling increases, and so does the wind, the same way the sea gets angry and crashes against the rocks, filling the hollows, and each wave is bigger and stronger than the next. All the lights are off. People are sleeping. Maria's house is quiet, quiet and dark. Only the lamp on Mother's desk is lit. Mother's also awake, like me, like Grandfather, whose light may not be on, but surely he's not asleep, and like Infanta.

Infanta can't sleep. When I go upstairs on tiptoe I hear her crying softly. A few minutes later when I am in my room I hear the last door in the hall opening, Aunt Theresa's. Her uneven gait makes the floor creak and you're sure she'll fall, her feet will get tangled in her night-gown, something will happen, and she will fall. But she makes it to Infanta's door, hesitates, and then goes in.

She is talking to Infanta now. These days she never lets her out of her sight. I can hear her whispering but I can't make out what they are saying. A shutter is banging in the wind. The whispering stops. Then it starts again.

When I went out into the hall and stood outside Infanta's door—that's just how it happened, I wasn't trying to overhear; besides, how are you supposed to sleep on a night like this?—I heard her saying to Infanta in a worried voice, "What did he want coming here again this afternoon?"

"He came to see me. He wants to see me..."

Infanta was crying as she spoke.

"I hope you treated him the way he deserves to be treated. That you kept your dignity and pride. Like we said, like—"

"I told him that he must not come back, that I didn't want to see him, that I would never see him again..."

Then Aunt Theresa's voice got very official and serious: "Now you are free, Infanta, free to reach that state of perfection."

And then, "How about we take up that peacock embroidery again tomorrow? It kind of got put aside these past few months."

And that night I understood why Mother went to visit the old man. The Polish grandmother sent her letters to his house, it was clear; besides that was the address on the envelope.

The next day I was in such a hurry to see him that I couldn't wait until the afternoon. Already at breakfast I couldn't sit still in my chair; I took a sip of milk and then got up to get something, sat down, took a bite of bread, went out on the veranda. Mother looked at me angrily. She didn't like my manners. "It's because she was locked up in her room for a week," said Aunt Theresa as if to excuse me. Her saccharine voice got on my nerves. I must take Infanta aside and tell her to stop listening to Aunt Theresa.

It's true, though, on Saturday I locked myself up and today it was Saturday again. Everyone was waiting for my decision. They hung on my every word, sneaking looks at me. But they were all proud and weren't about to ask. Only Rodia smiled at me in a knowing, teasing way. As far as she was concerned there was no doubt. I was in love with David, love-struck as she put it, and I would marry him. I couldn't accept this right away because I was still a girl and that's the way girls are, that's the way they should be about marriage, slightly ashamed. Mother didn't appear at all curious. She was dignified as always. I looked at her, at her tired eyes.

"Will you just stay put, Katerina? You're making me dizzy," said Mother.

It was as if the empathy I had for her last night suddenly dissolved and I became more and more stubborn, set on learning about her secret life. I thought of saying something to hurt her. Instead I decided to act totally indifferent—that's what really annoyed her—and so I kept on sitting, getting up, going out on the veranda, coming back in ...

Only years later would I realize how much my love for my mother was like a lover's: the stubbornness, the moments of hatred, and the limitless tenderness afterwards. And how my love for my father was the love of mankind.

"You are impossible!" my mother screamed. "Impossible. I pity the man you marry."

I then felt like laughing. Poor David! And the way I was holding my cup it slipped from my hand, fell onto the saucer, tipping upside down, spilling all over the tablecloth. I couldn't contain my laughter. All I could say is "It's nerves," and I ran out into the garden.

What a beautiful day! The lavender has dried up but the scent is still there. The roses are blooming again, and the chrysanthemums for the first time. The bees are tricked into thinking it is still summer. But the cicadas have stopped singing; only their shells are left scattered at the base of the tree trunks.

I found the old man writing *The Sea Captain*. He was seated at his desk in front of an open window, from which he could see the red rose bush that sometimes made him long for death. I began calling him from afar. He raised his head and smiled; under his thick white eyebrows his eyes were smiling.

"So you discovered the secret?"

And when I looked at him in amazement.

"One only has to look at you—that triumphant air ... Your neck is at least two inches taller than usual. As for your eyes ... Her neck too used to stretch when she was proud of something, just the way yours does."

He then began to tell me about the Polish grandmother, slowly and in a soft voice at the beginning, but as he went on he grew more excited ...

He met her around the same time Grandfather had—he and Grandfather were cousins—and both of them fell in love with her. She was beautiful, ah, so beautiful, no words do her justice.

"I met her first in Vienna. Remember how I told you about a lady who invited me to the opera and then made me wait two acts? When she came to Athens all the men fell for her and all the women hated her. It wasn't only her beauty, but her laugh so lively and spontaneous it filled up the space around her—it could fill up a whole meadow— and then, I'm not sure how it would happen, but each man thought she had paid special attention to him. After a dance everyone left with the hope that she was in love with him. She had such a free, open way of walking, of holding her head ... and when she scowled with astonishment because someone was rude to her ... She thought it was extraordinary when people didn't agree with her, when they didn't anticipate her slightest desire. And if you tried to give her any advice she would get angry, her neck stretching up and her eyes glaring. I remember how they would get greener and how they had a little of the evil of cats' eyes when you wake them by petting them from the head down. She loved life passionately, obstinately, as if she wanted to swallow it all, every second of it. Nothing was enough for her. She was never at peace. You should have seen her ride a horse, even the wildest, how she would run in the forest, how she would swim ... Even in the winter she would go swimming, and then her laugh would echo strangely on the beach. And if she fell from a horse she never hurt herself. She never got tired swimming. It was as if she had a mysterious pact with nature. And because of this nothing scared her. Wherever she went, Dimitris and I would accompany her. She always wanted both of us, she said it amused her the way we looked alike— in truth we didn't look at all alike. She seemed to prefer me, though. 'You should drop medicine and write novels,' she would say. I had just published my first book. 'As for Dimitris, tending the garden is plenty for him.' We had both fallen for her and this kindled a new animosity between us. The scales tipped one way one day and the other way the next. There was no time to be happy because of something she had said before she was saying the same thing to the other, making him happy instead. Then things would switch back again. It was enough to wear one down. It ruined our friendship forever. Suddenly one day she told me she was going to marry Dimitris and that she had decided this long ago. In the meantime I also got married and Andreas was born...I didn't see them for years. I just heard that she would go to Athens for days, for weeks, and that Dimitris was unhappy..."

The old man stopped talking for a while. Then he said, "*The Sea Captain* is going well. It's moving along."

His voice sounded strong and young. Then he lowered it again.

"I didn't see them, but I didn't stop asking after them. The tiniest detail of their life was interesting to me. I found out about the birth of Theresa and Anna..."

He stopped again. His voice was no longer animated, nor his eyes.

"No one could decide whether she was good or bad...Once I remember when we were walking in the woods, her dog, a magnificent German shepherd who adored her, went after a chicken. She called it once, twice, three times, but he didn't listen to her. She left Dimitris and me behind and ran to where he was, and before we could see what she was doing, she had beaten him so hard with the leather leash that he was wounded in two or three places and there was blood. The animal was in pain; he cried with his nose buried in his paws, not moving; he didn't try to get up. And she was still beating him, making him bleed more. I took the leash from her hand. Dimitris, a little farther off, had turned completely pale. 'I forbid you to interfere,' she screamed at me in a rage, and on the way home she spoke only to Dimitris. Then for days she nursed the dog—she loved it too much. It was a phrase she often said—'I love him too much.' She said it about animals, places, things, even about the smallest, most insignificant thing, a dress, for example. Perhaps because she loved life itself too much. Truly, it was strange, her insatiable passion for life. So much so that it was as if real people and the facts were not enough for her; she made up her own people, her own facts, and she would relate these make-believe stories as if they had really happened. And you had to know her really well to know that it was all made up, because when she told her stories she seemed to believe them herself. She had a simple and natural way of telling them. Only at the very end after the last word she would look at you inquisitively as if you were the one who had been talking, not her..."

"Tell me," I whispered, "tell me how the Polish grandmother is now."

"That I don't know. Even Anna doesn't know. In her letters she says that she is well, and a thousand other things—sometimes amusing, sometimes sad—it's impossible to know, though, what's true and what's false. As for her life, she doesn't write anything. She refuses to speak about it."

"It's really strange that she married Grandfather who isn't, how should I put it, strong..."

And then a little later, "But that's how Maria married Marios. And Maria has the same laugh. It fills up the space around her, Maria's laugh, it could even fill up a whole meadow..."

Silence.

"Only whatever happens, whatever happens, Maria will never abandon little Yannis. Nor Marios. Not the little Miltos. Little Miltos isn't born yet; he'll be born any day now. But Maria is sure it's a boy."

Silence.

"And Infanta has her beauty and her courage. Nothing frightens Infanta. She'll ride the wildest horse. She never gets tired swimming, and then there was that time she killed a snake before our eyes. She raised the stick and hit it on its head and later its tail kept moving all by itself. And I? I am only like her because of my neck and the lies I used to tell as a child..."

I was talking as if I was hypnotized. I had the Polish grandmother's face before me, and that was it, a face I had never seen.

"Do you know," the old man interrupted me, somewhat annoyed by my incoherent babbling, "any day now Andreas is coming. I got a letter from him."

I stood staring at the old man. I stared at him a long time.

"What's the matter? Aren't you listening to me? My son Andreas is coming."

As I took the road home the wind had changed direction; instead of a south wind, it came from the north, down from Parnitha, passing through the woods, and then coming straight to us, right into our chests, passing through us and leaving us feeling clean and light. It's almost frightening how light and clean you feel when the north wind blows.

But these days the wind also switched the other way from north to south. When that happens a fine, warm rain falls on the flowers, mixing with the pollen, and the world fills with scents. Autumn has come, I thought as I walked down Aniksi Avenue.

Now I knew a lot about the Polish grandmother and yet I knew nothing. Everything seemed vague, uncertain, her life a secret. And Aunt Theresa and Mother were cool and reserved, afraid that they might turn out like her, afraid of life itself . . . I wanted to know what the Polish grandmother's eyes were like now, and if they still got greener when she was angry. Perhaps she doesn't get angry anymore.

I must make a decision. I must tell David. I would like to be holding hands with him now and running, or to be together in the olive grove, even if it was a little scary, it wouldn't matter. "What's the matter? Don't you know I'm talking to you," said the old man. "My son Andreas is coming." Polish Grandmother, you, only you, would understand . . .

VII. THE SEA CAPTAIN

IT WAS morning when Andreas arrived at our property. At first all we saw was a carriage racing like mad—we saw it when it turned off of the road and came across the meadow at a fast clip, its wheels digging deep into the earth, staggering from one moment to the next as if it were going to turn over, its hood swaying this way and that, like the sail of a boat that you unfasten and re-tie when the wind changes so it almost touches the crest of the wave.

When the carriage stopped in front of the house its wheels were covered in mud, the horse was foaming at the mouth, his eyes wild, his hindquarters sweaty. Andreas's forehead was also a little sweaty. He was holding the reins and laughing. As for the driver, he was sitting in the passenger seat, cowering in the corner. "You almost killed me, sir," he said. "And you've ruined my carriage." "How much did it cost?" asked Andreas. "Such and such an amount." "Take the money." Andreas pulled out a huge wad of bills and gave them to him.

Nobody seemed surprised by Andreas's arrival. It was as if we had always known him. Mother and Aunt Theresa greeted him warmly. "The only thing," they said, "is that Grandfather must not find out. Because of the old animosity." But there wasn't much of a chance, since Grandfather had locked himself up in his room now for days reading his medical books from morning to night. Every once in a while he would get dizzy. He was no longer interested in the trees and plants; it was as if he had never loved them.

"Good morning, Maria, Good morning, Infanta, Good morning, Katerina," Andreas said as he passed through the wooden gate and we looked on in amazement. He came up the path under the pistachio trees without shaking a single branch, not at all like Mr. Louzis. He climbed up the stairs to the veranda, taking huge steps, and plopped himself down in an armchair. "It is really very pleasant here," he said, "one's ear gets a rest from the sound of waves."

He stretched out his legs, leaned his head back. He was tall and sunburnt. He wasn't wearing his uniform. He had on white pants and a white shirt with an open collar. He had white teeth. His laugh was strong, so were his hands. They weren't at all like David's hands. They were hairy, and they didn't change expression depending on what was being said. They just squeezed the chair's wooden armrests tighter. And then the iron ring on the fourth finger of his left hand would bother him, so he would take it off as he was talking, play with it in his right hand, toss it in the air, and then put it back on. "An astrologist told me that of all the metals, iron would bring me luck and of all the days, Friday. An astrologist, not an astronomer," he added, looking at me. "And during the shipwreck of Corsica that ring saved me. I'll tell you how another time. And in the harbor of Constanza..."

In the meantime he had turned to Maria. "I'm expecting little Miltos," she then said, "that's why I'm so big." And she remained there staring at him, her eyes wide open, so much so that we had to beckon to her to cut it out. But Andreas was also staring at her; he had left off mid-sentence, not caring what others thought. "That was when I was captain aboard the *Jupiter*," he said. And Maria repeated, "I'm expecting little Miltos."

Aunt Theresa was shuffling back and forth, laughing to herself, letting out little exclamations every once in a while. She seemed to admire everything Andreas did—even the way he tossed his ring in the air. She urged him to tell them about his adventures, not his sea adventures, but his adventures with women. For example, she had heard that once—here her laughter was totally indescribable—that after the shipwreck when his ship was being repaired in North Africa he would fly to southern France where..."the parties, the parties," she cried. "That's what life is for..." And then there was that woman in Algeria in Oran who spent the whole day in bed—a beautiful big soft bed—and only got up after sunset for a quarter of an hour. She would come back holding a branch of greenery and fall back into bed. Scents were her weakness. "I like scents, too," whispered Aunt Theresa, and she attempted to straighten her hair coquettishly... But she had very little hair, the poor dear, so her hand just slid over her white dandruffy scalp.

"Perhaps you met my fiancé on your travels? His name began with 'R' and he had shiny hair and thick lips."

Infanta then began to laugh.

"And Nikitas," she shouted, "Nikitas too had thick lips and I never kissed them. Nina, your wife, Nina, kissed them."

"My wife?" he asked with a certain curiosity. "Ah, yes," he said after a moment, "once I did marry a woman named Nina. It was all because of that letter, the one I tossed out of the airplane."

"Would you forget me as quickly, Andreas?"

Infanta got up and walked toward his armchair as if to show him how beautiful she was.

Why shouldn't he forget you, I was about to say...

In the meantime Andreas had gotten up, taken her hand, and they were running together in the garden. I got furious...

"You are impossible," I screamed after her. "You act as if all you care about is your embroidery with the peacocks. First it was Marios, then Nikitas, then David—yes, even David—I remember the way your eyes looked the night Maria gave birth when I told you about David. And now it's Andreas."

"It will only last until she gives birth to a little Yannis or Miltos." Maria said this. I turned and looked at her. We were alone on the veranda. Her face looked like a rose in bloom.

"Do you remember, Katerina, how Marios was before we got married?" she said slowly. "Now he likes to stay in Athens as long as he can, and sometimes at home he forgets I'm there. He whistles as if the room is empty when I am right there in front of him. Because there's a different sound—isn't that right, Katerina—when you whistle and you're alone than when there's someone else in the room... especially on the high notes. Listen, I had a dream last night, a dream about you. Over there where the meadow stops, right there in front of our eyes, the sea began, a sea that got immediately deep and was more green than blue. On the beach heather and thyme were growing. We were going down a mountain path, the two of us, when we saw it. We also saw a ship anchored there, a strange ship, rectangular and red, more like a raft with a huge white sail. 'Sister dear,' you said to me, 'I am going to travel.' And as soon as you said those words the path grew like a snake unwinding and went into the sea right up to the ship. You followed it without even looking at me. And by the time I had reached the ship and raised my eyes to see you, searching for you, you had become a white bird and you were flying above my face, but it didn't seem strange, and I said goodbye to you, and I had such a strong urge to travel, too, it was as if I had already left . . ."

"Maria, that's because I will travel, really," I cried. Softly though because they were coming back.

"The Black Sea was stormy, a devilish wind from the Levant turned my ship inside out . . ."

Infanta listened, eating up every word. They were even holding hands. *She wouldn't dare*, I thought to myself, and that calmed me down. He spoke loudly, perhaps so that we would also hear. And his gaze wandered from Infanta to Maria, from Maria to me. It was as if he was looking at all three of us at once. His eyes were sparkling; and sometimes the pupil shrunk, making the white appear bigger and other times the pupil grew and took on the color of the ocean before a storm.

"I can't stand it," whispered Maria.

"What do you think about when you are traveling?" asked Infanta then.

What a stupid question. Infanta's not very smart. I'm the smartest of the three.

"Dry and ironed clothes," answered Andreas.

"This day seems like a year," Maria whispered again.

"We'll see, we'll see which of you three will be the tall ship that opens its sails."

His voice was very strong now. I got up, leaving Maria on the veranda, pushing Infanta back . . .

"I am ready," I cried. "The rest want to go with you, but Maria can't and Infanta doesn't dare."

"At dawn I will wait for you by the cistern," he whispered so that no one else heard.

Early the next morning I found the words "I was just joking" written on the ledge of the cistern.

"Andreas has left," Aunt Theresa was saying.

It seems that my own crying woke me. And even though I knew Andreas hadn't left because he had never really come, I couldn't stop crying. It was all so beautiful.

"I've made up my mind," I told Mother as soon as I entered the dining room. "I will not marry David, I'll set off on a tour of the world."

Though I'm not sure how, as I said this my cup slipped out of my hand, onto the saucer, and spilled all over the tablecloth.

"You are impossible!" screamed Mother.

Everyone made it clear by their looks that they agreed with her.

The next day I learned from the old man that Andreas had stayed the night in Kifissia and that he had left very early that morning for a long trip.

VIII. THE STRAW HATS

THINGS must have happened something like that. I have tried to tell it in order without any lies. But then again, how is a person to distinguish what really happens from what one thinks is happening? Was Aunt Theresa's gait so uneven? And David's hands so expressive and feminine? And Andreas's eyes so startling? Oh dear, I forgot I've never seen Andreas, only dreamt about him. And did Mrs. Parigori really love David?

I imagine Maria will have more children. It's hard to tell what her fate will be, the same goes for Infanta and me. But certainly those three summers will play a role in our lives. I remember that first day of that first summer when we bought our big straw hats.

GLOSSARY OF GREEK NAMES

Stressed syllables are indicated by the presence of an acute diacritic (´).

Aghía Triáda	The name of a church as well as of its surrounding neighborhood. *Aghía* means "saint" or "holy"; *Triáda* means "trinity."
Andríkos	Diminutive of the name "Andréas."
Ániksi Street	*Ániksi* is the word for the spring season.
Áris	A common name. From Ares, the god of war.
Bouboulína	Laskarína "Bouboulína" Pinótsis (1771–1825) was a female naval commander who became a heroine in the Greek War of Independence. She was from the island of Hydra, where Liberaki spent her summers.
Deliyánnis Street	A street named after the Greek statesman Theódoros Deliyánnis (1820–1905).
Edipsós	The healing waters of Edipsós in Evia (or Euboea) have been known since Ancient times.
Eliá Avenue	*Eliá* means "Olive."
Elikóna	Also known as Helicon; a mountain to the north of Athens.
Feláha	A feminized version of *feláhos*, which is in turn derived from *fellah*, the term for an Egyptian farmer or peasant.

Helidonoú	A neighborhood near the girls' house; literally "female swallow."
Karaïskáki	Yiórgios Karaïskákis (1782–1827) was a legendary military commander and leader in the Greek War of Independence.
Kifissiá	An affluent suburb north of Athens.
Kostáki	A diminutive of the name "Kóstas" or "Konstantínos."
Koukoúki	An endearment used for infants derived from the word *koúkos* or "cuckoo."
Mavroúkos	A diminutive of the word *mávros*, meaning "black."
Mount Párnitha	Párnitha or Parnes is a part of a mountain range to the north of Athens.
Mount Pendéli	Another mountain north of Athens, Pendéli or Pentelicus is known for its Pentelic marble.
Oropós	A town northeast of Athens as well as the jail located there.
Óthonos Street	Named for Otto or "Óthon" the Bavarian prince who was the first King of Modern Greece (1832–1862).
Panaghiá	The term for the Virgin Mary, the literal meaning of which is "all holy."
Piraeus	The port of Athens.
Profítis Elías	Churches situated at the highest point of many parts of Greece are named after the prophet Elijah. The feast day of the church is celebrated on July 20.
Rodiá, Rodoúla, Rodítsa	*Rodiá* means pomegranate tree. *Oula* and *itsa* are diminutive suffixes for female names.
Spirétos	A form of the male name *Spíros*.

Syntagma Square	A square located in the center of Athens. *Syntagma* means "constitution."
Tatoï	A forested area (and airport) named for a former royal palace in the north of Athens. The palace was burned to the ground in 1945, at the start of the civil war.
Yangoúlas	Another form of the male name *Yángos* or *Yánnis*.
Zezína	The name *Zina* with the diminutive prefix *ze* appended.

TITLES IN SERIES

For a complete list of titles, visit www.nyrb.com or write to:
Catalog Requests, NYRB, 435 Hudson Street, New York, NY 10014

RENATA ADLER Speedboat*
ROBERT AICKMAN Compulsory Games*
CÉLESTE ALBARET Monsieur Proust
KINGSLEY AMIS Lucky Jim*
ROBERTO ARLT The Seven Madmen*
IVO ANDRIĆ Omer Pasha Latas*
ERICH AUERBACH Dante: Poet of the Secular World
EVE BABITZ Slow Days, Fast Company: The World, the Flesh, and L.A.*
DOROTHY BAKER Cassandra at the Wedding*
J.A. BAKER The Peregrine
HONORÉ DE BALZAC The Memoirs of Two Young Wives*
VICKI BAUM Grand Hotel*
SYBILLE BEDFORD A Legacy*
STEPHEN BENATAR Wish Her Safe at Home*
GEORGES BERNANOS Mouchette
CAROLINE BLACKWOOD Corrigan*
LESLEY BLANCH Journey into the Mind's Eye: Fragments of an Autobiography*
RONALD BLYTHE Akenfield: Portrait of an English Village*
EMMANUEL BOVE My Friends*
ROBERT BRESSON Notes on the Cinematograph*
ROBERT BURTON The Anatomy of Melancholy
MATEI CALINESCU The Life and Opinions of Zacharias Lichter*
CAMARA LAYE The Radiance of the King
J.L. CARR A Month in the Country*
LEONORA CARRINGTON Down Below*
JOAN CHASE During the Reign of the Queen of Persia*
UPAMANYU CHATTERJEE English, August: An Indian Story
COLETTE The Pure and the Impure
JOHN COLLIER Fancies and Goodnights
CARLO COLLODI The Adventures of Pinocchio*
D.G. COMPTON The Continuous Katherine Mortenhoe
IVY COMPTON-BURNETT A House and Its Head
BARBARA COMYNS The Juniper Tree*
BARBARA COMYNS Our Spoons Came from Woolworths*
JÓZEF CZAPSKI Lost Time: Lectures on Proust in a Soviet Prison Camp*
L.J. DAVIS A Meaningful Life*
AGNES DE MILLE Dance to the Piper*
MARIA DERMOÛT The Ten Thousand Things
ANTONIO DI BENEDETTO Zama*
ALFRED DÖBLIN Berlin Alexanderplatz*
DAPHNE DU MAURIER Don't Look Now: Stories
ELAINE DUNDY The Dud Avocado*
JOHN EHLE The Land Breakers*
EURIPIDES Grief Lessons: Four Plays; translated by Anne Carson
J.G. FARRELL The Singapore Grip*
KENNETH FEARING The Big Clock
FÉLIX FÉNÉON Novels in Three Lines*
SANFORD FRIEDMAN Totempole*
BENITO PÉREZ GÁLDOS Tristana*